Syphon

Guardians of the Fractured Realms

Chad Kunego

Printed in the United States of America
First Print Release, October 2016

What The...?!? Publishing
131 West Seneca Street, #109
Manlius, NY 13104

Library of Congress Control Number: 2016918746
What the...?!? Publishing, Manlius, NEW YORK

ISBN-13: 978-0692806449
ISBN-10: 069280644X

www.WhatThePublishing.com
business@whatthepublishing.com
www.ChadKunego.com
author@chadkunego.com

Formatting, cover design, by
What The..?!? Publishing

Dedication and Acknowledgements

Like most things in life, this book wasn't created in a vacuum, with that said I'd like to thank the following people:

My wife, Heather, for the encouragement and helping me polish this book until it hopefully shines. After 17 years, I finally found something that stuck.

Emily A.- My first beta-reader. Your thoughts gave me the confidence to keep working on this project.

Heather H. - Your suggestions and thoughts on this project helped refine what this book eventually became. For that, I'm thankful.

And finally, this book is dedicated to my Mom. I wish you could have lived long enough to see this book get published. You never stopped believing I could do whatever I put my mind to. I just hope you're looking down on me from Heaven, still rooting me on. I hope I made you proud in the end.

Thump...

He felt, more than heard, the sound reverberating around him. He couldn't see where he was. For some reason, he couldn't see anything. All he could make out were sensations of movement and pressure, of things sliding across his skin. Randomly, he felt hands trying to grab ahold of him as he spun away. His body slid smoothly through the resistance, instinctively changing direction in response to stimuli he couldn't detect.

Thump...

The air vibrated soundlessly, then he felt a new sensation. Pain. Momentary impressions of pain, barely noticeable at first but growing in intensity, flared up across parts of his body. It quickly faded, only to be replaced by more flashes of pain on other parts of his body. Confusion blossomed when he couldn't remember how he had come to be in this situation or what he was supposed to do.

Thump...

The pulses were coming more rapidly now as the world slowly started to resolve itself into flashes of half-seen distorted faces, of teeth snapping at his face while he continued to move. Something was coming, something malevolent. As he fought to free himself from the hands grasping at him, an overwhelming sense of dread grew behind him. Spinning himself around, a bloody demon with razor-sharp fangs lunged at him. As the world slowed to a crawl, he could see light glistening off the drool that coated the teeth and dripped off, falling toward the floor. The air seemed to thicken as he struggled to bring his arms up, trying to stop the creature from attacking him. With fangs approaching within inches of his face, he started to open his mouth to scream.

THUMP!

The demon's head exploded as his world disintegrated in a flash of white-hot fire.

His eyes snapped open. He lunged into a seated position before slamming his eyes shut again. The blinding light lanced into his skull, impaling his thoughts for a moment and causing him to recoil backward.

Thump… Thump… Thump…

He gradually became aware of the sound slowly working its way back into his consciousness. He took slow, deep breaths, trying to clear his thoughts. A massive pain was knotting up behind his eyes. Trying to focus his thought more, he felt his heart beat slowing down to a more normal pace. He struggled to make sense of what was happening to him. He felt the panic starting to rise before a sensation of warmth started to spread up his left arm. The comfort that accompanied the warmth allowed him to relax again, the pain behind his eyes quickly receded into the background.

Thump… Thump… Thump…

"Ohhh…"

Clenching his teeth, he realized he was scrunching his eyes tight against the glaring source of light. Struggling to relax even more, he vaguely heard a voice yelling in the distance. With renewed focus, he continued to collect his thoughts.

"He's waking up."

The sudden voice slammed into him, causing another wave of pain to cascade through his head, but it was less intense than the last spike of pain. Another pulse of warmth traveled up his arm. After another moment, he tried to open his eyes again. Squinting against the pain caused by the light, he tried to take stock of his surroundings. Begrudgingly, the room he was in started to resolve itself into something he could make sense of. He glanced to his right, trying to determine the source of the thumping noise. With a start, he realized it was the sound of fluid dripping from a bag of IV fluid.

Looking down at himself, he realized he was laying in what appeared to be a hospital bed. He caught movement out of the corner of his eye, causing him to abruptly shift his attention. Squinting in the direction of the movement, he noticed an older gentleman enter the room. By the lab-type coat, he assumed it was a doctor of some sort.

"Ah! You're finally awake I see!"

He winced at the volume of the doctor's voice. With a softer tone, the doctor spoke again.

"Sorry about that. Don't worry though, the sensitivity to sound should lessen shortly. My name's Dr. Greene. How are you feeling?"

He tried to look at the man through cracked lids, attempting to process what was being asked. After a minute, he realized the gentleman was staring at him with what he took to be an expectant look.

"Bright…" he replied, his voice cracking as his tongue stuck to the roof of his mouth.

He tried to swallow, but couldn't work up any moisture. The effort caused him to cough roughly.

"…Thirsty…"

"Well, that's to be expected. You've been unconscious for a good bit now."

He noticed the doctor glancing over his shoulder, nodding to someone he couldn't see.

Walking toward the bed, he unslung the stethoscope dangling around his neck. Adjusting the bed to an upright position, the doctor placed the stethoscope on various parts of his chest and back.

"Deep breath in. Hold it… Okay, breathe normally."

This went on for a few minutes before a nurse came in with a pitcher and a cup of ice with a straw in it. Pouring some water, she brought the cup over to him. He went to reach for it but was stopped short by something around his wrist. Looking down, he noticed he had a set of handcuffs on his right wrist along with a restraining strap. Wiggling his other hand under the blanket, he could feel another restraining strap on his left wrist as well. He started to feel panic rising only to have it fade again when another pulse of warmth traveled up his arm. After taking a long sip of water, he glanced back at the doctor, rattling the cuffs for emphasis.

"Oh… Those are for, uh, your safety as well as ours. When you were brought in, you started thrashing about pretty violently. You broke a nurse's nose before we were able to sedate you." He waved his hands when he noticed my eyes start to get wide, "nothing to worry about. He'll be fine. Anyway, as I was saying, you were brought in under some unusual circumstances."

"What happened to me? Was I in an accident or something?"

"Well…"

The doctor trailed off, a commotion out in the hall interrupted them. He glanced toward where the doctor was staring, trying to determine the source of the disturbance. He could just make out the nurses' station where a nurse appeared to be having an argument with a stocky guy in a suit. The lady standing next to him was staring intently toward his room. Looking back up at the doctor, he inclined his head toward the argument, raising his eyebrows in a questioning look.

"Yes… They're here to talk to you, if that's what you're inquiring about. As I was saying, you were brought here under some unusual circumstances. I'm not at liberty to tell you about it, but I'm sure the nice detectives will be more than glad to fill you in on the details."

He heard the sarcasm in the doctor's tone as he looked back at the two detectives. He wasn't sure why, but he knew that the stocky guy was right handed, carried a handgun in a cross draw holster, and had a backup around the inside of his left ankle. From the way he moved when the detective gestured in his direction, he could also tell that he favored brawling over other forms of combat.

As for the woman, after a quick glance, he could tell that she knew some type of martial arts. From how she unconsciously planted her feet to how she kept her weight balanced over the balls of her feet, he knew her mode of combat was more refined, something that favored movement and hand techniques. Of the two, he felt she was the more dangerous fighter. He wasn't sure how he could tell that just by looking at them briefly, but he was positive he was accurate on both counts. Before he had a chance to ponder it further, the guy became impatient and pushed the nurse out of the way before purposefully striding toward his room.

Glancing at the nurse, the doctor inclined his head toward the restraining strap on his left wrist.

"I believe we can remove that so our patient can hold his own cup, don't you think?"

Glancing once toward the door at the approaching detectives, she looked hurriedly back at the doctor. After a quick nod, she undid the restraining strap on his left wrist. Wheeling the table over to him, she placed the pitcher and cup within reach. Hurrying around the bed, she started undoing the restraining strap on his right wrist.

"WHAT THE HELL ARE YOU DOING?"

The nurse jumped and froze, her gaze snapped toward the detective with a slight look of fear in her eyes. The doctor laid his hand on her shoulder and nodded at the remaining strap before striding forward. While she started working on the strap again, the doctor replied.

"Oh come on detective! He's still handcuffed to the bed. What do you think he's going to do? Carry the bed away with him? Gnaw his arm off? He's still suitably restrained with your... your cuff on him. I just thought it would be better if he could hold his own glass of water instead of needing one of us to do it, unless you'd like to volunteer to have someone from your precinct do it?"

The detective started to take an angry step forward before his partner laid a hand on his shoulder.

"Of course. The handcuff is more than sufficient Doctor. My partner was just thinking about everyone's safety is all. He tends to get carried away about stuff like that."

He started to say something but she elbowed him in the ribs before continuing.

"Isn't that right, Frank?"

"Yeah, yeah... Let's get on with it."

Dr. Greene moved over to the corner.

"Don't stress him out too much or I'll have to ask you to leave."

Frank opened his mouth, glanced at his partner again, before snapping it shut.

"That's fine. We just have a few questions to ask your patient to try and determine what happened at the spot where we found him."

Glancing toward him, she continued.

"Hello, I'm detective Cora Blanchett and this," she said, motioning to her partner, "is detective Frank Giani. As we mentioned, we'd like to ask you a few questions if that's okay?"

He slowly nodded before she continued.

"First of all, when we found you, we couldn't find any identification on you. So can we get your name?" she asked, pulling a notebook out of her pocket and flipping it open, her partner mirroring the action.

He started to open his mouth to answer, then paused. A tinge of fear started to form before another pulse of warmth melted it away again.

"Uh…" he started, looking over at the doctor with a worried expression growing on his face. He tried again, concern starting to color his voice.

"Uh… I uh… I don't know… What happened to me? Why can't I remember…?"

"Likely story…" Frank muttered under his breath. Cora gave him a dirty look before focusing on the doctor with a raised eyebrow, vaguely waving toward him while he struggled to remember his name.

"Well, it is possible he could be suffering from some form of temporary amnesia," he began, flipping through some charts. "While the CT scans showed something odd…" he trailed off, mumbled something to himself. After a brief pause, he glanced back up.

"Other than reports of a lump on his head by one of the EMT's that brought him in, there's really no way to be sure whether it's temporary, permanent, or being faked. Assuming the EMT wasn't mistaken, then it's entirely plausible for the patient to be suffering from some form of memory loss due to head trauma." Looking over at him, he asked, "Do you know what day it is?"

He started to open his mouth, but then shut it while shaking his head no, concern flashing across his features again.

The doctor went down a quick list of questions before he looked back at the detectives.

"Well, from the sounds of it, he hasn't lost all of his memory or he wouldn't be able to talk to us. He seems to be able to move in a coordinated manner, so that part of his brain is functioning fine as well. Since the CT scans don't show any permanent trauma, other than a strange shadow we want to investigate with an MRI, I would assume it's just a temporary loss of memory. There's no way to be sure though since the mind is a funny thing. We'll just have to wait and see."

Giving his partner a dark look, Frank started to turn toward the door.

"So at this point he's a John Doe...? Seriously...? This is bullshit Cora and you know it. He's hiding something and I'm going to find out what it is. I wanna know why he was in that warehouse where we found him and why he was surrounded by dead bodies."

"Frank..."

Cora started to say something more when John Doe suddenly sucked in a sharp breath before he started coughing violently.

Everyone stared at him with varying levels of concern while his coughing grew increasing more violent. Doctor Green rushed over to him just as he gave one final, violent cough before wiping his mouth, a slight trail of blood streaked across his lips. He started to reach for the cup of water, but the doctor interrupted him.

"Open your mouth," he commanded, pulling out a pen light and gently grabbing his chin with the other hand, "let me take a look."

Dr. Greene shined the light in his mouth for a minute, turning his head from side to side before letting him go.

"Well, your mouth looks okay. Not sure where the blood came from since I don't see any lesions or cuts. I'll order up some more scans to check your lungs. Might be some internal damage we've overlooked since all the test results haven't come back yet."

Glancing back at the detectives, he waved his hand at them in a dismissive manner.

"My patient needs to rest. He's still recovering from whatever happened to him. Come back tomorrow."

Detective Blanchett started to say something, paused, then reached into her pocket before stepping forward.

"Here's my card if you remember anything," she said, laying her business card on the table next to the pitcher, "we'll be in touch."

As she spun away, he noticed her pause. As he reached for the cup of water, she glanced back over her shoulder to say something else. She cocked her head slightly when he gave a slight start after noticing the large piece of jewelry on his left hand for the first time. Quickly regaining his composure, he grabbed the cup before turning back to the detective.

"Since you can't remember your name, do you mind if we call you John for the time being?"

Taking a long sip of water, he nodded at her, noticing the thoughtful look she cast him when he replied.

"At this point, that seems to be as good a name as any."

Glancing back at the doctor one final time, she nodded before striding out of the room, her partner close behind her. Doctor Greene started walking toward the door, following the detectives before he stopped and looked back at him.

"Don't worry, I'm sure your memory will come back in short order. If you need anything, don't be afraid to use the call button."

He waited a few minutes after everyone had left before he looked down and opened his hand. Staring back at him was the blood-covered bullet he'd coughed up.

"Do you think we overdid the good cop/bad cop routine a bit?"

Cora glanced over at her partner as the elevator doors closed.

"Probably. So what was your impression of our John Doe?"

Frank scratched the back of his head before looking back at her.

"He's hiding something, I can just feel it. I mean, look at how calm and collected he was… When was the last time you saw someone that relaxed looking after losing their memory?"

"Yeah, I thought that was kinda strange too. The other thing I thought was strange was the readings that were showing on the heart-rate monitor. Did you happen to notice how low they were?"

"Nope, was trying to catch him in a lie, but I have to admit, if he's faking it, he's doing an impressive job of it."

"Yeah, it was weird. I've never seen someone in his circumstance so relaxed. When we came in, the monitor said his heart was beating at a steady forty-five beats a minute, so that, along with his build, makes him some sort of high level athlete. What caught my attention though was when we asked questions to try and get a rise out of him. For the most part, the only reaction I saw was maybe two or three beats that came faster, then it leveled back down to that unusually low pace. One of the times it spiked was when we asked him his name. Betcha he'd nail a lie detector test."

"Probably…"

"What do you make of that jewelry he's wearing? He kinda looked surprised to be wearing it."

Frank paused a second as they exited the elevator before continuing.

"Honestly, I'm not sure. It concerns me that they couldn't figure out how to remove it. It also bothers me that they stopped trying after burning out that first blade trying to cut it off."

"I'm with you. I don't like it when a suspect gets to keep something like that, but they did have a valid point. Their cutting blade didn't even scratch it and they ran a risk of causing an injury if they continued trying. I wonder what it's made out of."

"Don't know, but whatever it is, it's pretty tough. I've watched those cutting blades go through case-hardened metals before without a hitch, so whatever it is, it's a lot harder than anything I've come across before."

Cora opened the car door and climbed inside.

"Just another mystery to add to the pile I guess."

Frank nodded back.

"Looks that way."

He struggled to remember who he was. After several fruitless minutes, his anger finally spilled out. He flung the bullet across the room, frustrated with not remembering anything. Shocked, he watched it bounce off a couple walls in slow motion, seeing the metal deform with each impact, before landing in the bathroom garbage can.

What the? How the hell did I do that…

Shaking his head, he tried taking stock of himself. He figured he was probably around six foot or so and apparently worked out pretty regularly based on how muscular he looked. There wasn't a mirror he could look at, so he ran his hand over the smooth skin on his face.

Guess I shaved recently.

Reaching up, he ran his hand through his hair, which felt to be about shoulder-length and wavy. Bringing a lock of it forward to look at, he noticed his hair was black, like onyx, and shimmered under the harsh florescent lighting. Letting it go, he started examining the piece of jewelry on his left hand and arm.

Turning his hand left and right, letting the light play over it, he blew out a silent whistle while marveling at its craftsmanship. The overall design was of a finely-wrought dragon, varying in color from cobalt to icy blue. The size of the piece itself was surprising since he didn't even realize he was wearing it until he noticed it reaching for the water.

The head of the dragon covered most of the back of his hand while a sword appeared to be sticking out its mouth. Backing up the impression was what looked like a crossguard that spread across the back of his knuckles, giving the impression of a knuckle-duster. What would go for the hilt of the sword was a set of rings that traveled down his middle finger, ending just short of his fingertip, a blue gemstone covering the nail.

The neck, however, seemed shorter than he expected a dragon's neck to be, but he couldn't see all of it since the wings covered a majority of the neck and body area. The wings covered the entire length of his forearm and wrapped slightly around it while the dragon's tail coiled gracefully around his upper arm several times, ending just short of his shoulder. Turning his arm over, he saw that the legs of the dragon gripped his arm, the clawed toes interlocking with each other to keep it from coming off. It was so lifelike that he could almost imagine it having walked down and perching on his arm to take a nap.

While examining it, the word vambrace popped into his head, followed by a quick spike of pain.

How would I know what a vambrace is... Is my memory starting to come back?

After fiddling with it for a few minutes, he realized he couldn't figure out how to take it off. It fit snugly, like it had been crafted around his hand and arm instead of being slipped on.

All of it was fully articulated, moving fluidly when he flexed his hand, wrist, and arm. He also realized after a few minutes that it was also completely silent. There wasn't a hint of clicking joints or rattle of loose fittings. Looking closer, he could almost make out the glistening of the blue-tinged iridescent scales on the body of the dragon. With that level of detail and quality, he realized it had to be worth a small fortune.

Where would I get something like this? More importantly, how could I afford it? Am I rich?

While pondering the question, he noticed the eyes for the first time. Looking at them, he felt that whoever the artist was had outdone themselves. As he stared, it almost seemed like there was an intelligence behind the sparkling blue facets, glittering in the light.

If he had to guess, he suspected they might be sapphires. Based off the quality and detail of everything else, it wasn't that hard to believe.

Staring at the eyes, he felt like they were drawing him in.

"Time for your night meds."

The sudden voice snapped him out of his reverie. Looking up, he noticed the nurse that undid his restrains earlier. Cracking a smile, he nodded to her.

"Thank you for unstrapping me earlier. I felt kinda helpless."

"Oh, it wasn't any big bother. I honestly don't like it when any of the patients under my care have to be restrained. I mean, I understand if they're a danger to themselves or others, but from the sounds of it, all you did wrong was have the misfortune of was being in the wrong place at the wrong time... Or at least that's what I heard..."

She trailed off, focusing on exchanging the empty saline bag for a full one. Turning back to him, she handed him a small medicine cup with a few pills in it. He raised an eyebrow as he took the cup.

"Something to help you get some more rest. I can get you something for pain if you need it."

Fumbling slightly with the pills and the cup of water, he shook his head slightly.

"Honestly, other than a slight headache, I feel fine."

"Well, if it gets worse, just hit the call button."

"Thank you."

"No problem, I'll be back in a little while to check on you and refill your pitcher."

Smiling, he slipped his loose hand behind his head.

"I guess I could hang out here a little longer then... I'll see you later."

She chuckled slightly as she walked out the door.

"See you then..." she said, clicking off the room light.

His eyes snapped open. He wasn't sure why, but something was wrong, something that was causing the hairs on the back of his neck to stand on end. He slowly glanced around the dimly lit room, trying to figure out what had startled him awake. He almost felt a magnetic pull drawing his eyes toward the corner of the room farthest from the door and window. Focusing on the area, he began to notice indistinct movements coming from the shadows, almost like an afterimage. A strange chill slowly started traveling up his left arm.

"So Samuel, even after what happened to you, you can still sense me. I'm actually pretty impressed."

He jumped reflexively at the unexpected sound of the stranger's voice, his right hand clenching around the rail of the bed. As the speaker continued, he kept getting the impression that something wasn't quite right about the voice. He tried to put his finger on it, but couldn't quite determine the source of his unease. The sound played around him, the corruption in the speaker's voice became palatable, like something was rotting and decayed. The image that flashed through his head was of a midden under a hot summer sun.

"Come now… No greeting for an old acquaintance? My, my… the manners are the first thing to go when you get shot in the face, aren't they…"

The voice trailed off, the outline of a person began taking shape, coalescing from the shadows. The speaker approached him, their outline becoming more distinct. Grabbing a chair, they dragged it closer to the bed, the legs making a metallic hiss as it slid across the floor.

"Quite honestly, I'm a little disappointed. You see, my master spent several months planning that attack, expending quite a bit of effort coming up with it. You honestly weren't supposed to come out of that warehouse alive. But then that stupid bloodsucking mercenary just had to try and boost his reputation by being the one to finish you. I think you really did the world a favor when you tried ripping his heart out before his head exploded, but I'm getting off track here. Suffice it to say, if it wasn't for him grabbing you and then expiring messily in your arms, we wouldn't be having this conversation."

"Who are you?" he asked, trying to make sense of what the other person was saying. Even though the other person was only a few feet away, his features were still indistinct, like peering through a foggy window.

"You really don't know, do you? Maybe we were closer to our goal than we realized. Let's just say that it's not really that important at this point. What is important, however, is where we go from here."

His thoughts raced wildly through his head.

My name is Samuel? At least that's something. This guy knows me, but from the sounds of it, he tried to have me killed. He said I was shot in the face…? So why aren't I dead? Was that where the bullet I coughed up came from?

"Excuse me," the other person snapped, slamming his hand on the bed railing, "am I boring you? Really… some people…"

Samuel jumped slightly at the noise, trying to focus again on what the other person was saying to him.

"Sorry, just trying to come to grips with fact that you admitted trying to have me killed. Forgive me if I seem a little distracted."

"Ah… No worries. Happens more often than you'd think when talking to someone who survived an assassination attempt. Now where was I…?" he asked, trailing off while he tapped his finger on his chin.

"You were going to tell me why you wanted to kill me…?"

The sound of his abrasive laughter set Samuel's teeth on edge.

"Heh… Do you honestly think that, just by asking me, I'm just going to blurt out why my master wants you dead? What do you think this is… A movie? That you're going to trick me into some long-winded villainous monologue whereby you learn our whole diabolical plan? Then, through some unlikely happenstance, you'll somehow escape, only to return at some critical juncture to magnificently ruin it. My dear boy… The only thing that's going to happen is…"

Trailing off, he leaned forward, bringing his face to within inches of Samuel's face. Samuel sucked in a shocked gasp before gagging at the stench. The other person's face was a mass of writhing worms and other insects. The short whiff he got smelled of sulfur and decay. Trying to hold his breath, he attempted to press himself deeper into the mattress in a futile attempt to get away from the monster's face.

"Your death."

As the creature said it, Samuel felt an overpowering itchy sensation coming from his left finger. He absently started to reach over to scratch it before the handcuff stopped him.

"Oh no you don't!"

The monster grabbed Samuel by his neck and hoisted him off the bed. His right hand was yanked violently downward by the handcuff still attached to the railing, causing him to get jerked to a halt. Coming up short, the monster took a step back, quickly yanking Samuel with him. With a loud pop, the chain on the cuff snapped off.

"Here's the windup, and here's the pitch!"

Samuel felt his body start accelerating backward toward the window behind him. At the same time, he felt the world slow down to a crawl as he flew away from the creature, its evil-looking snarl etched in his mind.

I guess you really do have time to see your life flash before your eyes when you're getting ready to die. This'll probably be pretty quick though since I don't remember anything beyond a couple hours ago.

Without warning, the itchy sensation on his left hand became unbearable. Instinctively reaching over to scratch his fingers, he felt something take shape in his hand. As he slowly drifted away through the air, he was startled to find a handle forming in his hand. Intuitively, he pulled his right hand forward as he pulled his left back. Suddenly, an ice-blue crystalline sword materialized out of what appeared to be the dragon's mouth. Continuing the motion, he swung the blade around, connecting with the underside of the creature's wrist with a sound like glass wind chimes. The edge of the blade slid through the creature's wrist, lopping off the hand that he'd thrown Samuel with. Samuel was shocked that the sword sliced through it effortlessly. He had enough time to see the hand slowly start to drop toward the floor, encased in ice, before time snapped back into play.

As he sailed out the window, glass exploded into the frigid night air. The sword caught the side of the window sill as he went through backward, slicing deeply into the frame and cinder blocks, again without any noticeable resistance. It slightly slowed his backward momentum, but not enough to keep him in the room.

"OHHHHHHH SHIIIIIIT!!!!" he yelled as he sailed out the window.

As he started to fall, the sound of the monster screaming echoed into the night after him.

I'm gonna die!

That statement echoed through his mind as he dropped toward the sidewalk. He instinctively reared his sword arm back and swung it forward. Instantly, the sword's blade segmented and elongated, almost appearing like a bunch of crystal fragments held together by twin lightning bolts.

The sword stretched out toward the building, instantly embedding the tip and several fragments of the blade into the wall next to the window he had just flown out of. The blade continued to stretch, slowing his descent. Finally, it brought him to a stop several floors above the ground, in the process slamming him into the wall and knocking the air out of him. Trying to catch his breath, he looked back up at the blade. The lightning bolts had dimmed down to a muted neon blue and the blade was segmented into so many fragments that he quickly lost count of how many were visible.

Looking down, he estimated he was approximately six stories up. Looking back up, he quickly calculated that he'd fallen about ten stories before coming to a stop.

How the hell did I do that? Better yet, what the hell do I do now? If I climb back up, assuming I can figure out how, I'd most likely get thrown out the window again or worse. If I let go of the sword, I'll probably break my legs or kill myself anyway. Damned if I do, damned if I don't.

Without warning, the sword swung him away from the wall before coiling up and yanking itself out of the wall, pulling several chunks out with it. The segments snapped back, forming into a solid blade again while he fell the remaining distance to the ground.

He hit the sidewalk hard, pulverizing the sidewalk and sending small splintery cracks spider-webbing away from his feet. The blade of the sword chopped into the concrete next to him, leaving a huge gash where it came to a stop. Looking back up, he saw several softball sized chunks of wall dropping toward his head. He cringed, instinctively bringing his left arm over his head to try and protect it from the deadly chunks. He was suddenly buffeted by a blast of wind as the wings of the dragon flared out unexpectedly, causing the debris to bounce off the wings harmlessly.

Slowly standing on shaky feet, he watched the dragon shrink back down around his arm. He then felt a slight tug coming from his right hand. Looking down, he saw the blade segment again. The tip of the blade swung around, shrinking in the process as it heading toward his left hand. The dragon's head lifted slightly when the tip of the blade approached, and with a sound reminiscent of chains spooling off a boat, the blade retracted back into the vambrace. Finally, the pommel shrank back down and encircled his finger, to all appearances resembling a very elaborate piece of jewelry again. He clutched at his finger, trying to pull the sword back out, but it appeared to be simple jewelry again.

He noticed the dragon's eyes were glowing as the sword finished returning to its original shape. Examining the unusual glow, he was startled when it appeared to wink at him before it slowly faded out.

Who or what the hell am I?

Glancing around, he noticed the blanket from the bed he was in lying on the ground near him.

"Must have gotten tangled around my foot or something when that thing threw me," he muttered to himself absently. He bent over to pick it up before wrapping it around his shoulders.

I need to get out of here. I have no shoes, no shirt, a monster that's trying to kill me, and some bad-ass jewelry that winked at me. About the only thing going for me is I have hospital pants on instead of a hospital gown and a blanket to wrap up in. What more could go wrong?

Gradually, he could hear sirens in the distance getting closer.

I had to ask, didn't I?

Readjusting the blanket tighter, he took off at a slow jog. He wasn't sure where he was heading, but trying to explain to the police what had happened would generate more suspicions, including his level of sanity. Telling them he'd been chucked out a fifteenth-story window by a monster and landing without a scratch was going to be a pretty hard sell. At this point, all he knew was that the questions were piling up faster than the answers, and staying put wasn't an option if he wanted to get the chance to balance out the equation.

As he disappeared into the night, several thoughts kept looping through his head.

Who the hell am I, what did I get myself into, and how am I going to live through it?

"What the hell happened in here, and what is that horrible stench!"

Detective Blanchett covered her nose with her arm, trying to block out the overpowering smell of sulfur and decay that permeated the room.

"It looks like a bomb went off!"

Glancing up, a janitor shrugged his shoulders.

"Not really sure miss."

The janitor trailed off when Dr. Greene entered the room. Cora turned toward him as he approached.

"What happened in here, and where's our suspect?"

"We're still trying to piece that together. From the reports I'm hearing, about a half hour ago, loud noises erupted from this room, followed by breaking glass and a scream that raised the hair on everyone's head. By the time a nurse got in here, the room was in the condition you see it in now and empty."

"You," she said, pointing at the janitor. "Out, now. This is an active crime scene. Leave everything like you found it. Nothing leaves this room unless the CSI team clears it."

She started to turn away, but then looked back.

"Actually, can we get something to kill that smell though? It smells like hell in here, literally."

23

"I'll see what I can find," he said over his shoulder before walking out.

Turning back to the doctor, she continued.

"I wanna know what happened in here, and I wanna know now. How'd our John Doe get the handcuffs off, and how'd he get out of the room with nobody noticing?"

As she turned back toward the room, she looked back over her shoulder.

"And where's the guard that was posted outside this room, anyway? If you see him, tell him to get his ass in here. I wanna know why he left his post."

Turning her back on the doctor, she ignored his mumbling as she slowly walked over to the window.

"What the…?" she whispered as she studied the huge gash in the left side of the window frame. Looking closer, she saw it was a very clean cut. She made a mental note to ask the CSI techs what could make that cut as she leaned out the window. Looking down, she noticed some type of damage to the sidewalk, but she couldn't make out the details. Pulling her cell out, she punched the speed-dial.

"Frank, you here yet?"

"Just pulling in."

"Hey, I need you to come over to the sidewalk outside the suspect's window. Something happened to the sidewalk that I can't make out from here. Also, the room is a complete disaster. I'm gonna call the crime techs to have them go over this mess with a fine tooth comb. Call me back when you're outside."

Ending the call, she called the precinct to tell them to send the CSI lab rats to examine the room.

As she glanced around the room again, her phone rang.

"Hey, are you down there yet?" she asked, walking back toward the window.

"Yeah… Yeah I am, and you're not going to believe what's down here…"

"With the way this night's going, I'm not sure anything is going to surprise me…"

"Yeah, well this might. I'm looking at what appear to be footprints embedded in the sidewalk, along with a huge gouge along the right side. The gouge is about 5 feet long, straight, and it appears to get deeper the farther away from the footprints it gets. Looks like something sliced through it like butter."

She glanced at the gash in the window frame before leaning out the window to look at her partner again.

"That's not as crazy as it sounds. It looks like a bomb went off in the room and there's a huge gash in the frame... Also a clean-looking cut."

"Yeah, well that's not all. Inside the, uh, 'footprints', the cement is crushed to powder. There's a bunch of cracks all around the prints as well. If I didn't know any better, I'd say our perp jumped out the window and landed here barefooted, then walked away..."

"Yeah, well, I'd have to say you don't know any better. Nobody jumps out a fifteen story window, lands on their feet, then walks away from it. I'm a little rusty with the math, but I'd hazard a guess and say he would have been traveling over 60 miles per hour before he hit."

"Whatever, just have the lab rats look this area over when they get here."

She saw him look up toward her before gesturing toward the window.

"Hey Cora... Take a look to your left outside the window."

Leaning out further she glanced to the left.

"Holy..."

"What is it?"

"Something gouged the living shit out of this wall."

She tried to reach the hole, but it was just out of reach.

"Looks like we also need the techs to get ahold of a window washing platform. Something took several huge chunks out of the side of the building, and I'm suspecting whatever did that also took the nice gash out of the window frame and left that gash in the sidewalk as well."

"Excuse me..."

Cora jumped a bit at the sudden sound. She hadn't heard anyone come up behind her.

"Frank, I gotta go, someone's here."

She hit end and turned toward the door, only to find someone already moving around the room.

"Yes…? You shouldn't be in here," she said while examining the stranger. The woman before her stood about five foot eleven and was dressed in what appeared to be a black silk shirt, black leather pants, knee-high Doc Martens, and topped off with a black leather trench coat. All the black contrasted starkly with her pale white skin and fiery red hair that had cinnamon streaks running through it. Her hair was tied back in a ponytail with several stray strands dangling around her face.

"Can I help you?"

"I hope so… I was told there was an officer Blanchett here that might be able to help me. I'm trying to find a John Doe that was brought in last night…"

The stranger trailed off with a hopeful look on her face.

"I'm *Detective* Blanchett, and yes, we did bring in a John Doe yesterday. And you are?"

"I do so apologize detective. Where are my manners? My name is Sybil. Sybil Brennegan. Could you tell me more about your John Doe?"

"Oh…? Do you think you know him?"

"I kinda hope so," she said as she glanced around the room again. Cora noticed the woman only slightly wrinkled her nose a few times, in what appeared to be disgust, even though the over-powering stench still lingered in the room.

Interesting…

"What do you mean, exactly?"

"Well," she began as she started wandering around the room again, her boots making a clunking sound with each step, "I was supposed to meet a friend for dinner last night, but he never showed. Then I saw in the news this evening that a John Doe was brought here. The artist's sketch resembled my friend, so I hurried over to see if it was him."

As she talked, Cora noticed that she seemed to be investigating the room while trying to look indifferent. Her eyes lingered on the broken handcuff and the gouge in the windowsill momentarily, before continuing to scan the room.

What is she hiding? She seems to know more than she's telling me, but how to I draw it out of her?

"So does your friend have a name?"

"Samuel… Sam for short."

Cora pulled out her notebook again.

"So… This friend of yours, Samuel. Does he have any distinguishing marks, like scars or tattoos?"

"Hmmm…"

She paused for a second, tapping her finger over her lips as she looked up at the ceiling.

"Not that I ever recall seeing. He did have the most amazing emerald green eyes though."

As she said that, she absently brushed one of the loose strands of hair out of her eyes. Cora noticed something peek out from the sleeve of her trench coat. From the brief glance, it appeared that Sybil was wearing what appeared to be the same piece of jewelry that Samuel had been wearing. As her eyes moved back up to Sybil's face, she realized the other woman had noticed her stare. Before Cora had a chance to ask about it, her cell rang. She jabbed at the answer button.

"What? This better be good."

"What crawled up your ass? I just wanted to let you know the CSI rats were here. Did you want them to start down here or head up there first?"

"Have 'em start down there. Nobody's going to touch anything up here until we let 'em. On the other hand, those marks in the sidewalk might get contaminated if we don't check 'em first."

"Okay, sounds like a plan. What's go—"

Cora hung up on Frank, turning back toward Sybil to ask her about the jewelry. A quick glance around the room told her that she was alone.

"Sonofab…"

Cora ran out of the room and over to the charge nurse's station.

"Did you see a woman come out of this room a minute ago, wearing all black with a black leather trench coat?"

"Honey, with all these yahoos running around here tonight, I ain't had time to see anyone."

"Damn it."

Turning to head back toward the room again, she saw an aide running toward her, waving frantically.

"Detective, you need to come see this."

"Now what…?"

"It's that guard you were asking about. They just found him. He's dead!"

"Shit, the chief's gonna be all over my ass about this fiasco," she muttered under her breath.

Looking back at the expectant aide, her shoulders slumped as she waved in the general direction the aide had come from.

"Lead the way."

"Well look what we have here…"

Pain blossomed across the side of his face while the impact caused him to fall on his side. The pain made it hard to concentrate on where he was or what was happening.

"Ow… Dammit, this bum's got a head made outta rock or something…"

Before he had a chance to get his bearings, another foot connected with his face. His head bounced off the wall behind him. Stars flashed behind his eyes as he tried to remember where he was. He vaguely remembered sitting down in an alleyway to rest, and then the pain.

"Yo, you're right man, head like a brick."

Several more blows rained down on his head and ribs. Samuel did his best to protect his vitals, but was only partially successful. After a few minutes, the blows stopped.

"Is he dead? Come on… I was hoping for a little more fun than that. All we got out of it is sore feet."

As they talked, Samuel realized the pain was receding, allowing him to think coherently again. Opening his eyes, he assessed the situation. Standing before him were four men in their late teens, early twenties. He realized he could smell alcohol on them, and based off their movements, were slightly drunk. He also realized that they didn't have a lot of fighting experience based on how they held themselves.

"Hey, he's still conscious."

Turning their attention back, one started walking toward him.

"Who you eyeballing? Do you want some more of THIS?"

Samuel saw the thug rear his foot back for another kick. As the foot came forward, he instinctively brought his hand up, catching him at the ankle.

"Ah! Fuck! Leggo!"

Samuel twisted his opponent's leg quickly, trying to knock him off balance, but was unprepared for the sound of snapping bones before the guy fell down, clutching his ankle.

"HE BROKE MY LEG!" the guy screamed, clutching the injured part. "KILL THAT SONOFABITCH!"

As the other three started to rush him, he slammed his hand on the ground, popping him up into a standing position, his blanket falling to the ground.

"Holy shit! Look how jacked he is…"

Samuel took a step forward, causing the three men to involuntarily step back before they fanned out around him. The first guy rushed in, trying to take him out quickly with a haymaker. Stepping inside the arc of the punch, he grabbed him by the wrist and under the arm, twisting and dropping his center of gravity. As he pushed up with his right hand, he felt the man's shoulder separate as he went sailing over his head, slamming into the wall upside-down before dropping three feet to land on his head, crumpling into a groaning heap. Continuing his spin, he deflected the straight kick of the next man with his left arm. As the kick started to slide past him, he slid backward, wrapping his left arm under the leg, scooping it up so it rested on top of his shoulder.

Placing both hands on top of the knee, he quickly yanked down, hyper-extending it to the point it popped out of socket. As he stood up to face his final assailant, he felt a sharp burning pain in his side. He clumsily swung at the last guy as he stumbled away a few steps, grabbing his side. Looking at his attacker, he noticed blood dripping off the knife in his attacker's hand. Backing away from him slowly, Samuel glanced down and saw blood leaking through his clenched fingers. As he put pressure on the wound, the flow of blood gradually slowed. He also noticed the pain rapidly started to fade as well.

I need to take care of this guy before I go into shock.

Samuel turned his body slightly, showing his injured side toward his attacker, hoping he'd take the bait and try and attack him again. What he didn't expect was the reaction he got. His attacker glanced down at his wound, his eyes growing large before dropping the blade and running off in the opposite direction.

Huh...?

Samuel looked back down at the stab wound to see how bad the injury was. He knew he needed to put pressure on it again or he might bleed to death. Instead of a gaping wound, all he saw was a red line that faded as he watched.

How the hell?

His attention snapped back to his current situation as he made out the sound of sirens approaching from a distance. Quickly stripping the boots, shirt, and jacket off the unconscious thug he'd slammed into the wall, he threw it all in a pile on the blanket before tying it up into a bundle. Taking one last glance around, he took off down the alleyway in the opposite direction of the guy who stabbed him. As he ran, he tried to make sense of what had just happened and figure out how he'd been able to heal from a stab wound and beating within minutes.

"Holy shit!"

Cora jammed the call button on her phone again, staring in disbelief at the scene.

"Yeah?"

"Frank... Listen. Leave a couple of the CSI guys on that sidewalk thing, but have the rest come up here, pronto."

"Huh? Why? Thought you were worried about contaminating the scene down here?"

"Yeah, well, something just took priority. Russo's dead and it's a mess. Just get 'em up here, now."

"What! How?"

"That's the question. What I'm seeing here should be impossible. Just send the techs, okay?"

"They're on their way. This case is really beginning to turn into a cluster, isn't it?"

"Yeah, yeah it is. I even had someone up here inquiring about our John Doe, but she vanished into thin air. Said her name was Sybil and apparently our John Doe's real name might be Samuel. I didn't get the chance to see if she had a last name for him, but get this, it looked like she was wearing the same thing on her left hand that our boy was. When she realized I'd seen it, she pulled her vanishing act."

"Damn, do you think it's worth the effort to try and lock down the hospital to try and catch her?"

"With the way she got out of this room without me or anyone else noticing, I doubt she'd have any problems dodging our guys. Anyway, get up here as soon as you can, see if you can make any sense out of this mess up here."

"Sure thing, I'll just give the geeks their marching orders and I'll be right up."

Putting her phone back in her pocket, she looked back into the supply closet. What she was seeing in front of her just didn't add up. How it could happen without anyone noticing was beyond her. More importantly, how was it even possible. She'd just have to wait for CSI to tell her the details. Her eyes were almost magnetically drawn upward as she looked at Russo's body again. Granted, his head was dangling at an unnatural angle, but the bigger question was, how the hell did someone manage to pin him to the cinder block wall with two broken mop handles.

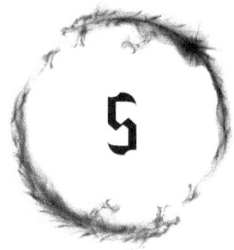

5

"So where we headed?"

"To an alleyway about twelve blocks from here."

"For what, exactly?"

"Well, after our boy disappeared, I put out the word to let me know if anything odd or unusual happened in the vicinity. Seems a group of guys got 'jumped' over there. Apparently three of the four weren't able to get very far. A dislocated knee here, broken ankle there. If it'd been any other night, I woulda just ignored it, but after the craziness we just went through and its proximity, I didn't think it'd hurt to check it out."

Cora stared out the window as Frank drove, trying to make sense of the whole evening. When they'd left, the techs were still trying to figure out how someone could drive a wooden broomstick through someone's body, let alone a cinder block wall. It just didn't make sense. Sure, she'd heard about stuff like that happening during tornadoes, but this was inside a janitor's closet less than fifty feet away from the nurses' station. How could something generate that much force in a broom closet? Better yet, how come nobody had heard it? It seemed every question only led to more questions instead of answers.

"Cora?"

Pinching the bridge of her nose, she glanced over at Frank.

"Sorry, lost in thought. You were saying?"

"No problem. Was just thinking about your mystery woman. You said she disappeared?"

"Yeah, one minute she's walking around the room, then you called. By the time I looked back up, POOF, she's gone. I'm not sure what to make of it. When I'd been talking to her, she was making lots of noise walking around the room with those boots of hers. When I turned away for a second, I never heard her leave. So either she was playing me by purposely being noisy while walking around, or there's something very bizarre happening here."

"Bizarre you say?" he asked as he ran his fingers through his hair, "there hasn't been one thing normal about this case since we picked it up."

"Let's start with what we know," he said, ticking off items on his fingers.

"We have an unconscious guy found in a warehouse, no marks or identification on him, surrounded by over thirty bodies, wearing a piece of jewelry that probably costs more than I make in a year and, as far as we can tell, is impervious to damage. The whole place is covered in cuts, gouges, claw marks, bullet holes, and all sorts of strange puddles of goo and other crap our guys can't identify.

"Now our prime suspect, who conveniently has no memory of who he is or what happened, escapes his handcuffs, has his room torn apart, more strange gouges that might be from the same thing that gouged up the warehouse, and everything points to our suspect jumping out a fifteen story window and hitting the sidewalk hard enough to pulverize it before casually strolling away to parts unknown. I think 'bizarre' is putting it mildly, don'tcha think?"

Cora chuckled under her breath. Her brusque partner had a way of succinctly describing everything that'd happened so far. As best she could tell, there wasn't anything about the entire case that made any sense so far. With all the strange stuff they've had happen with this case so far, she could tell it was starting to bother her partner. Since the incident at the hospital, she felt he was becoming a little apprehensive about the case, which was saying a lot. She knew he didn't like to talk about his experiences in Force Recon and she wasn't inclined to pry. All she knew was, he'd seen some rough stuff over there, so for him to get agitated, it meant he'd now traveled into crazy-parts unknown.

"So what do we know of these guys who were 'jumped'. What makes you think it has anything to do with our boy?"

"Well, for one thing, for getting jumped, they have very specific, very localized injuries. The one guy had his ankle snapped like a twig. Another had his knee dislocated. The third had his shoulder separated along with a probable concussion, probable neck injuries, and possible brain swelling. The one with the concussion was also stripped of his shirt, shoes, pants, and jacket. The fourth guy had no injuries whatsoever."

"Yeah, not your typical sneak attack. Sounds more like they got in a fight with someone and bit off more than they could chew. I have to agree. If they'd been jumped, they would have had a bunch of other injuries, not just stuff that would have taken them out of a fight quick…"

Cora trailed off as she saw the lights from the cruisers parked at the entrance to the alley. A couple of ambulances were parked nearby, preparing to transport the injured guys to the hospital. As they came to a stop, she looked over at her partner.

"Alleyway or perps?"

"Rock, paper, scissors? I win, I get alley, you win, I get perps, deal?"

"Deal."

After a quick game, Cora headed toward the alleyway, leaving her partner cursing under his breath. Cora smiled to herself, thinking about how she had picked up his tells a long time ago, allowing her to beat him fairly regularly. He wouldn't even play poker against her anymore. Stepping under the police tape, she nodded at the patrolman.

"So what've ya got?"

Nodding back toward one of the squad cars, he then pointed down the alleyway.

"Well, that one there was seen running from the mouth of the alley and headed south until he got picked up by one of the units that was responding to the disturbance. Witnesses reported hearing a fight happening in the alleyway. From the looks of it, these four perps appeared to be having a game of kick the bum when the tables got turned. Apparently, after beating on him for a few minutes, they stopped to talk, then one of them started yelling at the homeless guy again. That's when things went sideways for 'em."

"One of the witnesses said they heard the start of the confrontation and had wandered down the alley and hid when they saw the homeless guy getting assaulted. They also saw the homeless guy block another kick to his head by grabbing the guy's leg and twisting it so hard that they heard it snap. That's when he took off. From there, the fight only lasted about another minute. The guy we caught was babbling about stabbing the homeless guy before dropping his knife and running off. There's some blood in the alley, but not what I'd expect to see if someone was stabbed badly."

"What about the one that was stabbed?"

"Not sure. We tried to find a blood trail, but other than the puddle and bloody footprints that only went several feet in the opposite direction, we couldn't find anything."

"Did the witness give any type of description of the victim?"

"I believe their exact words were, 'he was so ripped he made Bruce Lee look flabby.' Beyond that, only that he had dark colored hair, possibly of Mediterranean or Arabic descent."

Cora glanced around the alley. Looking back at the officer, she nodded toward the scene.

"Mind if I take a quick look around?"

"Be my guest. I'm stuck until they get someone over here to take over the crime scene anyway, so knock yourself out."

"Thanks."

As the officer walked away, Cora turned back to take a closer look at the area. The scene seemed to match up with their theory. There wasn't any evidence indicating there'd been a brawl here. As she picked her way through the scene, she tried to visualize the chain of events. As she looked around, something caught her attention. Walking over to the wall, she pulled her cell out.

"Frank?"

"Yeah?"

As she bent down, she pulled a latex glove out of her pocket to pick up what she'd spotted.

"Our boy was here."

"How can you tell?"

As she stood back up, she motioned to a nearby officer to bag up what she was holding.

"Easy, I just found his plastic ID bracelet from the hospital."

6

"Well, it took a bit of persuading, but the only guy that managed to remain upwardly mobile finally admitted they'd tried to jump the guy for fun. Apparently it didn't go as planned and the tables got turned pretty quickly. Based off their description and the medical band you found, it was our boy from the hospital."

"Well," Cora started, rubbing the back of her neck, "it appears our boy didn't forget how to fight. From the sounds of it, after getting surprised and stomped on for several minutes, it only took him about a minute to dismantle three of his attackers."

"Sounds about right. I can't say I'd have been able to do that on my best day, even if I wanted to. Even without being jumped, I probably wouldn't be able to take out three assailants that quickly. It's really beginning to sound like he's someone I wouldn't want to go toe-to-toe with, especially if he's the one responsible for the mess at the warehouse."

Frank paused for a minute, looking around before lowering his voice.

"What do you make of that guy saying he stabbed our guy? I saw the knife. The entire blade was coated with blood, along with his hand and the front of his shirt where he tried to wipe it off. Based off just that, I'd say our boy could probably make it a few blocks before blood loss and shock took him out. The funny thing is, this guy's saying he saw the wound close up and stop bleeding while he watched. That's why he ran. Remember when you were talking about the strangeness of this case? Well it just took the shuttle into X-files territory, minus Scully."

"Not so sure about that… That redhead from the hospital might just qualify."

They headed to the car while they spoke, talking over the oddities of the case up to that point. As Cora started to get in the car, she noticed a flash of red at the mouth of the alley. Doing a double-take, she noticed a tall redhead heading away from the alleyway.

"Frank! I think that's her!" she shouted as she slammed the door and took off running.

"Wait!" Frank yelled, trying to climb back out of the car quickly, but Cora was determined not to lose their best lead again. As she started closing the distance, she noticed the other woman had picked up her pace a bit. When Cora had gotten within fifty feet of her, the woman ducked into the next alleyway. Breaking into a sprint, Cora reached the alleyway a few seconds later. Heading in, she noticed the other woman had broken into a jog, heading toward a tall chain link fence at the far end.

I need to catch up to her before she has a chance to climb that fence.

As she gained on her, Cora thought she saw Sybil smirk when she glanced back over her shoulder.

"STOP!"

I got her now. There's no way she's gonna be able to climb that fence before I catch up to her.

As she got closer to the fence, Sybil did a quick stutter step, then leapt upward, clearing the eight foot fence with room to spare. Landing on the other side, she landed feet first. As her feet hit the ground, she tucked and rolled forward before springing back to her feet.

"What the f—"

The other woman turned around and faced Cora, confirming it was the same woman from the hospital.

"Now, now detective… watch the language."

The other woman walked closer to the fence, running her fingers across the links.

"Detective, for your own safety, I suggest letting this case slide. You're way out of your league."

Cora pulled her pistol out, leveling it at the other woman.

"Don't move. You're wanted for questioning. What you're going to do is climb your way back over this fence so we can continue our conversation down at the station."

"Now why would I climb over this fence? I might rip my coat. So unless you're going to shoot an unarmed person through the fence, I believe we're done here."

"STOP!"

The other woman slowly started to back away from the fence.

"Heed my warning detective, back off this case."

"CORA!"

Cora turned her head slightly so she could yell over her shoulder.

"I'm over here Frank!"

She cast a quick glance over her shoulder to determine how far away her partner was.

"I've got her over—"

As she glanced back, she realized the woman was gone again.

"DAMMIT! HOW THE HELL DOES SHE KEEP DOING THAT!"

"Whoa… What's wrong? Where is she?"

"Frank, if I didn't know any better, I'd think we're dealing with a ghost…"

"Huh?"

As she holstered her gun, she glanced around the empty alleyway again.

"Frank, she jumped this fence like it was nothing, then disappeared when I glanced over my shoulder at you, all without making a sound. So if that isn't some spooky shit, I don't know what is. Oh, she also told us to drop the case for our own safety…"

"She threatened you?"

"I really couldn't tell, honestly."

"Well, based off everything we've seen so far, I'm almost inclined to agree with your mystery woman…"

Cora gave him a dirty look before walking back toward the car.

"Come on… Let's get out of here before a chupacabra hops out of a dumpster or something…"

She heard Frank snicker under his breath.

"Right behind ya Cora… Right behind ya…"

"Where to? The precinct, or back to the hospital?"

"Let's head back over to the hospital. Maybe those knuckleheads'll be more talkative after being patched up some."

Frank cast her a sideways glance.

"Maybe…"

"What?"

Frank was quiet for a minute. He looked over at her, then back at the road, before continuing.

"Cora, we've dealt with a lot of weird cases… plus I've seen some crazy shit when I was in the military, but this is a whole new league of weird. I'm starting to get a bad feeling about this case."

"Frank, I—"

"No, hear me out. I've worked with a lot of high-speed operators with my time in recon. Guys that enjoyed going into bars and starting fights for the fun of it. What I saw in that alleyway would have made those guys jealous. Assuming this was our boy…"

Frank held up his hand to cut her off again.

"Assuming this was our boy, then he's in a whole different league of skill. The amount of strength and skill needed to eliminate the threat against him borders on the impossible. If that one perp isn't exaggerating, then he did all this AFTER they'd given him a beat-down for several minutes."

"Yeah, so our guy's pretty tough. We've seen meth-heads do stuff like that before."

"Just think about it. Here's a guy that supposedly has no memory but somehow escapes his hospital room. Someone who, by all appearances, did it by taking the express route out the window wearing nothing but a pair of scrubs and possibly a blanket before taking off into the night. A night, I might point out, that was in the mid-teens.

"A few hours later, instead of finding him frozen in some alleyway, our guy gets blindsided by a group of miscreants that play kick the can with his head. But instead of leaving a body behind, the 'bum' destroys most of them in under a minute with surgical strikes before getting stabbed. Then he disappears again to parts unknown without leaving a blood trail.

"I've seen a four-man fire team accomplish similar results in that time frame, but our guy did it by himself. Our guy was stabbed but still managed to strip one of his attackers and escape with a non-existent blood trail. If we don't find this guy within five blocks from here, then I really don't want to tangle with him in a dark alley, gun or no gun."

Cora didn't know how to respond. The fact that Frank was that spooked about this case was enough to make her consider her words carefully before saying anything. He'd been her partner for a few years now, and she'd seen how he handled himself in a confrontation. One time, she'd watched him dismantle a three-hundred pound biker wanted on suspicion of murder and drug possession, by himself, after the guy came at him with a bat. If he could do that but was concerned about tangling with a suspect that he probably outweighed by at least twenty pounds, then she needed to re-evaluate what was happening here.

"Frank, I hear ya, but this was dropped in our lap. We can't just slack off on it. Something bad's going on, and from the looks of it, the body-count is only going to keep going up. So unless you have a better idea, we need to keep working this case until we catch a break."

"Yeah… Let's just hope that break isn't our necks…"

Cora and Frank entered the emergency room. Looking around, Cora spotted the nurse's station and strode over and flashed her badge.

"Three men were brought in earlier. One with a broken ankle, one with head, neck, and shoulder injuries, and one with a screwed up knee. Do you know what rooms they're in?"

The nurse glanced at them before consulting her computer screen.

"Yeah, the one with the knee injury is in surgery right now to repair some torn tendons and ligaments. Probably going to take a couple hours or so. The one that had the head and neck injuries is up in the ICU to keep an eye out for brain swelling. The broken ankle guy should be over there, in room 103a."

"Any idea why there isn't a uniform outside his room?"

"None whatsoever. Might have to do with the fact that, until they put a cast on him, he's not likely to get too far."

"Thanks."

Looking over her shoulder, Cora nodded toward the room.

"Guess we'll start with that one."

Nodding in agreement, they both started walking to toward the room. As they got closer, they could make out groans of pain.

"Where's that damn Doctor? My ankle's killing me!"

"They're busy… but how about telling us what happened earlier while you're waiting," Frank said as they entered the room.

"Who the hell are you?"

Cora pulled out her badge as she responded.

"Concerned citizens. Who're you?"

"I ain't got nothin' to say to no cops."

Frank wandered over, bumping into the side of the bed closest to the broken ankle.

"Ow, Shit! Watch where you're going man…"

"Oh… Clumsy me. Always running into stuff…" Frank replied as he bumped the bed again.

"Damn it!"

"What'd you say your name was again?" Cora repeated as she pulled out her notebook.

"Fine, my name's Kyle… Now would you tell your partner to stop bumping into the bed? That shit hurts."

"I'll see what I can do," she said as she cast a glance at Frank.

"So tell me Kyle… What exactly happened in the alley tonight?"

"We got jumped, that's what happened."

"Really…? From what I heard, you and your buddies decided to hassle a homeless guy and wound up getting your shit broken off…"

"Man, that's bull… Where'd you hear that crap from?"

"Frank, who was it that told you that?"

Frank made a big production out of pulling out his notebook and flipping to the right page.

"Hmmm… Oh yeah, looks like it was your pal, Pete. Seems he was the only one to get away from the 'brawl' without getting a scratch on him. How do you suppose that happened, with your group getting jumped and all…?"

"Sonofa…" Kyle trailed off, mumbling a bunch of curses.

Frank leaned in close to Kyle, bouncing his hip off the side of the bed again.

Kyle sucked air through his clenched teeth, his face starting to go pale.

"So how is it that he got away if you got jumped? Seems a lot more likely that you started a fight that went against ya, based off the evidence we've recovered from the alleyway."

Cora watched Kyle's face as her partner grilled him. She noticed that his tough expression was starting to falter.

"Listen. Tell you what," Cora said, appearing lost in thought.

"You tell us what we wanna know, and we won't run you down to booking tonight. If it's good enough, we might even be inclined to put in a good word with the D.A.… maybe have them try and toss out the charges…" she finished, arching an eyebrow as she glanced back at Kyle.

She watched his expression closely as she said it, waiting to see if he'd rise to the bait. After a moment, she could tell he was wavering.

"This is a one-time offer Kyle. If we walk out this door with nothing, then you're going to get booked on aggravated assault charges, possibly attempted murder. Tell us what happened, and it might all go away… Minus the broken ankle and all."

Cora waited another few seconds before looking over at Frank.

"Hmmm… Looks like it's gonna be option number two…" she said as she started to turn toward the door.

"Okay, wait… wait… Fine, I'll tell ya, but remember you promised ta get rid of the charges."

"If it's good, then sure, we'll talk to the D.A.," she said as she flipped to a blank page and got ready to write.

"Fine, this is what happened. We saw this bum…"

"So whatcha think…? Think he was telling the truth?"

Frank scratched his chin absently.

"If he was, then this guy continues to impress. To break a man's ankle one handed? I sure as hell couldn't do it. Dislocate, maybe… assuming I could get in the correct position and apply the right leverage. But to flat out break it? That amount of torque is well beyond what an average person can generate."

"Yeah, I've only seen that happen once when someone landed badly in aikido class. So, our guy is significantly stronger than he let on when he was cooped up here. I'm guessing he stood a good chance of being able to break that cuff we left him in, but then the question remains. Was he alone when he did it, or did he have help. If he had help, did either of them have anything to do with Russo's death? And how does Sybil play into all of this?"

"More questions without answers. God, this is turning into one big cluster…"

"Yeah, no shit. Let's say we call it a night since the other two won't be able to talk until sometime later this morning."

"That's about the only good thing I've heard so far today…"

7

Samuel slowly woke to the smell of food cooking. Eyes snapping open, he sat up quickly and looked around, trying to determine where he was. Seeing no immediate threat, he took another, slower look around. He noticed several disheveled people standing in what appeared to be a cafeteria line. As he watched, he saw a few more people in mismatched clothes come in through what he assumed was the front door, before heading over to stand in line.

"Better head on up before all the grits is gone."

Turning around, he saw an older gentleman approaching him, or more specifically, toward him on his way to the food line.

"Where am I?" he asked as he stood, joints popping randomly as he stretched.

"You's at the Main Street homeless shelter. I was here last night when they brought you in. Seems you was unconscious jes' around the corner, so a couple people hep'd carry you in. Was right nice of 'em ta do it too, seeing as how it got below freezing last night and all. Based off what you was wearin', you probably woulda froze ta death if they'd hadn't found ya. Now if ya'll excuse me, I'm gonna get some grits and bacon before they's gone."

As the man wandered over to the food line, Samuel took stock of his situation. He was wearing a pair of boots that were too big for his feet, a pair of worn but durable jeans, and a shirt and jacket that were a bit too small. Considering his options, his stomach reminded him that it'd been quite a while since the last time he'd eaten anything.

Come to think of it, when was the last time I'd eaten anything? I hadn't really been hungry when I first woke up at the hospital, and seeing as how I took an impromptu flying lessons shortly thereafter, food hadn't really been at the top of my list up until now.

Getting up, he headed over to the stack of trays and grabbed utensils before making his way through the line. By the time he'd hit the end of the line, his tray was almost overflowing with food. Heading over to the tables, he noticed the gentleman that had talked to him earlier sitting at the far corner of the room. Since he hadn't talked to anyone else, he headed over to sit with a vaguely friendly face.

"Did ya get some grits?"

Samuel smiled back at him, pointing to a spot on his tray.

"Yes. I also got some oatmeal as well."

As he put his tray down, the other guy whistled.

"If you wasn't a guy, I'd ask if you was expectin."

"Yeah, I might a gone a bit overboard, but I don't really remember the last time I ate, either."

"Well, then. Let's save the chit-chat for after the vittles. Oh… Almost forgot. Name's Hank. Hank Iam… The Great."

Hank waved his hand around theatrically as he said it. Then he held his hand out to shake hands. Samuel smiled as he let the other man's hand go.

"I'm Samuel, or at least I think it's Samuel."

As he took a bite of food, Hank raised an eyebrow.

"Well, yesterday I woke up in the hospital with no memory. Now I'm here with no real memory of how I got here, either. Had a stranger that might have known me call me Samuel, so that's about all I got going for me at the moment."

"Well, ain't that somethin."

Hank chuckled before stuffing some grits in his mouth.

"That's an understatement. So what's the 'The Great' in reference to?"

"Oh, used to be a performer. Like Houdini, only greater. People's used ta called me the Great Iam"

As he said it, Hank made a grand gesture, a plastic flower appearing in his outstretched hand. Samuel thought he saw a slight sparkle in the other man's eyes, but it vanished too quickly for him to be sure.

Must be my imagination acting up again.

"So what happened…?"

A sad look washed across the other man's face.

"People's lost interest 'n me. How's 'bout we pick dis up after we've eatin'?"

"Sounds like a plan."

With that, Samuel dug into his food.

Samuel looked back up at the chow line, debating whether to go back up for seconds. Glancing back at Hank, he saw him yank his hand behind him. Cocking his head slightly, Hank chuckled.

"Was just gettin' 'em outta sight before you think about eating 'em too… I ain't never seen someone put food away like that before."

"Yeah, honestly, I'm not sure where I'm putting it all either. Maybe they added a stomach while I was at the hospital or something."

He'd said it jokingly, but by the sudden change in Hank's expression, something wasn't right.

"What's wrong?"

Samuel noticed Hank had started edging away from him.

"I was just kidding. I don't have a second stomach."

Hank stared at him for a few more minutes before color started returning to his face.

"I've heard the government does experiments like that on people all the time. They help out the grays with their agendas and stuff."

"Grays?"

"Yeah, the grays. From Andromeda…? Don't tell me you've never hear of 'em… They liked ta take cattle afore they decided humans was more interestin'. Got the man involved with their secret projects an' stuff. That's how the government gets new technology. They let the aliens do things to peoples in exchange fer flying saucer technology an' stuff."

"Well, I'm pretty sure I haven't run into any aliens, or at least none that I can remember over the past couple days that I actually can remember."

It's kinda funny, but that actually makes more sense with what I've gone through since waking up in the hospital. Aliens came back to continue their experiments on me. Can see it now. Alien hybrid... Film at eleven.

Samuel smiled to himself. As he did, he realized Hank took the expression wrong.

"Mark my words. Them aliens are around, and if you're not careful, they might get ya."

With that, Hank got up and hurried toward the front door. Samuel started to head after him, but decided not to.

It might be better if I let him go. As it is, he's suspicious of me. Last thing I want to do is make him terrified of me. Besides which, they're still serving breakfast.

Grabbing his tray, Samuel headed back up to the food line.

Samuel eyed the food line again. For some reason, even though he was full, he still felt hungry. As if to add emphasis to the thought, his stomach growled at him.

I know I can't eat any more right now, but for some reason, I'm still starving. I ate enough food to feed at least four or five other people. Maybe the aliens did stick a second stomach in me or something...

He smiled at the thought.

"Hello there. Glad to see you have a, uh, healthy appetite, especially after the condition you were in when they found you."

Snapping out of his reverie, Samuel glanced up at the newcomer. Judging from the way he was dressed, he assumed it was one of the people who ran the place. Deciding it was probably better not to make another food run, Samuel pushed his tray slightly away as he turned on the bench seat.

"Hello."

"Mind if I sit down?"

"Uh... Sure, no problem."

Samuel gestured awkwardly at a spot next to him.

"Thank you. My name's Carl and I'm one of the people who help run this place. I was here last night when you came in. Considering how cold it was last night and your condition when you arrived, I just wanted to check in on you, make sure you're alright."

Samuel paused to consider what he was going to say before responding.

"I'm doing okay, I guess. Don't really remember a lot from last night. I remember getting jumped and escaping somehow. Next thing I remember, I'm waking up here, starving."

A quick look of concern flashed over Carl's face.

"Are you hurt? We have some EMTs on staff that volunteer here. If you'd like, I can see if one of them can look you over and make sure everything's okay, make sure there's no serious injuries or anything."

"Thanks, but I think I got away before they did anything permanent. I'm just glad I woke up somewhere warm."

"And with food, based off what I saw you inhale. Did you at least get a chance to taste it?" he asked, a big smile on his face.

"Nah, I figured I'd taste it later," he said, smiling back.

"Well, I don't want to take up too much of your time, but if you need anything, either myself or one of the staff would be more than happy to help you however we can. Also, if you're interested, we have some connections with various work programs to help you get back on your feet…?"

Samuel could hear the question in the other man's voice. Looking down at himself, he realized that he looked like any of the other homeless people that he'd seen here.

Now that I think about it, I actually am homeless. I have no clue who I am and no source of income. I also doubt I'd be able to sell this thing on my arm, even if I wanted to. It might be a good idea to take him up on the offer.

Reaching a decision, Samuel stretched his hand out. As the other man returned the gesture, Samuel responded.

"I might just take you up on that offer later. I don't suppose you have anywhere I can get cleaned up, do you? And maybe directions to the nearest library after that?"

Carl raised an eyebrow.

"Sure, we have showering facilities. I think we might also have some clothes that might fit you better as well, along with laundry facilities. If you plan on coming back tonight, I'm sure we can clean what you have by the time you come back from the, uh, library."

Nodding his gratitude, Samuel stood up while grabbing his tray. Motioning for Carl, he replied with a grin.

"Lead the way, if you wouldn't mind."

8

Samuel felt significantly better after getting cleaned up and putting on clean clothes that fit better. Doubling up on the socks let the boots fit better as well. Thankfully, nobody had asked him about the strange jewelry he had on his left arm. Trying to explain why he had it while being homeless would have led to his amnesia problem, a problem that might expose his desire to hide from the police while he tried figuring out what was going on and who he was.

Up ahead, he could make out the sentinel statues Carl had told him to look for at the top step of the library. He stomach was still feeling distended from breakfast, yet he was still hungry. He couldn't figure out what his body was craving even after the huge amount of food he'd eaten earlier.

As he approached the steps, a weird feeling, almost like ants crawling across his skin, played across the back of his neck. After a few seconds, the sensation went away, but not before he realized it had slowly shifted, like it was coming from a specific direction or object that was moving. It had only lasted a few seconds, only long enough to determine the general direction the sensation had come from. He leaned against the side of the steps for a few minutes to see if the feeling came back, but after a few minutes, he shrugged his shoulders and went inside.

As he stepped inside, he got déjà vu, along with another weird tingling feeling as he crossed the threshold. Looking around, he tried to figure out what had triggered the feeling again. Had he been here before? Or was it just a general impression from going into a library in general? Either way, he had a reason for being here. Hopefully, it might jog his memory, assuming he'd been here in the past. Heading toward the front counter, he noticed the librarian had her back to him. From the look of it, she was in the process of sorting the returned books on a cart. Samuel cleared his throat.

"Excuse me… miss?"

The woman held up her hand, signaling him to wait a moment as she finished shuffling some books before she turned around. For a split-second, her eyes widened. Samuel thought it looked like she recognized him, but she adjusted her glasses before smiling.

"Yes? How may I assist you today?"

"Uh, yes. I was hoping you'd be able to point me to where you keep recent copies of the local newspaper?"

Adjusting her glasses again, she gestured off to a corner of the library.

"The periodicals section is over in that direction. You'll find that we have the previous week's copies of several local periodicals there, along with other regional and national papers as well. If you need something further back, we also keep the past five years' worth on computer. If you need any assistance, don't be afraid to ask myself or one of the other librarians here. Is there anything further I can assist you with at this moment?"

"No thank you. I, uh, think that will be good for now."

Samuel started to walk toward the periodical section, but decided to ask her if she knew him. As he turned back, he noticed she was staring at him but quickly looked back down at the cart of books, accidentally knocking several books off. He quickly turned and strode away.

Smooth… real smooth, now she's probably embarrassed. Maybe she thought I was cute or something. Now it'll probably be awkward to talk to her. It probably wasn't a look of recognition anyway. Maybe once I figure out who I am and what's going on, I'll come back and ask her out on a date. Kinda hard to do that right now, being homeless and all.

Samuel took a couple steps before another thought occurred to him.

Wait a sec, do I already have a girlfriend? Or what if I'm married? I suppose either's a possibility at this point. Just gotta keep my mind on the task at hand.

Shaking his head, he made his way over to the periodicals section, looking for the local papers from the past several days. After a few minutes of searching, he found what he was looking for. Grabbing the stack, he wandered over to a table and sat down. He spent the next half hour pouring over the previous week, trying to find any mention of the incident he was supposedly a part of. A couple days back, he noticed a small blurb about a disturbance in a warehouse that police were called to, but not much else. Yesterday had a small article about a murdered police officer at the local hospital, along with a mention that one of the patients was missing and wanted for questioning.

That's probably me. If they find me, I'll probably wind up in a dank cell for the next twenty years.

Samuel glanced around and found a small stack of notebooks laying out along with several pens. Grabbing a notebook and pen, he sat back down. He copied down the sparse info the paper gave about the warehouse, intending to check it out later when it got dark. Hopefully he could find the address by then. As he put the stack of papers back, he noticed the head of the dragon poking out of his sleeve. Pulling the sleeve back down, it got him to thinking. It had to have come from somewhere. Maybe one of the local jewelry stores could take a look at it and possibly give him an idea of where it came from or who might have made it. After all, it was just his imagination that it had come to life last night. Being thrown out a window and surviving must have played tricks on his mind. So that meant someone had to have made it. With so little else to go on, it was worth a shot. Maybe a local jeweler might just be able to point him in the right direction.

After putting the newspapers back, he wandered around the library for a few minutes until he found the reference section, hoping to find a phone book there. He didn't want to embarrass the librarian again when he was perfectly capable of finding information on his own, especially since he had noticed out the corner of his eye that she kept staring at him when she thought he wasn't looking.

Finding a phone book, he flipped through the yellow pages until he found a list of jewelry stores. Scanning down the page, he found a space ad for a store that specialized in gothic and cosplay jewelry.

That sounds promising.

Jotting down the address, along with several other stores in the area, he set the phone book back down on a nearby table. Glancing back up, he noticed the librarian looking at him again. When she noticed him looking again, she spun around and headed over toward a door that he hadn't noticed before. As she went in, he had the strange feeling that the door was important, but he couldn't figure out why. As he stared at it, he suddenly got the impression that the air around the door was shimmering, like heat coming off a hot surface. As he continued to stare, he started to notice what appeared to be a slight blue glow coming out around the door frame. Before he could study it further, he heard a voice off to the side.

"Excuse me… Are you finished with this?"

Turning to look at the speaker, he stumbled back a few steps. Standing before him was what appeared to be a tall, gaunt looking man with pointed teeth, solid white eyes, and long, pointed ears. Blinking rapidly and rubbing his eyes, Samuel continued to back up.

"I say, are you all right sir?"

Samuel looked back at the man again. Standing before him now was a relatively tall gentleman dressed in a suit. He still appeared to be gaunt, but not overtly so. He still felt a slight sense of menace from him, but wasn't sure why.

"Yeah, I'm okay. I've just had a long morning is all."

"Quite all right."

Samuel noticed him gesture with his head toward the phone book.

"Oh, yeah. I'm done with that. Be my guest."

"Thank you kindly."

As the gentleman reached for the phone book, Samuel got a bizarre double image of the guy standing before him. One was of the thing he'd first seen and another, almost transparent image of the guy he had just been talking to. Shaking his head, he glanced back at the door, but it just looked like a normal door again. Tucking the notebook and pen in his pocket, he headed for the front door. Maybe some fresh air would help with the hallucinations he was having. It would also explain why he thought the dragon was alive. After all, the doctor had implied he might have a brain injury.

"Cheerio!"

He glanced back at the man/thing waving to him. He waved back and headed toward the exit. He started wondering if he should turn himself back into the hospital so they could check to make sure he wasn't suffering brain damage, either from the fight last night or possibly what caused him to end up in the hospital with amnesia in the first place. After all, he had coughed up a bullet. The only reason he decided against it was, other than the strange visions and odd sensations, he felt fine.

If they get worse, I'll have to turn myself in. There's no sense of me dying to find out who I am. They'll be able to figure out who I am eventually. But I'll cross that bridge when the time comes. Until then, I need to figure this out on my own.

Trying to cross the threshold again, he felt the odd tingling sensation, along with a slight physical resistance. It wasn't enough to stop him, but it was enough to be noticeable. Feeling an urge to look behind him, he noticed the door the librarian had disappeared through opening again. The librarian stepped out, followed by a couple of strange guys dressed all in black with black trench coats. Feeling exposed, he dodged to the side of the door before glancing back in. He saw the librarian glancing around, gesturing at the two men. Looking frustrated, she started making gestures toward the door he'd just left through.

As they started heading in his direction, Samuel spun around and ran down the stairs, catapulting himself down the last several steps. He sprinted to the right and heading toward a nearby parked car. Ducking behind it, he glanced back toward the library door. Standing at the entrance were both guys, intently scanning the area. Ducking back down, he swore he could feel their gaze pass over the car. Pulling himself down into a tight ball, he hoped that they wouldn't spot him. His arm seemed to get hot for a moment, then went back to normal. After a few minutes, he glanced back around the car. The men were nowhere to be seen. Taking a chance, he got up and sprinted away, effortlessly dodging people as he put distance between himself and the library. As he ran, he wondered what that creature had been, who the guys were, and what the strange tingling sensations he kept getting meant.

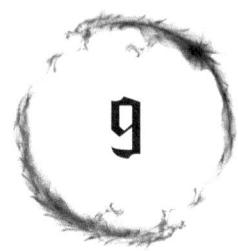

9

Cora read through the preliminary lab results from the warehouse incident again.

"Frank, does any of this make sense to you?"

Frank glanced up from his copy to look at her before looking back at the file.

"Nope, not one bit. Maybe we should head down to see if they can explain it so it makes sense."

Cora glanced back down at the report. If what she was reading was accurate, then most of ash and dust that had been found at the scene came back as cremated remains, or something very similar to it.

"Even though the ash resembles the material recovered after a cremation is performed, it's missing some of the mineral content normally found in cremated human remains. They don't give an estimate of how many cremated bodies worth of ash they recovered though."

"Well," Cora said as she typed something into her computer, "assuming the ash they've recovered was, in fact, from cremated bodies, a quick search says that the average cremated body weighs between four to six pounds. The report mentioned they recovered at least a hundred pounds of the stuff and they're still recovering more, so…"

Cora punched some keys on a calculator.

"Looks like somewhere in the ballpark of twenty bodies' worth, give or take. Think there might be a local funeral home involved? Or maybe a vet if it turns out to be animal remains?"

"Maybe, but it's unlikely to be animal remains. I mean, how many people actually pay to cremate their pets. I'm leaning toward it being human remains since we also found intact bodies there."

Frank paused a moment to consider what she said.

"Well, I could see a funeral home or crematorium sneaking one, maybe two bodies out, but twenty bodies worth of ash? I don't buy it… This is something else."

"What about someone making their own crematorium?"

Frank set his folder down, rubbing the bridge of his nose. Looking back up, he replied.

"Cora, with all the weird stuff happening so far in this case, the fact that I'm considering the possibility of a perp building their own crematorium seems almost mundane. Honestly…"

Frank got a strange look on his face. Then he picked up the folder and studied it a few minutes. Cora waited while he work through what he was thinking. She was fresh out of ideas anyway. After a few minutes, he looked up.

"You said that the amount of ash worked out to around twenty bodies, right?"

"Yeah, so?"

"And from this report, there was an additional forty-some odd bodies scattered around the warehouse as well, correct?"

"Yeah, where you going with this Frank?"

"Hear me out. Right now, the rough estimate is around at least sixty bodies in that warehouse, right?"

"Yeah…?" she said, waving her hand in a hurry up and finish gesture.

"Well, where did they all come from? Why haven't we had a huge number of calls coming in reporting 'Johnny' missing, or 'Sandy' never coming home from her party?"

"You know, now that you mention it, that is kinda strange. With that many bodies, you'd think we'd would of gotten at least a few calls about it, but I haven't heard anything over the past couple days. How could that many people, cremated and otherwise, go unreported this long?"

"What if a majority of them were homeless people? Maybe this is the end result of an underground fight club or something. Ya know, kinda like bum wars, but without the losers walking away from it? That would explain the cremated remains as well. Maybe they just didn't have time to torch all the bodies..."

Cora saw a pensive look on his face.

"What?"

"If my theory's correct, and the more I roll the idea around my head, the more solid it seems... if it's correct, then what does that make our suspect?"

Cora looked at him questioningly as she crossed her arms.

"I don't follow."

"Well, he was either a willing participant, which means he's a murderer, or an unwilling participant, which means he's a victim. Without his memory, it could go either way, but if he's faking his amnesia, then maybe he was covering for someone. Someone who paid him a visit in the hospital room and tried to silence him. And that strange woman you've come across twice, Sybil was it? She's involved with it somehow. Maybe she's one of the organizers..."

"If all that's true, then we need to find this guy quick before whoever killed Russo catches up to him and gets rid of another loose end."

Cora headed out to start checking out homeless shelters, after winning another round of rock, paper, scissors. Her partner was left investigating funeral homes and crematoriums. She just hoped her partner didn't catch on someday or use something more random, like a coin-flip.

Based off the list she'd compiled, it'd probably take the better part of a couple days. She was actually surprised at the number of shelters, soup kitchens, and food pantries scattered across the city. She spent a few minutes weighing her options. Starting with the shelters closest to the warehouse might turn something up. If this group was smart though, and she had to assume they were, then the best bet might be to start at the ones furthest from the warehouse since that would generate less scrutiny.

Another thought popped in her head. Assuming he had been telling the truth about not remembering who he was, her suspect might actually show up at one of those shelters as well. With that thought in mind, she turned on her GPS and set the address for the shelters closest to the hospital. As an afterthought, she cross-referenced with the ones closest to the alleyway disturbance. She found three that not only fit the criteria of being close to both the hospital and the alleyway, they were nearly in a direct path her suspect would have taken if he'd kept traveling in the same direction away from the hospital. With that, she hit the navigate button and headed out.

10

After jogging for several blocks, Samuel figured he'd put enough distance between himself and the strange guys at the library. The whole situation seemed bizarre but, strangely enough, it felt somewhat familiar as well. He could feel the memories dangling just out of reach, like a spider's web over his mind. Trying to focus on the men he saw, he tried to figure out why they felt so familiar.

Without warning, a stabbing pain ripped across his mind, causing him to stumble. As the pain intensified, he took faltering steps into a nearby alleyway, trying not to draw attention to himself. Staggering away from the mouth of the alleyway, he slumped to the ground. He focused on the pain, clenching his head between his hands. His head felt like it was going to explode as the sound of blood rushing in his ears intensified. After a few minutes, the pain lessened as he started getting disjointed images flashing through his mind. The most vivid memory flash was of him fighting a woman with red hair, dressed in similar attire as the men at the library. He could almost feel the impact vibrations as he used his sword and vambrace to deflect multiple sword strikes from her, almost hearing the metal singing as the blades slid across each other.

As the images started to clarify, he was startled back to the present by the sound of someone begging to be left alone. Cursing the interruption to what felt like recovered memories, he started to settle back down to concentrate when he realized he recognized one of the voices.

"Hank…?" he whispered.

Slowly standing back up on wobbly legs, the pain in his head started fading as he glanced around. Not seeing anyone at the mouth of the alleyway, he focused again on the voices. Turning, he headed deeper into the gloom, warily choosing his steps, trying to be as silent as possible. About fifty feet in, he came to an intersection. Pausing to listen, he turned right. After another twenty feet, he could make out several guys surrounding Hank, pushing him around and occasionally hitting him, causing him to fall and groan before they hoisted him back up to continue the harassment.

"Are ya sure you ain't got no money? We'll stop if you can give us just a few bucks or so… Or maybe some drugs?"

Samuel felt a simmering rage begin boiling up inside of him. He knew firsthand what it felt like to have a bunch of punks do that, and he'd be damned if he was going to let it happen to someone he knew, even if it was only this morning that they'd met.

"Come on fellas," Hank pleaded, "I ain't got nuthin'. I was just scavenging for stuff in that dumpster. I didn't mean nuthin' by it. I'll leave right quick if you'd let me."

"Nah, I think the boys and I are gonna show you what happens to people who come in our territory and don't pay the tribute."

Without warning, one of the guys sucker-punched Hank in the back of the head, knocking him to the ground, groaning in pain. At that signal, the rest of the guys started kicking and punching the incapacitated man.

"Hey, how about you pick on someone able to fight back!"

All of them stopped at once to look at Samuel in surprise. As they stared, he started walking toward them. They glanced at each other before glancing at the semi-conscious man at their feet.

"Oh yeah, and who are you then?" one of the guys yelled at him.

"I'm the one who'd going to turn you into something resembling leftover roadkill if you don't leave now."

"Really now," said another man, kicking the downed man hard before turning to fully face him, "so it's just you that's gonna turn us into roadkill, is it?"

Glancing around, the speaker picked up a chunk of wood from a broken pallet. With that, the spell was broken and the rest of the men quickly found other bits of pipe and wood to use as improvised weapons.

As Samuel continued to walk toward the men, he glanced at the arrayed makeshift weapons.

"Last chance to walk out of here…"

"You know what, you're a funny guy," the leader said before glancing over his shoulder.

"You hear that guys, this nice fella's giving us a chance to give up before someone gets hurt. What do you thi—"

The man abruptly spun back around, violently swinging the wooden plank in a powerful overhead arc at Samuel's head.

Without thinking, Samuel nonchalantly swung his left arm up to block the makeshift weapon. With a loud crack, the board splintered over his upraised arm. Shaking the splinters off his sleeve, his steady stare burned holes into the other man bulging eyes.

"Well, I did warn you, didn't I?"

Samuel knelt down beside Hank. Gently turning him over, he could see his face was a mass of cuts and bruises from the assault the men had administered. Glancing around at the broken bodies littered around the alleyway, groaning in pain, he mentally debated what to do. Reaching a decision, he gently squatted down to picked Hank up in his arms, surprised at how light he felt.

"Please, don't hurt me anymore," Hank mumbled, fading in and out of consciousness.

"Hank, it's me Samuel. I'm going to to bring you to someone who can help. Just try to relax."

Struggling to open a rapidly swelling eye, Hank tried to focus on him.

"Su… Sus… Samuel?" he asked weakly.

Samuel could tell the injured man was struggling to form a coherent though based on the deep furrows breaking across his forehead.

"Yeah Hank," he said gently, "it's me, Samuel. I'm going to get you back to the shelter. They have medical people there who can help you."

Standing up, Samuel tried to get his bearings. Almost without effort, a mental map came up in his mind's eye on how to get back to the shelter quickly and without gathering undue attention. It felt like another one of his lost memories returning, but he couldn't take the time or effort to focus on it right then. His biggest concerns were getting Hank to medical help and getting away from the aftermath his rage had caused before the cops came.

Pulling Hank a little tighter to his body to help lessen the jostling, he took off at a gentle jog, trying his best not to bounce his injured friend.

Samuel kicked the door to the shelter open, accidentally breaking the latch and causing the door to slam against the wall.

"I need help over here!"

Several pairs of eyes looked at him.

"I need help! Now!"

Shaking off their shock, several of the workers scrambled over to him.

"What happened?"

"He got jumped! That's what happened. Where can I set him down?"

"This way," one of the workers said, moving away at a rapid pace.

As Samuel followed her, a couple of the others began to follow him.

"Everyone, get back to work. I'll take it from here."

Samuel glanced over to see Carl rapidly heading toward him, shooing him on.

"Don't slow down, keep following Blythe. She's taking you to what doubles for our infirmary."

Picking up the pace slightly, Samuel continued following after Blythe.

"Wait right here," she said, leaving him in a room near the showering area. Reappearing a minute later, she unfolded a cot before motioning him to set Hank down.

"Can you help me get his jacket and shirt off?"

"Yes… We need to be careful though. I think some of his ribs might be broken."

After a few minutes of getting him partially undressed, checked over, and situated comfortably, Samuel stood up to stretch. Catching Carl's glance, the other man motioned for Samuel to follow him.

"Is he going to be okay?" he asked Blythe quietly.

Rubbing the back of her neck, she looked up at him.

"It's still really early to tell, but I think he's just got a lot of bruises and superficial cuts. I don't think his ribs are broken, but they may be cracked. My biggest concern is internal bleeding though. I'm going to call one of our EMT volunteers to see if they can swing over quick to give him a once-over, see if he's serious enough to take to the hospital or not."

"Thanks for helping him."

"No, thank you for bringing him here."

He glanced at Carl again, who was starting to look a little annoyed.

"Let me know if there's anything else I can do to help," he said softly before turning to follow Carl out.

Carl headed down the hall and turned in to a small office, clicking the light on before motioning for Samuel to sit. Closing the door behind them, he walked around a desk before sitting down, looking at Samuel for a moment before speaking.

"So tell me, what happened? I only heard a bit about him being jumped?"

"Yeah, about six or seven men were attacking him. I stopped them."

As he started talking, Samuel had a chance to really think about what had happened. One minute, he was fine, the next minute, he was filled with rage at the treatment of his friend. Why he felt he could stop them, in hindsight, was pretty far-fetched. But in the moment, he knew, beyond any doubt, that the men posed no threat to him. Honestly, he didn't even really remember the fight past the board breaking over his arm, only that there was pressure and movement, and then the stillness that follows a battle.

Stillness that follows a battle...? Where did that thought come from?

"So," Carl began, "you mean to tell me that you scared away six or seven men? By yourself?"

"No..." he said, steel suddenly appearing in his voice, "I said I stopped them."

Reflexively lurching back in his seat, Carl's eyes widened for a moment before regaining his composure.

"What do you mean by stopped, exactly?"

"Well, by now the ambulance should have carted them off to the emergency room to get some bones reset is my guess..."

"You actually fought with them...? And wo—"

"Listen, I've really had a rough few days. I saw someone I knew getting hurt, with a real possibility of being killed, just for being in the wrong place at the wrong time. When I saw it happening, something snapped inside. I approached them, told them to leave before they got hurt. They thought it was funny and decided a better idea was to try and jump me instead. They learned their idea was flawed. In my opinion, they got what they deserved. End of story."

Samuel watched as the other man's mouth opened and closed silently several times before he spoke again.

"So, just so I understand this correctly and that there's no misunderstanding, you saw your friend being—"

"Hank."

"Excuse me, you saw 'Hank' being jumped by several men. You told them to leave instead of trying to take them by surprise, got in a fistfight, and won?"

"Pretty much, except they'd picked up boards and pipes and stuff before they tried to attack me. Are we through here? I've had a long day already, my friend's hurt, and I'm starving again. If you don't mind me asking, when's dinner?"

"Uh... Dinner's in a, uh, half hour or, uh, so..."

"Thank you."

As he stood up and reached for the door, he turned back to Carl.

"Take good care of my friend, please."

Samuel walked out of the office, leaving Carl with his mouth hanging open.

11

Cora was beginning to suspect she got the short end of the stick after visiting her first two shelters. How those shelter workers could stand to be around so many people who either didn't bathe regularly, had some form of mental illness, were former cons, just fell on hard times, or some combination of the above she'd never be able to figure out. Some of the regulars had surprised her with their intelligence or observational skill, but they were overshadowed by the others that had invisible friends or thought the aliens were going to be coming back any day.

A few even started getting agitated when they found out she was a cop, stating they kept getting hassled by other cops. She couldn't help but wonder if Frank was having an easier go of it talking to funeral directors. While she considered the likelihood of switching jobs with Frank, her phone rang.

"Yeah? Cora speaking."

"Cora, it's Frank. There's been another alleyway incident."

"Seriously? How bad?"

"Nine guys. None of them upwardly mobile. Multiple bone fractures. Evidence this time of weapons use, but something isn't quite right about the whole scene. Unless I'm missing something, only the perps in the alley were using weapons. Their injuries are consistent with unarmed strikes as far as I can tell. None of them were in any condition to answer questions though. If this is still the work of our suspect, then my assessment of his prowess just took another significant jump. A lot of their improvised weapons show evidence of being bent or broken. How that's even possible is a little worrisome, quite honestly. If our suspect wasn't using weapons himself, then how was he breaking their weapons? I've seen kyokushin stylists break bats over arms and legs on the internet, but not bending steel pipes. It's not adding up."

"On my way. I'll be there in twenty."

"Make it ten if you can… See ya soon."

"So what's the story this time?"

Frank shook his head, "would you believe an almost carbon copy from the last one…?"

"How so?"

"Some gang-bangers were hassling a homeless guy that was scavenging in their territory. They felt they needed to tune him up for trespassing. Then our guy shows up, some words were exchanged, then this mess was left. Some uniforms are canvassing the area, but I'm gonna guess that there's no witnesses."

"You're probably righ—"

Cora and Frank turned to see a younger officer jogging up.

"Hey, we lucked out this time. Apparently one of the store owners got sick of having their fryer grease stolen, so they set up a security cam that covers a good portion of this area. I reviewed some of the footage, and you're not going to believe it. Almost looks like they were filming a movie with the moves this one guy has."

"Let's go take a look then," Frank said as he started walking in the direction the other officer came from.

"Gotcha one better. The owner burned us a copy," she said, waving a disc at them.

"Good job."

Frank turned toward Cora.

"Should we stop for some popcorn to go with this movie?"

12

"Oh. My. God!"

Cora paused the fight footage. She cast a sideways glance at Frank before she hit play again. He sat there with his mouth hanging open.

"How is that even possible?"

Frank's mouth twitched. He looked over at Cora and worked his mouth, but nothing came out. He gestured at the screen and cleared his throat.

"That's impossible…"

Cora rewound the scene, then played it again in slow motion. Although the footage was a little grainy since it wasn't a great security cam, she knew it was Samuel when he blocked the 2x4. When he swung his arm up, she could see the flash of light reflect off the metal jewelry he wore on his left arm. Where he'd learned to fight was unknown, but there was no denying he was an extremely well trained, and an incredibly tough fighter. After blocking the 2x4, you could tell that Samuel had said something to his shocked attacker. Then he'd dropped down while throwing simultaneous palm strikes at his opponent's legs, snapping both femurs at the same time. From there, it took him slightly over a minute to incapacitate the remaining eight men with similar results: broken improvised weapons and multiple broken bones.

"Did you see how that piece of pipe bent around his arm? How come his arm didn't break? Or move for that matter. Every time he blocked something, it was like they were hitting a wall."

"That's what scares me. One thing's clear though. He definitely has the capabilities and skills needed to have killed all those people at the warehouse, but we still can't confirm he's our guy."

Frank paused for a minute.

"What?"

Frank stared at the screen, lost in thought before he responded.

"I just had a very disturbing thought. If Samuel isn't our guy, it'd mean there's someone else out there capable of this level of destruction who took our boy out…"

"Shit… That's not a very comforting thought, but the bigger question is, why did we actually find him there? He didn't have any visible injuries. Hell, they only suspected head trauma due to being unconscious for nearly a day after they brought him to the hospital. Granted, he looks tough enough to have taken a hell of a beating… But no injuries? I don't think anyone can be that good…"

Cora trailed off as she stared at the screen. She hit the rewind button and played the video again.

"Frank, did you see that?"

"See what?"

She rewound the video again, slowing it down even more. She let it play again before she paused it.

"That."

Frank squinted at the screen, staring at it for a minute before turning back to Cora.

"What am I looking at? I don't see anything other than him dislocating that other guy's shoulder like it was dry kindling."

"Exactly!"

"Huh…? I don't follow you."

Cora rewound it again and played the fight back, frame-by-frame.

"Right there…"

"Cora, I still don't see what you're trying to show me."

"Look at how Samuel's positioned the guy…" Cora said, pointing at the screen.

"That guy's neck is laid out like a Thanksgiving turkey. If you watch our guy's hand, it's obvious he was going in for a kill-shot. It's only at the last minute right here," Cora pointed to the screen again, "that he redirected the strike to dislocate that guy's shoulder. He had him dead to rights and changed his mind, mid-strike. A strike, I might add, that was going too fast for either of us to follow at normal speed."

"Yeah! You're right. He did change the angle of his strike. Rewind the fight again."

Cora rewound the fight again, playing it back frame-by-frame again. After going through it again several times, they both sat back in their chairs.

"He gave up a killing shot every time for a crippling shot instead. Don't get me wrong, he's still a very vicious fighter, but it's obvious from this footage that our guy doesn't kill indiscriminately."

"That's what it's lookin' like, but that doesn't rule him out for the warehouse slaughter. Maybe he had a good reason, in his own mind, to turn them into greasy smears."

"I don't know... Something doesn't feel ri—"

"How about we ask him if he had a reason, after we catch him? All I know is that he was found in the middle of a slaughterhouse, and since he escaped from the hospital, he's been the cause of at least twelve people going to the ER, including the other three from yesterday. The longer he's out there, the higher the body count's getting. At this rate, he's going to have the hospital full by the end of the week."

"Yeah, you're right," she sighed, "since it's going to be several hours until we can interview those guys, let's say we get back to checking out the funeral homes and shelters. Feel like swapping for awhile."

"Nope."

Cora though she caught a slight smile on Frank's face when he said it.

Cora sat in her car, staring at a city map she'd just picked up at a nearby gas station. She put a dot where the hospital was. Then she put dots at the location of both fights. She put a dot where the warehouse was, but could tell it was well outside the radius of where the rest of the dots were.

"Where are you hiding…?"

So far, the dots covered an area roughly around five miles square. It was a lot of area to cover by herself, but she would guarantee Samuel would be found holed up somewhere in that area. The big question was, what was he doing. He wasn't acting like a fugitive. Most fugitives wouldn't be leaving a trail of bodies everywhere they went. They would have made a bee-line out of town. Instead, he was leaving behind a mess wherever he went.

"I wonder…"

Cora pulled out her smartphone and opened a search bar.

>can someone lose their memory and still be able to fight?<

Cora spend a few minutes refining and reviewing her results.

So it's possible to lose your memory, but still keep your reflexive skills. This whole time, we've been thinking that he was faking his memory loss, but what if he wasn't faking it. What if really can't remember who he is…? If I was in that situation, what would I do?

Cora started at the map, trying to get into Samuel's head. As her eyes trailed across the page, they came to a stop.

Of course, the library. He knows that he was found at a warehouse and bodies were involved, so there's a chance he might try and look it up. If that's the case, maybe he might go to the warehouse, hoping something might jog his memory. At least that's what I think I'd do in his situation.

Cora put her car in gear and headed out toward the library, following her hunch.

Cora pulled up to the front of the library and parked. Glancing up the steps, she couldn't ever remember being at this library before. Then again, she hadn't been in a library since she was in high school, so that didn't mean much.

I wonder how much longer this place can keep going, with things like the Internet and online bookstores allowing such easy access to information. Not really much reason to go to one anymore.

She got out of her car and headed up the steps. As she climbed, she examined the metal statues at the top of the stairs. Whoever had made them did an amazing job. They appeared almost lifelike. The muscles of the centurions almost looked like they were getting ready to flex at any moment, hurling the spear they were holding at some perceived threat. The chain leading down from his other hand to the seated lion looked just as real. She had to resist the temptation to see if the fur cast into the iron was as smooth as it looked.

Cora shook her head as she smiled.

Yeah, sure. The 'fur' on that iron statue is really going to be all soft and fluffy. It's really been a long, weird week so far…

Cora opened the door and headed in. For some reason, the hair on the back of her neck stood up, almost like a cold draft had blown across the skin. She shivered slightly, then adjusted the collar on her jacket before heading over to the counter.

As she approached the desk, she looked around for someone to help her, but it wasn't until she was at the desk that she noticed someone squatting down behind the counter sorting something.

"Excuse me."

The lady behind the counter jumped in surprise, rapidly standing up as she adjusted her glasses.

"I'm sorry. How may I be of assistance?" the librarian asked, smoothing out the front of her white blouse.

"Yes, I was wondering if you could help me… Ms. Renault?" she asked, glancing down at the other woman's name tag as she flashed her badge.

"I was wondering if you've seen someone here within the past day or two…"

Cora noticed a slight tightening around the other woman's eyes as she asked her question, filing the information away for later.

"I would be glad to be of assistance, Officer—"

"Detective."

"Excuse me, detective… As I was getting ready to say, I would be glad to be of assistance, but a lot of people come in and out of here all day, so I'm not sure I'd be of much help."

Cora glanced around the library, noticing security cameras located strategically around the room.

"I couldn't help but notice you have a bunch of cameras around the place… I don't suppose I'd be able to take a look a—"

"No!"

Cora's eyes opened slightly wider in a questioning look at the other woman's interruption.

"Excuse me again, Detective. What I meant to say is that those cameras are just there for show. They're not actually functional. The board thought it might help deter possible theft if our patrons thought they were being recorded… not that we have a lot of theft here to start with I might add. It also helps us get a slight discount on our insurance rates as well, I believe."

"Okay…" she said slowly, "anyway, I have a picture of the person we're looking for."

As she said that, she pulled out her smartphone and pulled up a picture of Samuel while he was lying unconscious at the hospital.

"This is a shot of him before he disappeared. We just have a few questions to ask him to clear up something he was a witness to a few days ago. We believe he's in danger, so the sooner we can find him, the better."

The librarian gave the picture a cursory glance before looking back at Cora.

"I'm sorry, detective. I can't say I've seen him before. But now that I know law enforcement is looking for him, I'll be sure to contact you if he comes in to read the latest copy of the Enquirer."

She raised one of her eyebrows, "Is there anything else I can be of assistance with, detective?"

"No, thank you," she said as she put her phone back in her pocket, "I think that'll be all for now."

Cora pulled out one of her business cards.

"If you hear anything," she began, handing the card over to the other woman, "please give us a call."

Reaching out like she was picking up a dead mouse, the librarian gingerly took the card out of Cora's hand.

"Absolutely."

As Cora started to turn around to leave, she caught a flash of movement near the back of the library. All she caught was a flash of what appeared to be a black trench coat disappearing behind some shelves.

She glanced back at the librarian again.

"Thank you again," she said before she hurried back toward the shelves where the person had disappeared. As she reached the bookcase, she cast a quick glance around the corner. She caught a flash of someone turning another corner, dressed all in black and wearing a watch cap. She rushed over to the next isle, trying to catch up with the other person. As she got to the corner, she noticed the person was only halfway down the aisle.

She picked up her pace, breaking into a jog. Before the person had a chance to reach the next turn, she reached out and grabbed their shoulder.

"Hey, I wanna talk to you," she said, spinning the other person around.

"Excuse me?" he said. "Do I know you?"

"Oh… Sorry, I thought you were someone else," she said as she examined the man standing in front of her. He was dressed exactly like Sybil was, with a neatly trimmed goatee and mustache. She was getting ready to excuse herself when she caught a flash of light from his right hand. Glancing down, she noticed a now familiar looking piece of jewelry. She reached out quickly, trying to grab his hand, but he smoothly moved his hand out of the way.

"What, may I ask, are you trying to do?" he asked, a hint of humor tinging his voice.

"That thing on your hand. Where'd you get it?" she demanded.

"Pardon me?"

"That jewelry, where'd you—"

The sound of a pile of books crashing to the ground caused her to turn her head to look behind her for a second.

"As I was saying," she said as she turned back, "where…"

The man was gone.

13

Samuel sighed. He'd already been up to the food line several times, but he was still hungry. From the feeling in his stomach, he was pretty sure he was getting ready to rupture something, so he wondered why was he still thinking about another trip through the food line.

"He's stabilized. The EMT looked him over, and other than maybe a few cracked ribs and a possible mild concussion, he should recover fine."

Samuel glanced up to see Blythe standing next to him. He absently thought about how cute she was with her blond pixie-cut hairstyle.

"I'm glad to hear that. Is he conscious yet?"

"No, we gave him a mild sedative to help him rest and start the healing process. He's probably going to need a couple days bed rest, but judging from the injuries and marks on him, it could have been much worse. Lucky for him I think, all the extra clothes he was bundled up in helped protect him from the worst of it."

"Yeah, it looked pretty bad when I stepped in."

"I know, I kinda caught a little bit of your conversation with Carl. He's still sitting in his chair with a 'deer caught in the headlights' look. How'd you beat them, anyway?"

Samuel looked down at his hands. How had he known he could beat all those guys without getting hurt? It wasn't anything he'd thought consciously. It was more of a deep-seated feeling. He never doubted he could do it, but he still couldn't remember why he knew how to fight so well. He glanced back up at Blythe, a slightly puzzled look on his face as he shrugged his shoulders.

"Honestly, I really don't know. I just felt this incredible rage build up inside me when I saw Hank getting beat on. After that, I just kinda flowed through them all, almost like an afterthought," he said as he absently ran his left hand through his hair.

"Wow! That's some serious jewelry. What are you doing here if you got something like that?"

Samuel quickly readjusted his sleeve, self-consciously trying to cover it back up.

Blythe's face started to go slightly crimson as she watched him.

"I'm sorry, that was pretty insensitive. I didn't mean for that to come out like that, though. I've just never seen anything like that before. I know a few people I cosplay with who'd give up their first-born for something like that."

Blythe eyes opened up wider for a second before reaching into her pocket.

"I'm not supposed to wear these while working, but I thought you'd appreciate it," she said, sliding something onto her fingers. When she pulled her hand away, she held the other one up, wiggling her fingers in front of him.

"See, not as cool as what you got, but I like it."

As she wiggled her fingers in front of him, Samuel examined the jewelry she'd put on. She had slipped on four rings that looked like medieval plate armor that covered the entire finger, except for the tips. Connected to the rings were finely wrought chainmail chains in a four-by-two pattern that ran up her hand and connected to a helm-mail style slave bracelet.

"That's pretty cool," he said, gesturing for her to sit down next to him. He took a deep breath before continuing.

"Honestly, I don't know where I got it from," he said, turning so he could partially hide his arm while pulling his sleeve up, "I kinda had it when woke up in the hospital yesterday with a case of amnesia. Other than my name, which I'm still not sure about, I don't remember anything about myself other than I seem to know how to fight really, really well."

Samuel slid his sleeve back down as he looked back up at Blythe. She had a downcast look on her face as she looked back up at him as well.

"That's so sad. Do the doctors think your memory'll come back on its own?"

"They couldn't say. They weren't sure what caused it in the first place, and I kinda had to, uh, leave before all the test results came back."

"You should go back. They can't keep those test results from you if they've already taken them. Maybe they'll tell you something."

"I'm not sure. I had to leave under some bad circumstances, so I'm not sure if I want to go back just yet and poke the bear."

Blythe sat back, looking like she was thinking about something before she leaned forward again.

"I know!" she said excitedly, "I get off work here in around an hour. You seem like a nice guy, so if you want, I can take you to meet some of my friends. They might be able to tell you something about your jewelry that might jog your memory."

Samuel turned the idea over in his head a few times. He didn't really have any better leads to follow right now since the jewelry store he wanted to check out would probably closed by the time he found it. Glancing back up, he noticed the cheerful look on her face slowly start to wilt.

"You know what, that sounds like a great idea. I don't have anywhere else I need to be…" he said with a smile.

Blythe's face lit back up.

"That's great. Don't go anywhere. I'll swing back by to grab you before I leave. This is going to be awesome."

Blythe got back up, practically prancing away. He noticed her stop for a second, almost as an afterthought, to pull her rings and bracelet off, sticking them back in her pocket before she bounced away toward the kitchen.

Blythe pulled up in front of an old warehouse building in the industrial section of the city. As Samuel looked around, she turned off her car. Samuel wasn't sure why, but the building seemed familiar.

"I know, it doesn't look like much, but the landlord is really nice and there's a lot of space for us to do LARPing."

"LARPing?" he asked with a raised eyebrow.

She glance over at him like he'd grown an extra eye.

"Yeah, live action role-playing? You mean you've never heard of it?" she asked before her eyes went wide again.

"I'm so sorry. I'm such an idiot. Of course you wouldn't have heard of it. You've got amnesia."

Blythe quickly got out of the car, but not before Samuel noticed her face going bright red again.

"You know, I might have amnesia," he started off as he exited the car, "but I'm not a kid, either. I'm not going to take offense at silly stuff like that. Relax."

She cast a glance out of the corner of her eye as she walked quickly to the front door.

"Oh… Uh… Okay…"

Samuel smiled to himself.

This oughta to be interesting.

As she unlocked and opened the door, Samuel could make out the sounds of metal clashing against metal and banging on wood. Blythe reached into her purse, fumbling around for something. As she fumbled, his vision rapidly adjusted to the darkness.

"I'm sorry for how dark it is in here, but the landlord makes us pay for the electricity since he gives us such a break on the rent," she said as she continued to fumble in her purse.

"I know that flashlight's in here somewhere," she whispered under her breath.

Samuel came up next to her, glancing in her purse.

"It's okay, I can see pretty well in here," he said as he reached his hand into her purse, his hand lightly brushing against her's, "but I think this is what you're looking for."

She jumped slightly at his touch before replying, "You can see in here…? I can't even hardly see my own hand in front of my face…"

Her voice trailed off as he placed the flashlight in her hand.

81

"Um… thank you," she stammered before clicking the light on and headed toward the noise.

After a few minutes of walking and stepping around pipes and miscellaneous equipment, they came to a large open space. Samuel quickly glanced around, taking in the surrounding area. He realized with a start that he was analyzing the area in case he had to fight there. Looking back toward Blythe, he looked over the group of people she was approaching. A quick mental calculation told him there were thirty people in the group in various forms of armor. As he approached them, he realized a lot of the weapons and armor were props designed to look like the real thing. The three guys who had been sparring when they'd entered had steam drifting up off them in the chill air.

"Hey Blythe, who's your friend?" one of the women called out as they got closer.

"He's a guy from the shelter I work at. He—"

"Oh, no! Blythe's brought home a stray," one of the guys who was sparring quipped, elbowing one of his partners.

"Ha, ha. Very funny Clifton," she said sarcastically.

"Damn it Blythe, you know I hate it when you call me that. It's Cliff, not Clifton."

"Oh, so sorry," she said dryly.

"She's got your number Cliff," the guy he originally nudged said, returning the gesture.

"Ha Ha. Just for that, I'm not going to go easy on you during our next bout."

"Sonofa—"

"Joe! There's ladies present!" Blythe snapped.

Everyone was quiet for a second, then one of the other women quipped, "Yeah, ya ass. There's F'n ladies present."

With that, everyone broke out laughing. From the sound of it, it was a well-worn joke.

Cliff set his longsword in a rack and strode over.

"Don't mind us, we're just a rowdy lot," he said as he extended his hand.

Samuel returned the gesture. He could feel Cliff trying to squeeze his hand hard to test him, so he squeezed a little in return.

"I'm Cliff, as you're already aware of," he said, rubbing his hand.

"Thanks. I'm Samuel. Nice to meet you."

He glanced around the room, making eye contact with everyone.

"It's nice to meet you all, actually."

"So what brings you amongst us this fine evening?" Joe said with a theatrical bow.

"Uh, Blythe, actually..." he said with a smile. Several people chuckled.

Blythe piped up, "You guys gotta see the jewelry he has. It's amazing!"

Everyone paused for a moment to look at him.

"Uh, didn't you say he was from the shelter?"

A girl slapped him in the back of the head.

"John, stop being an ass. That was pretty insensitive."

"Jeez, I didn't mean it like that. I just figured that if he was like most of the people at the shelter, he would have sold anything of worth for food or alcohol or something..."

The girl got up, making a point to shoulder John as she moved past him.

"Don't pay any attention to John. Apparently he was raised by woodland creatures, so he was never taught manners. I'm Karen by the way," she said as she approached.

"No problem, nice to meet you," he said as he shook her hand gently.

She looked back over her shoulder, "Look guys, a true gentleman. I think we should keep him around to show you louts how to act around a lady."

"When we get some ladies here, it might come in handy..." someone piped in from the back.

Karen cast a dirty look at the group before turning back to Samuel.

"So, Blythe says you have an interesting piece of jewelry... Mind if we take a look?"

"Sure, I'm hoping to get some answers about it, actually."

Karen looked at Blythe, casting her a questioning look.

"It's so sad. He lost his memory, so he doesn't know where or how he got it. I told him you guys might some ideas."

As they were talking, Samuel took off his jack and pulled up his sleeve.

"HOLY CRAP!"

John sprung up and came rushing over, elbowing Karen out of the way as he reached for Samuel's arm. Everyone else followed and jockeyed for position, trying to get a better look.

"Everyone… Back. Up. There's plenty of time for everyone to look at it, but you're going to crush the guy if you don't give him some room!" Cliff bellowed above the commotion.

Reluctantly, everyone except Cliff, Blythe, Karen, and John slowly wandered back to where they were sitting, casting quick glances over their shoulders. John tentatively reached toward Samuel's hand again before pausing.

"May I?"

Samuel held out his arm as he nodded.

"Damn! Look at the detail on this thing. If it wasn't metal, I'd swear it was alive at one point. Look at the realism of those scales."

"And look at the level of articulation," Karen said while pointing at several joints, "I can't even see where the pivot points are. Whoever made this was a master. I'd love to meet 'em some time."

She looked over at John.

"Could you imagine if we could get some of their pieces in our bookstore? People would go crazy. I doubt if very many could afford craftsmanship of this level, but even if we just had it as a showpiece, it'd be the focal point of the entire store."

"Damn straight."

Karen looked back at Samuel.

"I don't suppose you'd mind taking it off so we could take a look at the underside of it?" she asked hopefully.

"Heh, about that, I haven't been able to figure out how to remove it, actually. That's part of the mystery."

"Really…?" they both said at the same time, "you have no idea how to take it off?"

"Yeah… Like Blythe was saying, I really don't remember how I got it. I honestly don't remember anything before a couple days ago. So how I got this, or who I am actually, is one big mystery. The only reason I know my name is because someone told me what it was."

"Man, that's gotta suck…"

"Yeah, it does," Samuel said as Karen cast John another dirty look.

"What?" John asked.

"Nothing," Karen replied.

The two of them spent the next ten minutes examining the jewelry, trying to figure out who might have made it and how to remove it. Finally, Cliff said.

"Okay you two, enough gawking over it. Let everyone else get a chance to look at it."

"Fine… fine," he said, waving his hands toward Cliff in a placating gesture before turning back to Samuel.

"If you don't mind though, I'd like to look at this again after I'm done getting my ass handed to me. I wanna take some notes down. Something about that jewelry looks vaguely familiar. I wanna see if I can figure out where I've seen it from. Might give us an idea where you might've gotten it from and maybe even who made it."

As he started to turn away again, he spun back while reaching into his pocket.

"Oh! I'm such an idiot. Hold your arm out again," he said as he pulled something out of his pocket.

Samuel held his arm out again as John pulled out his cell phone and snapped a few pics.

Cliff glanced at the group before he pointed at Blythe.

"Blythe, you're up!"

"Aw, do I have to?"

"You know the rules. If you're going to be here, you need to spar. You managed to skip out last time we got together."

Blythe glanced back at Samuel before reluctantly getting up and heading over to the weapons rack. She glanced at the arrayed weaponry before grabbing a nondescript rapier off the rack along with fencing gear. Turning around, she headed toward the sparring area.

Cliff turned toward the group and gestured.

"Karen, you're up as well."

Samuel watched as Karen hopped up and quickly retrieved an Epee and fencing gear before moving to the other end of the sparring area. After taking their places, Cliff stepped toward the middle of the sparring area. As Samuel watched, he noticed that while Karen aggressively swung her sword through the air to limber up and test the balance of the sword, Blythe appeared reluctant to use hers.

After getting in position, Cliff nodded to both women.

"Are you ready?

After waiting for an acknowledging nod from both women, he stepped back to the edge of the sparring area.

"Salute!"

At the command, both women raised their blades in front of them before dropping them down to point at the floor.

"FIGHT!"

At the command, Karen lunged forward, attempting to stab Blythe in the chest. At the last instant, Blythe swung her blade across her body, point down, while twisting so her left shoulder drifted back. Sliding her left foot back to continue her counter-clockwise turn, she lightly deflected the epee, causing it to barely miss her as she performed a molinello on her left side. As she rotated the blade, she angled the cutting edge so it would cause a slice across her opponent's neck, but just before it touched, Blythe pulled the strike and stepped back into an upper guard position.

The speed and precision that Blythe had performed the block and counter-attack was fast enough that Samuel doubted anyone else had noticed that Blythe had actually won the pass. Leaping back, Karen brought the point on target again and stabbed out. Samuel noticed that Blythe instinctively swung her blade around to deflect again, but then pulled back enough to allow Karen to score a point.

"Point! Karen one, Blythe Zero."

Both women stepped back to their starting positions before clashing again. Again Samuel noticed that Blythe could have easily won the clash, but instead allowed her opponent to just barely win the clash. As far as Samuel could tell, Blythe should have easily been able to dominate the fight, but instead chose to allow the other woman to win. After the final point was scored, both women saluted each other and removed their helmets.

"You almost had me a few times."

"Yeah, but you're so good with that epee. I just can't seem to keep up with it."

As Blythe gestured at the other woman's blade, Cliff walked over.

"Blythe, I keep telling you, you need to be more aggressive. If you had pushed your attacks harder, you might have been able to score against Karen this time. Once we're done here, I'll give you a few exercises that should help."

"Okay..."

As Blythe walked back toward him, Cliff looked around again.

"John, you're up next..."

"Who am I sparring against?"

Cliff thrust his thumb against his chest.

"Me," he said with a smirk.

"Aw crap. Can you at least try and take it easy this time? The last sparring session we had left bruises for almost a week."

"Well, that's to help motivate you to get your guard up faster," Cliff said with a good-natured smirk.

"Fine, fine," he mumbled as he turned back to me.

"Thanks. Wish me luck..." he said as he slowly walked to the sparring area.

"This should be entertaining..." Blythe whispered in Samuel's ear.

Cliff and John slid their padded helmets down over their faces.

"Ready?" Cliff asked.

John's only reply was a feeble nod.

"En Garde!"

Samuel sat mesmerized. Even though he couldn't remember any of it, he KNEW he knew how to use a sword. He could spot opening and feints and felt he could easily hold his own against either of them. The fact that, during his hallucination, he'd somehow pulled a longsword out of his jewelry was another reason he thought he might be familiar with swordplay.

"Want to try your hand at it?" Joe asked, catching him off guard.

"Who, me?"

Joe smiled as he replied, "sure. I've been watching you over here and noticed you were imitating some of the techniques they were using up there. You're more than welcome to give it a shot. We promise to take it easy on you."

"Uh, okay… sure," he said as he got up.

As Joe led him over to the sparring area, Samuel said, "for some reason, I think I might know something about sword-fighting. I can't say I really remember anything, but something about it just feels really familiar…"

As he trailed off, he spotted a long sword that resembled the sword he pulled out of the dragon's mouth on his wrist. He walked over and picked it up, examining it and checking its heft.

"Ah, the gentleman knight's best friend, the longsword. That metal practice one might be a little heavy for you if you've never used one before, but we do have some wooden replicas, along with some shorter swords as well…"

He trailed off as Samuel started experimentally swinging the sword around. As he moved, he just immersing himself in the flow of movement that somehow felt right. He lost track of time as he flowed through different combinations before finally coming to a stop in a defensive position. Letting out a deep breath, he turned around to face everyone.

Everyone had varying levels of shock on their face. He suddenly felt self-conscious as he looked back at them.

"Did I, uh, do something wrong?"

Everyone jumped slightly at the sound of his voice before Blythe responded.

"Dude, that was awesome. And beautiful as well. You just started swinging that sword around through forms that I've never seen before. I couldn't even follow half the stuff you were doing. You've been going at it for like, five minutes or so…"

Samuel tried to recall exactly what he'd done for the past five minutes, but all he could remember was feeling like the sword was a part of him as he moved. Feeling slightly embarrassed, he started to put the sword back down.

"Oh HELL NO!" Cliff said, causing Samuel to freeze, snapping his attention over to him.

"If you think you're going to get out of sparring with me after that little impromptu demonstration, you're nuts. From what I just saw, you're years ahead of anyone else here except for maybe Joe there."

"Damn straight! From what I just saw, I'm not even sure I could hold my own against you, and I've been doing this for over ten years," Joe added.

Samuel was loath to put the sword down, but was concerned as well that he couldn't remember the display he'd just done. What if he forgot himself and hurt one of them.

"Any time now, or are you just chicken?"

Samuel glanced back up at Cliff. From his expression, Samuel could tell that he was just doing some good-natured ribbing, but Samuel was still hesitant.

"I promise not to hurt you…" Cliff replied again sarcastically.

Samuel felt a pinprick of anger well up inside himself.

"Fine. I promise I'll try not to hurt you either," he replied with a slight edge in his voice.

Cliff took a slight step back, his eyes going wide slightly before recovering.

"Get him suited up Joe. Let's see what he's got."

Samuel started having second thoughts as he adjusted his stance in the sparring ring. Against both Cliff's and Joe's insistence, the only padding he'd agreed to put on was the chest padding and the helmet. Everything else felt too bulky and restricting to him. He glanced at Cliff and noted three different openings in his defense, but wasn't sure yet if they were intentional… Or feints.

"Last chance… You sure you don't want to wear any of the arm or leg protection?"

"I'm good. I take full responsibility if I get hurt."

"Don't say we didn't warn you…"

Samuel adjusted his feet again, resting on the balls of his feet. Bringing the sword up, he waved Cliff over with a come-here gesture.

"Whenever you're ready…" he said, smirking at Cliff.

"Fine! En Garde!" he snapped, lunging forward with a quick horizontal slash at Samuel's left side.

Samuel instinctively swung his sword vertically to the left, performing a point-up inside deflection. Continuing to move, Samuel started to turn clockwise as he reached his left arm over the locked blades, grabbing Cliff by the wrist nearest the crossguard. Pushing slightly upward and outward with his left hand, he slid his blade under and across, slashing Cliff across the stomach. Continuing the motion, he flourished the blade before bringing it forward, pretending to pommel strike him in the head before doing a front stomp kick to Cliff's chest, causing the other man to stumble backward several feet.

Everyone held their breath while their eyes bounced back and forth between the two combatants.

"Uh… touché?"

Everyone burst out with applause and cheers.

"Wow. I've never seen Cliff get bested that easily before!"

The chatter went on for a few seconds before Cliff snapped, "I was just taking it easy on him. Let's see how he does when I'm serious."

This time, Cliff approached more carefully, doing feints and tentative attacks, in an effort to determine Samuel's defenses and reflexes. As they jockeyed back and forth, Samuel started to loosen up and enjoy himself. Cliff hadn't offered really any sort of challenge, so Samuel wasn't in any hurry to counterattack just yet. He wanted to just soak in the feeling of moving smoothly, sword in hand, while defending himself from attacks that weren't really a threat.

After several minutes of having all his attacks rebuffed, Cliff stepped back out of range, letting his guard drop slightly. Samuel noticed that Cliff was gulping in huge draughts of air while he himself didn't even feel slightly winded yet. He was still surprised to find that he was in such good shape, even though he'd been able to jog nearly twenty minutes carrying Hank to get help.

Without warning, Cliff let out a yell while surging toward him, wildly swinging his sword in aggressive arcs and jabs, the air whistling as it cut through the air. Without thinking, Samuel responded, dodging, deflecting, and blocking all of the sword-strokes Cliff was launching at him.

After one aggressive flurry, Samuel realized he had gotten careless, letting his sword get out of position, moving it to the right while the attack was coming at his left side again. He knew there wasn't enough time to reverse the momentum of the sword and get it into position to block the strike without compromising his balance. Doing so would leave him open to another riposte. Instinctively, he snapped his body clockwise to the right while pulling his right arm in, accelerating his sword in another flat arc, rotating his wrist to turn the blade in a counter-clockwise motion while his arm continued to whip the blade to the right. Turning his arm over, he whipped the blade up behind his back vertically, the tip pointing toward the ceiling as he dropped down to one knee.

The blades clashed, throwing off sparks before Cliff reared back again for a powerful overhead strike. Samuel reversed the grip on his sword while he swung his left arm up, arresting the descent of his opponent's blade by clashing just above the crossguard while his body spun back around in a counter-clockwise motion, bringing the pommel of his sword up on the outside of Cliff's wrist. Yanking back and downward forcefully, he stripped the sword out of Cliff's hands while he swung his right foot around, sliding it behind Cliff's leading foot. Shifting his weight, he slammed his shoulder into Cliff's chest, causing him to fall backward. As both Cliff and his sword started to drop to the floor, Samuel's left hand blurred, grabbing the sword in a reverse grip. As Cliff landed on his back, Samuel sprung skyward while executing an inverted X-block, landing with his feet on either side of Cliff's chest before dropping forward. His knees pinned the other man's shoulders while pressing the edges of both blades on either side of Cliff's neck. He slid the crossguards together, locking Cliff's neck between them, the edge of both blades intersecting across his throat and pinning his head to the floor.

"I yield! I yield!" Cliff yelled.

Samuel rocked back on his feet and sprung up and glided back a few steps while casually flipping both blades around so they were both pointing upward in his hands. Everyone in the room was hushed, afraid to break the tension that was almost a physical presence rolling off Samuel in waves. After a few seconds, he shifted the sword from his right hand over to his left and stepped forward again, holding his hand out. Cliff glanced at it, then glanced at Samuel's face. With a slight nod, Samuel continued to hold his hand out to Cliff. The tension drained out of Samuel's face and shoulders as Cliff swung his hand up, grasping Samuel's hand in a tight grip before Samuel effortlessly pulled him to his feet. Meeting his eyes again, Samuel nodded to the other man before breaking into a smile.

"That… was fun."

Everyone noisily let out their collectively held breath.

"Man, I'm so sorry. I didn't mean to attack you in anger like that. Honestly, I've never gone up against someone with your skill level before and it was so damn frustrating. I haven't been manhandled that badly in a sword-fight since I first started training. If it wasn't for your unbelievable skill with a blade, I probably would've seriously hurt you back there. I know I acted like a rank amateur, letting my emotions get the better of me. I really screwed up, but I hope you'll accept my apology," he asked as he held his hand out.

Samuel reached out and gripped the other man's hand again. Giving it a vigorous shake, he replied, "Hey, no harm, no foul. I'd also like to apologize if I hurt you with my riposte."

Letting Samuel's hand go, he rubbed his butt.

"Other than a sore ass and a severely bruised ego, I think I'll live," he said as he broke into a smile as well.

"That was one hell of a fight though…" he said as Samuel handed his sword back.

"Sure was," Samuel replied as he draped his arm across Cliff's shoulders as they turned back toward the rest of the group.

As everyone rushed over to congratulate them on the fight, Cliff looked back over at Samuel.

"Honestly dude, when you finally get your memory back, you've gotta introduce me to your instructor. You were doing stuff I've never even seen before. I'm not even sure how to defend against half of it."

"Are you okay? Did he hurt you at all?" Blythe asked, examining Samuel all over for injuries. It might have been his imagination, but he felt she was examining him a lot more thoroughly than expected.

"Yeah, I'm fine. It was really fun, actually. I just wish it'd helped my memory come back."

Joe came up and kept looking back and forth between him and Cliff, his mouth hanging open.

"Holy shit! That was amazing. I've never seen anyone move like you do Samuel. You seemed to know where Cliff was going to strike before even he knew. In all the years we've been sparring against each other, and even against some of the other people who come to his gym, I've never seen anyone fight Cliff to a standstill, let alone beat him. I don't think I saw him get past your guard even once. I'd love to spar you, but I don't think it'd even be a challenge…"

Joe got quiet for a second.

"I know… How about you spar against both me AND Cliff. I bet you'd still be able to beat the two of us without breaking a sweat, but I'd just love to see you in action like that, assuming you're willing…" he said, a hopeful look on his face.

Nodding at Joe, he replied, "Well, assuming Cliff's interested in it as well," he said, casting a glance at the other man and getting a slight nod in return, "then I don't see why not. Even though I can't remember how I learned how to use a sword, I'd love to try and figure out what my limits are. Who knows, maybe the challenge of fighting two skilled opponents might help me remember something."

Joe let out a whoop as he jumped in the air. Samuel chuckled under his breath at Joe's antics. Out of the corner of his eye, he saw John moving toward him with a purposeful stride.

"Did that jewelry get damaged from blocking that strike?" he asked as he got close enough to be heard over the rest of the crowd.

"I don't think so," Samuel replied as he glanced down at it. "It's taken quite a few hits before without any visible damage."

"Can I take a quick look at it to be sure?"

"Uh, okay," he replied as he held his arm out.

"Remarkable. There isn't a ding or scratch on it. What the heck is this thing made out of? Even high carbon steel should have shown some type of surface damage, blocking that heavy of a blow."

Karen came over while John continued to examine it for any signs of damage.

"You know, the way you used that thing, I'm not entirely sure it's just supposed to be a piece of jewelry. I think that thing might be a fully functional vambrace, or at least that's how you're using it. If skippy here is right about there not being any damage, that would indirectly reinforce that possibility as well. You swung it up to block that sword strike with such practiced ease that I suspect it's been used in that role too many times to count. That was completely unconscious reflex action there."

She glanced back down at the vambrace again. A slightly puzzled look came over her face.

"Hey John?"

"Yeah?"

"Weren't those gemstones in the eyes an almost cobalt blue when we looked at it earlier?"

"Yeah, why do you a—" he said as he looked at the eyes again. "What the…?"

"Could it be the lighting?" she asked, turning his hand back and forth.

"Maybe. Without knowing what kind of gemstones they actually are, it's hard to tell if it's a natural effect."

"Huh?" Samuel asked.

Karen looked up at him, pointing to the eyes on the dragon's face.

"When we first examined those gemstones, they were almost a dark sapphire blue. Now they seem to be approaching almost aquamarine in color. Just very odd is all."

"But that is a mystery for another day. Let's celebrate the fine battle we just witnessed!" Joe said, still bouncing around in excitement.

The three of them looked at each other before nodding, walking back toward the rest of the crowd.

15

Cora drove around the city aimlessly, going over what had happened at the library in her head. She knew that the librarian was hiding something, but what was she hiding exactly? She felt sure that the librarian had recognized the picture of Samuel, but was she protecting him, or was she just one of those people who felt strongly about not helping law enforcement? It was hard to tell with how tight-lipped she'd been during the conversation.

And what about that guy she had talked to? As far as she could tell, he was dressed nearly identical to Sybil. Plus he'd had the ability to vanish the same way. Were they following her, or was the library an important location for them and she just happened to stumble upon it? She pulled over and turned the car off before pulling out her map, going over the different locations again. As she studied it, she realized that the library was nearly at the center of the city. So it was slightly more likely that it was the location, and not her being followed, that accounted for that guy being there.

As she sat there, her driver side door swung open unexpectedly. Before she had a chance to react, a hand slid down the left side of her body, yanking her gun out of its cross-draw holster. Trying to grab the hand that took her gun, she got stuck in her seatbelt. She heard a slight tap on the roof of her car before the passenger door swung open. Spinning her head back, she came face-to-face with her own gun pointed at her face.

"Go ahead and close your door and get situated."

Cora moved very slowly and deliberately, closing the driver side door before getting adjusted behind the wheel. She started to glance to her right, but the barrel of the gun flicked.

"Hey, no peeking just yet. Let's just go for a nice little drive instead, shall we?" the voice said.

Cora started the car and gently pulled into traffic. As she merged in, she asked, "Where are we going?"

"Oh, no place in particular detective Blanchett. Oh, and don't worry, I'm not going to shoot you. That was just to get your attention before you tried something stupid. I'm just here to offer my suggestion a little more, how shall I phrase it, forcefully than I did last time," the voice said as she lowered the barrel of the gun.

"YOU!" Cora exclaimed, her face hardening into a mask as she started grinding her teeth.

"Oh, there's no need for all that. Now while I don't particularly care, and your dentist will absolutely love to bill you for it, the only one who's going to suffer is you if you keep grinding them like that. Now where was I? Oh yes, your continued insistence on trying to track down Samuel. You're sorely ill-equipped to deal with him or anyone who might be after him. If I was able to get the drop on you so easily, you don't stand a chance against any of the others."

"How about I pull this car over and I show you how capable I am of handling you."

Sybil's voice sounded like fine crystal as she laughed.

"Oh detective Blanchett, if there was time, I would take you up on that offer. I honestly find your bravado very refreshing. But there's something coming that our group needs to deal with and we can't have you interfering with us. A lot of people are going to die if we can't correct it quickly, and Samuel is the key to it all."

Cora risked a glance over at Sybil. She noticed she was holding her gun casually in her right hand. More importantly, she wasn't wearing her seatbelt. The other woman continued talking, apparently unaware that Cora had glanced at her.

"Once this crisis is over, I might pay you a visit again and maybe, just maybe, fill you in on some of the things that go bump in the night that your kind are so blissfully unaware of."

"Our kind?" she asked, a puzzled look on her face.

"Oops, I do believe I've said too much, I'm afraid. Be that as it may, please listen to me this time when I tell you to stop looking into this matter. Otherwise, I can't be held responsible for what might happen to you."

While Sybil had been talking, Cora had gradually been speeding up. Looking over at the woman, she asked, "is that a threat?"

"Oh no dear, that's actually what one would usually consider a warning. A threat would imply an outcome our group would possibly enforce. A warning indicates a probable outcome that has nothing to do with us."

Cora looked over at Sybil. As she stared, she saw out of the corner of her eye the on-ramp to the expressway, including the barrels of water lined up to help slow vehicles that missed the ramp entrance. Taking a deep breath, she stomped the gas pedal.

"I don't take kindly to threats OR warnings," she snarled, pulling her seatbelt tight just before the impact.

"Seriously detective?"

She vaguely felt the impact. Instead, she heard a loud explosion and then blackness. She came to, the airbag pressing against her face as she struggled to maintain consciousness, willing herself to recover faster than Sybil. For some reason, she was having difficulty moving. With a start, she realized she was having problems breathing as well. As she fought to recover, she heard the other woman talking from a distance.

"My poor dear… That was really uncalled for. I was getting ready to leave anyway, but your gesture as to how far you're willing to go hasn't gone unnoticed. I suspect that I'll be seeing you again soon, regardless of anything I say to you."

Cora heard the sound of tearing metal and snapping plastic before she felt the woman's hands on her face and neck. It felt like she was doing a quick check to make sure she was okay. Then she felt the other woman's hands on both sides of her face. A feeling of warmth spread out from her hands, soothing the cuts and scrapes she had sustained in the accident. The warmth built up to a scalding intensity in her neck before fading away, flowing through the rest of her body. The splitting headache she had started to subside. Without warning, she reflexively sucked in a huge gasp of air.

"That should hold you until the paramedics can get here, my dear. Ta ta for now."

Sybil touched the side of her face again.

"Sleep..."

Suddenly, an overpowering wave of exhausting rolled over her. She fought hard against it, but she could feel herself losing the battle this time. As she started to drift off, her head rolled to the right. She heard the screech of tortured metal again as she watched the other woman force the passenger door open. It reminded her of the sound the jaws of life made when tearing into a vehicle. She blacked out for a second before her door was ripped open to the same deafening screech of metal being force beyond its capabilities. Then the noise was gone, leaving her in silence. As the blackness finally overtook her, her eyes focused on two things that left her puzzled. One was her gun neatly disassembled and unloaded on her passenger seat. What was more baffling was the left hand print that was embedded almost an inch deep into the dashboard.

16

The next thing Cora became aware of was the steady beep of something to her left. As she struggled to make sense of it, she tried to reach for the sound to make it stop. Moving her arm caused a spasm to travel up her arm, leaving a trail of fire in its wake. Becoming more fully aware, she realized her whole body ached. The sudden return of pain caused her to groan.

"Cora? Cora, can you hear me?" she heard the voice and knew it was familiar, but she was having trouble thinking. She distantly heard the voice yelling in the distance.

"Nurse! Get the doctor, I think she's starting to come to."

She felt someone grip her hand gently.

"Cora, just lie still, the doctor's on his way."

Cora tried to make sense of that. Doctor? Why was a doctor coming for her? What was going on? Why did she hurt so much?

Suddenly, the accident snapped into focus in her mind's eye. The pain… the confusion… her difficulty breathing… and that woman. Sybil had been in the car with her and was the entire reason she risked crashing her car. A car accident… She'd been in a car accident. That's why she was in so much pain, and why a doctor was coming. She struggled to open her eyes to see who was talking to her.

"…Frank?" she croaked out. Her throat felt like she'd been crossing a desert for the past week.

"Shhhh. Just relax. You're lucky to be alive."

"Water...?" she croaked out hopefully, closing her eyes as the effort to hold them open became too much.

She felt a straw touch her lips. She weakly sucked on the straw, cold water dribbling as much down her throat as it was down the front of her chin. Trying again, she was able to get a much larger swallow of water down her throat, easing the scratchiness. As she continued to sip, she felt her strength starting to return. She let go of the straw before opening her eyes again.

"How long have I been out?" she asked, her voice slowly becoming stronger. She looked up at Frank as she asked, seeing the concern etched on his face.

"They brought you in about four hours ago," he said softly, "from all the damage your clothes and your car sustained, they thought you were in critical condition. It wasn't until they cut you out of your clothes that they could tell that you were practically unscathed. They were at a loss to explain where all the blood came from, though. They're saying you're lucky to be—"

He paused as he heard someone clear their throat behind him.

Dr. Greene stood in the doorway, visually examining her before approaching the bed.

"Ah... Ms. Blanchett, so good to see you conscious again. How are you feeling?"

"Like I've been gargling sand while crawling across an electric fence."

"Well, now. I quite expected you to be doing much worse, truthfully. You gave us all a fright when you came in earlier, but it looks like you might actually be able to leave as early as tomorrow. Honestly, we're just keeping you overnight for observation and make sure you get rehydrated. I must advise you though, once you get out of here, remember to drink more fluids. With as dehydrated as you were, I'm not surprised you passed out and crashed. You're lucky to be alive."

Cora laid quietly while the doctor gave her a quick examination. She responded quietly when he asked the standard questions, like if that hurt, or could she feel this poke or prod. Finally, he stepped back away from her, scratching a few notes on her chart before looking back at her.

"Everything seems to be in working order still. I'm frankly still amazed at how well you're doing. I've seen people pulled out of minor fender-benders have worse injuries than you. You must have had a guardian angel riding shotgun tonight. Anyway, we should have the rest of the results back shortly. Try and get some rest if you can."

Frank glanced at her when she involuntarily clenched his hand at the mentioned of a guardian angel.

Dr. Greene turned around and headed toward the door. Before he left, he paused and turned back toward her.

"Do you need anything more for the pain?"

Cora though about it for a moment. She realized that, other than the initial pain she had upon waking up, she didn't hurt anywhere.

"No. Thank you. I think I'll be fine for now."

"Really...?" he trailed off. Turning around, he headed out the door while mumbling to himself.

"Remarkable..."

Cora watched Frank stare at the door before getting up. He walked over to the door, looked both ways, then shut it behind him as he came back over to the bedside.

"Okay, spill it. What the hell happened out there?"

"Huh?" she asked, confusion spreading across her face.

"The good doctor there might believe you passed out at the wheel, but I'm not buying it. I was only a few blocks away when the call came in, so I was the first one on the scene. Your car looked like it was ripped open by the hulk or something. I could actually make out the hand prints on the driver side door where someone had grabbed the door and pulled it back like a sardine can while pressing their other hand against the side for leverage. I also saw your gun sitting neatly disassembled on the passenger seat and another hand print crushed into the dashboard. It looked like a bomb had gone off in there with all the damage, so don't give me a 'Huh?' when I ask what happened. So talk."

Cora was taken aback by the anger tinging his voice as he spoke. In all the years he'd been her partner, she'd never heard that level of concern or anger in his voice, especially directed at her. Taking a deep breath, she tried to put the events in order.

"It was her again. She was in the car with me. She'd gotten the drop on me and was holding me at gunpoint, with my own gun."

Frank dropped down heavily into the chair as she continued.

"How did she get your gun away from you? Where were you?"

"That's just it. I was sitting in my car. Frank, she moves like he does, possibly faster. I had pulled off the road to look at a map I've been plotting everything on. The next thing I knew, the car door had been yanked open and my piece pulled out of its holster. By the time I had turned my head to the left, she was already in the passenger seat with the gun pointed at my face. I heard a slight tap on the roof, so I'm pretty sure she somehow jumped over the car..."

Cora took another sip of water before continuing.

"She started telling me again about how outclassed we were and basically threatened me this time if I didn't back off. She also mentioned something bad happening soon, something that Samuel was a key part of. That's about when I rammed the barrels, hoping it'd either kill or at least incapacitate her enough to arrest. Apparently it didn't turn out so well. The last thing I remember before passing out was being unable to breath, her touching the sided of my face, a burning sensation in my neck, then her telling me to sleep. I vaguely remember seeing my gun and the hand print, but I thought it was just a dream. Next thing I know, I'm waking up here."

As she finished her story, she glanced over at Frank. He had a really weird expression on his face, but she was at a loss to understand why.

"What's that look for...?"

"Cora, don't take this the wrong way, but let me ask you a question... Have you ever broken your neck or back in the past?"

Cora looked at him like he'd grown an extra ear.

"Why on earth would you ask me such a bizarre question? Of course I've never broken my neck. Do you think I'd be standing," she paused to look down at herself, "Okay, laying here if I'd broken my neck sometime in the past? If I'd had, I'd be sucking food through a straw right now. Why?"

Frank rubbed the back of his neck before responding.

"That's kinda what I thought, but I didn't want to say anything to the doctors until I had a chance to talk to you first. The crime scene techs stated there was a catastrophic failure of the seatbelt locking mechanism, along with a delayed deployment of the airbags. From the evidence they've collected, you had been snapped forward at the waist, which should have dislocated the L4 and L5 vertebrae. As you whipped forward, your neck was slammed against the steering wheel, deforming it by at least five inches. You can actually see the shape of your neck bent into it. That impact should have shattered your C3-C5 vertebrae and crushed your windpipe."

"Instead, everything is fine. The odd thing is, the X-rays show that those same areas appear to have sustained extensive damage in the past. The doctor is guessing, based on the level of fusion, that it happened around six to ten years ago. He's at a loss as to how those vertebrae fused back together so perfectly. As far as he could tell, those vertebrae were shattered into chunks the size of marbles at one point, but there's no signs of pins or surgical fusion to account for the repairs and healing. There's even less explanation as to how they were able to hold together after the significant trauma you exerted on them again today during the accident. So my question to you is, if you never broke your neck or back, then how do you account for injuries that appear to have been healed nearly a decade ago?"

"I… I can't. Or at least I can't explain it without getting myself locked up for a seventy-two hour psych hold. The only thing I can come up with, no matter how implausible, is that Sybil somehow healed me. As for the rest of it, I'm at a complete loss."

"That's about what I suspected. It's why I told the Chief that we wanted off this case. It's just getting too dangerous, and after your accident tonight, he agreed."

Frank paused to take a deep breath.

"As of right now, we're officially off this nightmare."

17

"LIKE HELL WE ARE!" she yelled, bolting up in bed before vertigo forced her to flop back, the throbbing behind her eyes from the sudden movement accentuating the point.

"Yes, we are. Even though your body doesn't bear out the evidence, you should have died tonight. There's no other way to look at it. It's either lottery-winning level of luck, cosmic intervention, or some other form of miracle that you're still able to suck air, let alone being able to get up under your own power without any injuries to show for it."

"Well, you can tuck tail and run, but I'm not giving up on this case. Even if I have to work it in my off-time, or do the Hollywood cop cliché of taking vacation days to investigate, I'm not going to stop. I'm so—"

"Damn it Cora! I lost way too many friends fighting over there. I'll be damned if I'm going to lose another one right here if I can help it!"

Cora stared at Frank. She was at a loss for words. Before she could open her mouth, she saw him wipe a tear away.

"Cora," he said in a softer tone, "I care for you. A lot. It's kinda scary, actually. The thought of you getting killed trying to find this Samuel guy is more than I can take. For the first time in a long time, when I saw you unconscious in a nearly shredded car, I was at a complete loss for what to do. I don't like that feeling. I've spent a long time, and a lot of effort, trying to build up routines that'll let me have some semblance of order no matter how hairy the situation becomes."

Frank paused as he raggedly sucked in a breath.

"This case though… This case is so far outside of anything that makes sense, I feel like I'm trying to swim through quicksand. No matter how hard I struggle, I just feel like I'm sinking deeper and deeper into a mess that I'm not going to be able to survive. And, by all rights, you didn't survive tonight. But something intervened and brought you back to me. I'm not going to let that gift be in vain. So yeah, we're off the case. If you want to continue chasing it down, then you're going to have to do it without me. I'll put in a request for a new partner if I have to, but I done with this. You should think strongly about leaving it alone as well. I'm sorry if you feel like I'm letting you down, but I've hit my limit."

Cora stared at him as he got up and walked out of the room, closing the door softly behind him. If he'd looked back, he would have seen the tears that started streaming down her face as well.

As she thought about it, Cora got angry.

How dare he do this to me? Behind my back even! He did it without even asking me! For that matter, where does he get off trying to guilt me into dropping this case?

She stewed for a bit before buzzing the nurse. A few minutes later, a nurse came in.

"What can I get for you? Do you need something for pain?"

"No, I'm good. What I'd really like is a notebook and a pen if you have one?"

"Sure, no problem. I'll be back shortly."

As she waited, she alternated between being pissed at Frank, going over in her head everything they'd learned, and everything that'd happened to them over the past few days. One thing she was sure of now was, the library was important. It was no coincidence that, shortly after her visit and run-in with that guy, Sybil should pop up and hop in her car. Her thoughts were interrupted by the nurse coming back into the room.

"Here you go miss. Is there anything else I can get for you?"

Cora could tell that the nurse was either stressed out from work or was just annoyed with her for bothering her for such a simple request, but she really wasn't in the mood to apologize, not after her blow up with Frank.

"No thanks. This'll be perfect. Thanks again."

"No problem. You already know how to use the call button, so if you need anything else, don't hesitate to buzz me."

Cora nodded, already lost in thought as the nurse left the room. She started scribbling out notes of what she already knew. Then she scribbled out what she suspected. Her third list was for questions she didn't have answers for. That list took significantly longer. When she was done with it, it was a lot more confusing than the previous two. The final list was a time-line with locations for all the events leading up to tonight.

She tore the pages out and spread them out over the little table she managed to pull over from the side of the bed. Looking them over, she started to scribble out more notes.

"Why is the warehouse so far outside the area of where everything else happened?"

There just wasn't enough info to work from. A majority of what she had was from the inferred movements of Samuel, so she wasn't sure how much weight to give them compared to the overall picture.

"Damn it… I need my map. I know I'm missing something, but what?"

She could feel herself getting tired again as she struggled to keep her eyes open. Stifling a yawn, she looked back at her lists. She kept tapping on the library. Every time she came back to it, the library seemed to become more central to everything that was going on. She had nothing to base the feeling on, but somehow it just felt right. Another yawn forced its way out, nearly bringing tears from the intensity of it. Rubbing her eyes, she started to write another list of things she needed to check out once she was discharged from the hospital, regardless of Frank's threat. The primary thing was to go stake out the library. Maybe she'd get lucky and spot one of her suspects there. Then she'd be able to either call for backup or possibly even get a warrant to investigate the premises.

She kept going over her notes as her eyes started to droop. She tried to follow her hazy thoughts, to make more connections, but against her will, she drifted off to sleep again.

Cora woke with a start. It took her a minute to identify what had woken her. Glancing to her left, she found Frank sitting in the chair, shuffling through the small stack of notes she had compiled before she passed out. She sat there without speaking, watching him flip back and forth through the papers, his furrowed brow the only indication of how hard he was concentrating. She tried to repress a smile when she noticed he had gotten out his own notebook, comparing his notes to the ones she had made, glancing back and forth between the two sets. Occasionally, he'd shake his head and either jot something else down in his notes, cross something out, or add to the notes Cora had written down earlier. His sudden voice startled her as he glanced up at her.

"I guess it's safe to assume that, based off all these notes you wrote down, my threat of getting a new partner didn't change your mind about continuing to work this case. Since you're going to be so pig-headed about it, I guess I'll come along for the ride and watch your six. I haven't ever abandoned a partner before, so I guess it'd be kinda stupid to start now. So tell me, oh seeker of the hidden mysteries, what exactly do you plan to do once you get out of here?"

Cora tried her best to hide her smile, but it suddenly hit her how much she really wanted Frank to be with her on this case. She realized that, in hindsight, she might not have been able to continue following this case if she didn't have Frank protecting her back. There wasn't anyone else in the squad she trusted more than him. Meeting his stare, she gave a slight nod.

"I think the first thing is to do a little more digging into that library for starters. There just something off about it, but I can't put my finger on it other than the guy I cornered there. He pulled the same stunts as Sybil. I also don't think it's a coincidence that Sybil found me so soon after my visit, so at the very least, they probably know each other. Either that or the level of luck going on makes me think I should get a lottery ticket or something."

"Yeah, but I think you mighta used up all that luck surviving your crash, so I think the lottery ticket'll be a wash."

Cora chuckled before continuing.

"You're probably right. Anyway, I also think we should go back to the warehouse and check it out again. If this Sybil chick is to be believed, there's something more sinister going on than our original suspicion of homeless people being forced to fight to the death. What that might be, I'm at a loss, but it won't hurt to check again and see if we might have missed something."

"Sounds about right. I think the crime scene techs are done sifting and collecting all the evidence there. Since we know how weird all this is, maybe we'll spot something they overlooked. In the meantime, might I make another suggestion since I can't get you to stop chasing this fool's errand?"

She cast a dark look at him.

"What?"

"Might I suggest wearing body armor and carrying more firepower on you? If these people are as tough as you're saying they are, I think we need to go in armed for bear. And not a little tiny black bear or Winnie the Pooh. I'm talking the mutant, rabid grizzly bear that'd strike terror into Godzilla if he ever came across it."

As another broad smile broke across her face.

"Ya know what, I think that's the smartest thing you've said today."

He replied by balling up a piece of paper and chucking it at her head.

18

"That was unbelievable!"

Samuel glanced over at Blythe. He had to admit, he was pretty impressed with himself as well. He'd just spent the better part of an hour sparring against two, three, and at one point, four other partners. Even against such heavily stacked odds, he was still able to beat them without getting hit. What surprised him more, however, was that he felt more energized and rested now than when he'd first arrived. With a start, he realized he also didn't feel quite as hungry as he had since leaving the hospital.

"Yeah, I kinda surprised myself as well. Didn't know I was that good with a sword, or even dual-wielding for that matter."

"Yeah, Cliff said he'd never seen anyone handle two long swords like that before. Joe had experience with a sword and parrying dagger, but the way they went on and on about it, wielding two swords of the same length is pretty rare."

"I'm not sure why, but wielding two blades seemed even easier than just the one. It somehow felt more natural than just using the one sword, although it did impair my ability to use my jewelry as a shield."

"Well, you sure as hell looked impressive doing it. You flowed like quicksilver through them. It seemed like the more people you fought, the smoother you moved through them. I talked to your sparring partners when you took a break. They all said that it felt like you weren't even there when they went to hit you. Your blocks, for the most part, were so soft that they didn't even realize you'd deflected them until their blade missed you by inches. Speaking of which, did any of that jog your memories at all?"

Samuel shook his head.

"I wish. I could feel something rattling around just below the surface, but the harder I tried to remember, the further away it felt. I know that I can handle swords for obvious reasons, but I don't know how I know. The less I thought about it, the easier it became. It was weird, like fighting with swords was more natural than walking or something."

Blythe surprised him by giggling.

"What's so funny?"

"You almost sound like the description from a book I read when I was younger about a village of swordspeople," she said, getting a far-off look on her face. Shaking her head, she continued, "anyway, the main character was from a tribe or clan that basically taught their kids from the crib how to become expert sword-fighters. One of them was worth ten or more regular swordsmen. If they were real, you'd fit perfectly into their society perfectly."

"Speaking of which, what about you? I couldn't help but notice you repeatedly downplayed your skills. You pulled back every time you had an opening. I also noticed how you purposely let other's hit you. Why?"

Samuel watched as she ducked her head slightly before looking at him out of the corner of her eye.

"What? No… You're wrong. I'm just not that good is all…"

Samuel cocked his head slightly as he looked over at her again.

"Uh… Okay, if you say so."

Samuel puzzled over why Blythe would purposely play down her skill level.

She's obviously a much better fighter than anyone realizes, but she hides it in front of her friends. Guess that's just one more mystery I'll have to worry about later.

Leaning back into the car seat, he sunk into his own thoughts. With his skills at fighting in general, and sword-fighting in particular, he'd obviously had a lot of training. Even though he looked like he was in his mid-twenties, he was easily able to fight off people who'd been practicing sword-fighting for at least ten to twenty years. How does someone become so skilled with swords at such a young age? As he thought about it, he realized he was making an assumption. Namely, that he was in his twenties. Granted, that's how old he appeared to be when he looked in the mirror, but since he lost his memory, there was no way to be sure exactly how old he really was. Maybe he lived such a healthy lifestyle that he was in his thirties, or maybe even early forties. There was no way to be sure until his memory came back.

"Samuel?"

"Huh…? Sorry, lost in thought. You were saying?"

"Oh… no problem. I was, uh, asking if you planned on staying at the shelter tonight?"

"Honestly, I hadn't thought about it, but since I don't really have a lot of options, it's either there or the street. So yeah, probably going to crash there."

He glanced back over at her, watching her drive. From the expression on her face, he could tell she was trying to make up her mind about something. Appearing to come to a decision, she looked over at him.

"Well, I was kinda wondering… I know we don't know each other very well… but…" she paused for a moment, her breathing increasing slightly. He wasn't sure because of the low light, but he thought her face was getting flushed. Turning back to him, she suddenly blurted out, "would you like to stay at my place? You know… Until you get back on your feet and your memory returns?"

As soon as the words left her mouth, her eyes snapped forward to stare at the road they were driving on. Her breathing was coming in short, rapid inhalations and exhalations, like she'd just finished a short sprint. She had said it so fast, and without any warning, it took moment for him to process what she'd said.

"I mean, I understand if you don't want to and everything. We really just met and all. So if you wa—"

"Honestly, I would love to stay at your place instead. I'm going to hazard a guess and suspect it smells a tad bit better than my other choices, to say the least," he said lightly, trying to put her at ease.

She blinked a couple times, her mouth hanging open in mid-word. Her jaw worked a couple times before any sound came out.

"Oh… OH! Um, sure. Cool… Well, I live not too far from here, so we'll be there in a little bit."

Judging from the look on her face, Samuel realized she was severely flustered. If he had to guess, he suspected she hadn't expected him to say yes, so when he did, she wasn't sure what to do.

"Thank you for such a generous offer. You didn't have to, but I really appreciate it."

"Uh… no problem… I mean you're welcome…"

"Are you sure about this?" he asked. "You seem to be a little tense about the situation."

"Oh, I'm sure," she blurted out, her face getting even more flushed, "I'd love to have you stay the night… I mean… Oh… that didn't come out right."

She took a few deep breaths before she continued.

"What I meant to say was, you seem like such a nice guy, I'd feel bad about you having to sleep down at the shelter. Not that it isn't a nice shelter and everything, but I would hate myself if I just left you there when I could do something about it."

Samuel looked smiling as he responded, "As long as you're sure about it, I'd be glad to uh, stay the night."

He had to quickly grab the door handle when she nearly swerved off the road.

Blythe nervously fumbled with the lock for a minute, but Samuel pretended not to notice. Instead, he made a show of looking around the hallway as she finally unlocked her apartment door and went inside. He heard the lights click on as he followed her inside.

"I know it's not much, but unfortunately it's all I can afford right now. I'm still going to school, so between that, a couple part time jobs, and volunteering at the shelter, it's the best I can do."

Samuel glanced around the apartment quickly. It was a pretty cramped space, with a small kitchenette that flowed into the tiny living room. The couch looked well-used but in good condition.

As he looked around, he noticed Blythe trying to covertly clean the place. Noticing his look, she hid some clothes behind her back.

"I didn't get a chance to straighten up before I left this morning," she said, trying to kick something under a small desk. "It's usually not this messy."

"It's fine. Don't worry about it," he said, purposely turning away from her. He could hear her trying to stuff the items she'd been trying to hide into some nook or cranny that was close by.

Glancing back at her, he noticed her still trying to stuff more stuff into nearby crevices.

"If you can point me in the general direction of sheets and blankets, assuming you don't mind, I'll go ahead and make up the couch for tonight."

"Oh, of course. Sure," she said distractedly while continuing to stuff miscellaneous items in random spots. "They're in that closet over there," she added, waving toward a small door. Glancing at the door, he noticed a sword hanging on the wall.

"Blythe?" he said, stopping in front of the sword.

"Yeah?"

He reached out, almost touching the blade before pulling his hand back. He admired the sleek lines the blade cast. Without knowing why, he knew this sword was wielded differently than the longswords he'd been practicing with earlier.

"Is it okay if I touch this?"

"Sure, go for it. It's not near as heavy as the ones you were playing with earlier. Not really wielded the same way either…"

She trailed off as Samuel pulled the sword off the wall and started using it in a way that felt most natural to him. He instinctively used the red tassels dangling from the pommel to blind an imaginary foe as he gracefully swooped and pivoted with the blade. For some reason, he felt it was normal to point the first two fingers of his off-hand like a secondary blade as he continued to glide across the apartment.

"How do you know that form? I've been studying it for nearly a year and I don't look anywhere near as graceful as you do performing it."

Blythe's voice snapped him out of near-trance he'd been practicing in. With a sigh, he hung the sword back up on the wall.

"I wish I knew. Like earlier, I just flowed into how that sword felt like it should be handled. For some reason, I just knew it wasn't used like the swords from earlier. What kind of sword is it, anyway?"

"Well, depending on whether you use the Cantonese or Mandarin name for it, it's called a Gim or Jian. Most people just call it a Tai Chi sword though."

"Tai Chi?"

Blythe nodded as she took the sword off the wall again. Moving through a few graceful moves, she demonstrated some of the form he'd just performed.

"Yes, sometimes called Tai Chi Chuan. It's a form of internal martial art that's supposed to help develop internal power, or chi."

Hanging the sword back up, she demonstrated a different form.

"This one's called the simplified 24 form, what most people start out learning."

Samuel watched as she slid from one posture to the next. He could sense the power of the movements as she worked her way through the form. As he got lost in watching her perform, he suddenly noticed an odd shimmering-effect starting to form around her. The intensity seemed centered around a spot just below her belly-button and slowly suffused outward, forming an almost shimmering field extending several inches from her body. Before he had a chance to make sense of what he was seeing, she finished the form and the shimmering affect contracted back to her abdominal area.

Reaching into the closet, she pulled out a hand towel and wiped her face, which Samuel noticed had started glistening with sweat.

"It doesn't look like much, but it definitely gets your motor running while relaxing you at the same time. Kinda weird, actually."

"It looks like a pretty powerful form of self-defense, too."

Samuel noticed Blythe's face sag slightly.

"Yeah... I guess so. Not really why I started taking lessons though."

"Oh... Then why'd you want to learn it?"

Blythe's expression darkened before glimpses of sadness poked through.

"I had anger issues when I was younger. My parents thought Tai Chi would help calm me down, especially after..."

Samuel looked at her as she trailed off. After a moment, he cleared his throat.

"Blythe?"

She blinked before looking at him again. She had a slight edge in her voice as she handed him the blankets and sheets from the closet.

"I'm sorry, I'm kinda tired and I need to get up early for work tomorrow. If you need anything, just let me know. Goodnight…"

Before he had a chance to say anything else, she quickly turned around and walked into her bedroom, closing the door behind her.

19

Samuel awoke with a start. It took him a few seconds to remember where he was. Sitting up on the couch, he glanced around for the source of the noise.

"I'm sorry. I didn't mean to wake you. I was trying to be quiet while I got ready for work," Blythe said, poking her head from the bathroom.

"No problem. From what I can tell, I appear to be a pretty light sleeper. What time is it, anyway?"

Samuel heard gargling from behind the door. After a few seconds, she replied.

"It's a little after six in the morning. I have to be to work by seven unfortunately. If I didn't need the money so badly, I would have called out today."

"That's fine. There's some stuff I need to look into today anyway."

"Really? You're welcome to stay if you want. I only have to work 'til one today. After that, I have classes but they don't start until three. So if you're interested, maybe we can get some lunch together?"

Samuel could hear the hopeful tone in her voice.

"Sure. But you might want to consider bringing something home from the store. From the amount of food I seem to be able to pack away, I might eat your next month's rent if we eat out somewhere."

Samuel could make out the sound of fabric sliding across skin as he heard her giggle. Looking over as she stepped out of the bathroom, he watched as she finished pulling a shirt over her head before tucking it into her jeans. She caught him looking at her and smiled.

"Yeah, about that. I've seen you eat. Where do you put it all, anyway? I've never seen anyone eat like you before. Hell, I've never even seen two people eat the amount of food you pack away. How you don't rupture your stomach I'll never know."

"I'm not sure myself, actually. All I know is, since I've gotten out of the hospital, I've been constantly hungry. Even after I eat all that food and I know I can't eat another bite, I'm still hungry. What's odd though was I wasn't that hungry after sparring yesterday."

"Yeah, that is kinda odd. I know they say you should try to eat right after working out because your appetite is suppressed, so maybe that has something to do with it…?"

"Eh, maybe. Just one more mystery about me that I don't have answers for. So where do you work today?"

"I'm waitressing down at a local coffee and bistro shop. I cover the breakfast and lunch crowds. The tips aren't as good as they would be if I could work the dinner shift, but I have classes then. I'm hoping next semester I'll be able to work the dinner shift and maybe get ahead a bit. Anyway, you said you had some stuff to do today?"

"Yeah, I was thinking about visiting a few different jewelry stores and see if they might have any ideas about where this thing could have come from," he said, shaking his left arm in the air, "or who might have the skill to make it."

"Makes sense. Speaking of which, I'll try and get ahold of John and Karen, see if they've found anything yet. It's still really early right now. Since we were out pretty late last night with them, they probably went home instead of going back to their store. But you never know with those two. You'd think they were married the way they bicker sometimes, but at other times, they're so different that it's a wonder they can run a store together."

Samuel watched as she went back into the bathroom to do her hair.

"Of the two, I'd bet that John would stay up half the night trying to research that thing of yours, but I doubt Karen did much more than a cursory glance before going to bed. She's usually the first one to the shop in the morning while John has a tendency to keep the shop open late because he's lost in something he's researching."

"Well, hopefully they'll turned something up," he said as he got up and moved toward the bathroom, "because this not remembering stuff is getting really old, really fast."

He stopped at the door and waited for her to look up. She jumped slightly when she realized he was standing next to her.

"Sorry, I didn't mean to startle you."

"Nah, it's okay. I just didn't hear you sneak over here is all," she said.

"Would it be okay if I got cleaned up?"

"Sure…"

Samuel caught her looking him over out of the corner of his eye.

"You know, you're not that much different in build than my ex although you look a little beefier than he was. I still have some of his stuff that I haven't chucked out that might fit you."

She brushed against him as she squeezed out of the bathroom, heading toward her bedroom.

"There's towels and washcloths on the shelf over the toilet, so feel free to hop in the shower whenever. Unfortunately I don't have a spare toothbrush, but I'll pick one up when I stop to get us food at the store."

Samuel paused to look at himself in the mirror before pulling his shirt off over his head. As he was pulling off his socks, he heard a loud gasp behind him.

"Oh my God… I hate you so much right now."

He turned around, trying to figure out what he'd done wrong.

"How the HELL do you eat like a horse and still keep a six, no, eight-pack like that? I eat one damn cupcake and it goes straight to my ass!"

Realizing she wasn't really mad, he replied, "Well, in defense of the cupcake, it looks really good hanging out in your pants like that."

He made it a point to stare at her ass for a few seconds before she got red and threw some clothes at him.

"That's just wrong," she said, fighting back a giggle.

He glanced back down at her butt again as he wiggled his eyebrows.

"Yeah, I'm pretty sure I like cupcakes…"

With that, she started laughing. Samuel grinned at her before he closed the bathroom door.

"Will you be here by the time I get out?" he said through the door.

"Probably not. I'm going to leave a spare key on the counter for you so you can let yourself back in if you get back before I do."

"Thanks. I really appreciate that. While we're on the subject," he said, poking his head out the door, "I have the address of a couple of the places I want to check out today. Do you have any idea where they might be?"

He reached down on the floor and pulled the notebook out of his pants pocket before holding it out the door, waving it at her. As she took the notebook, she turn away quickly and walked over to the couch. Looking behind him, he realized one of the mirrors over the sink was open, giving her a perfect view of his backside in the reflection. Closing the door quickly, he got ready to turn on the water.

"One of these places is only a couple blocks away. The rest of them are probably around twenty to thirty blocks away, but all in the same direction. I'll write some directions next them so you can find them if you have time. I'll leave it on the table for when you get out."

"Thanks!" he said loud enough to be heard over the running water, "what time should I be back by?"

"Like I said, I get out at one, so I should be back by two at the latest. Anyway, I need to get going. Anything else I can get you before I leave?"

"Nope, thanks again so much, you've been great. Although…"

He paused for a second before poking his head back out.

"I don't suppose you could bring back some cupcakes, could you?"

"You're impossible!" she said as she threw a pillow at him as he ducked back into the bathroom.

Chuckling, he yelled through the door.

"See you later!"

"Later."

He heard the door close as he stepped into the tub. From the sounds of it, today was going to be a busy day.

Samuel looked at the clock as he came out of the bathroom. It was almost seven o'clock, so he still had at least an hour before any of the stores opened. He wanted to be back before Blythe got home, so with that in mind, he decided to hit one of the more distant stores first. He figured he'd be able to cover most of the distance before they opened, so he could at least be somewhat productive.

He realized that Blythe might have either overestimated how big her ex was, or had underestimated how big he was. The shirt was pretty tight, straining against his arms and shoulders. The waist on the jeans were a bit loose, but the thigh area was pretty tight as well. He hoped they would stretch out some as he wore them, or there was a chance he was going to bust a seam somewhere.

He looked over the list of jewelry stores. If he jogged, it'd probably only take a couple hours at most to reach the most distant one. He thought back to how easily he'd been able carry Hank while jogging and figured he'd be able to go faster since he wasn't carrying anything. With that in mind, he drank his fill of water and headed out, grabbing the spare key on the way by. As he closed the door, he got a strong feeling of being watched. He glanced around trying to find the source of the feeling, but the only thing he noticed was someone heading down the staircase. It didn't feel quite the same as the weird feeling he had the other day. That feeling had just seemed like something was there, while this sensation had almost felt menacing. He wasn't sure what to make of it since it had already faded away. Shrugging, he scratched the back of his neck before pulling up his hood and headed down the stairs.

Reaching the street, he glanced around to get his bearings. The last thing he wanted to do was forget where the apartment was, especially since he already had memory problems. Just to be safe, he scribbled down the street address. Suddenly, the hairs on the back of his neck jumped to attention again, causing him to spin around. He noticed a guy turning the corner at the end of the street, just before the feeling faded again. He wasn't sure, but it kinda looked like the guy he saw walking down the staircase a few minutes earlier. He thought about trying to catch up to the guy before dismissing it.

Guess I can get paranoid just like everyone else, apparently.

Shaking his head, he started off in the opposite direction.

"Nope, sorry. Never seen anything like that before. I'd love to know who made it though, I'd hire 'em on the spot, or attempt to buy up some of their inventory at the very least. If you're ever interested in selling that piece, let me know. Based off the workmanship alone, I'd be willing to offer you something in the low to mid five figures. That of course would depend on what that thing is made out of... I don't ever remember coming across anything like it in my fifteen years of running this place. Might be one of them new alloys I'm always hearing about."

"Thanks for your time then," he said as he headed for the door.

"No problem. The pleasure's all mine. It's not very often that I see something come through that door that impresses me, and let me tell you, that thing impresses me. I couldn't even hope to come close to that level of workmanship. That's not something you learn in a regular apprenticeship program or something, either. That's a multi-generational, secrets handed down to a select few type of skill level. Anyway, you keep in touch. If you remember who made it for you, you let me know?"

"Sure," he said as he walked out the door. As he put his hood up, he happened to glance back into the store. He noticed the owner was picking up the phone. When he realized he was being watched, the owner turned his back to the front door. Samuel stared at the back of the store owner's head for a few more seconds.

That seemed kinda odd... More paranoia on my part? Now that I think about it, I wonder if the cops have put out a poster of me or something...

Shrugging his shoulders, he started heading back toward the apartment. He'd already hit two stores and left empty handed. He knew he didn't really have time to stop at any more that were in the area, but if he started back now, he figured he'd get back early enough to hit the jewelry store right around the corner and still get back to the apartment before Blythe arrived. He wanted to get back early enough to wind down a bit and figure out his next plan of action before she got home. He hadn't really learned anything new yet, but hopefully the next store might shine some light on where this thing on his arm came from.

As he walked, he started thinking about Blythe, trying to figure her out. She was a nice person, and he was definitely attracted to her. It almost felt like a static tingle whenever he was around her, but it didn't feel right starting something with her when he didn't know anything about himself. But then the question became, how long would he wait for his memory to return before he moved on with his life? He might never remember anything from his past.

As he contemplated the situation, he started to notice a weird feeling, almost like he was standing in front of a large fire. He glanced in the direction the sensation seemed to come from. At the same time, he felt the metal on the vambrace start to tingle. Without warning, he noticed a shimmering affect surrounding a couple walking down the street. As the tingling got stronger, he noticed their appearance starting to expand away from them, almost like an afterimage, revealing that the couple was dressed like the people from the library.

He quickly ducked into an alleyway and jogged a little way down before hiding behind a dumpster. He wasn't sure why, but he knew they were extremely dangerous. As they passed the mouth of the alleyway, the woman glanced down it. Samuel could almost feel her gaze travel across the area. As her gaze washed over his hiding spot, he suddenly had another flash arc across his mind. It was another memory of the woman in black with red hair. He was fighting against her again. He could almost feel the impacts as she forced him backward against her onslaught. They were both fighting with the weird sword and shield that his vambrace turned into, but he couldn't remember why they were fighting. As she came in for a killing blow, his memory faded out again.

He sat there gasping as the vivid memory replayed through his mind again. Both times, the memory had been physically draining, nearly staggering him with its vividness. What concerned him was that the memories were about two separate fights he'd had against her.

Maybe she's the reason I can't remember anything. Maybe she finally beat me and left me for dead...

Samuel shook his head.

I can't get lost analyzing a memory while those people are in the area. Both times I've seen them, I've gotten the impression they're barely contained chaos. I need to get out of here first, then I can try to make sense of why I keep recalling memories of that woman trying to kill me.

Peeking back around the dumpster, he checked to make sure they weren't still looking his way. Not seeing them, he took off at a quick pace in the opposite direction. At the opposite end of the alley, he quickly glanced both ways before taking off. All he knew was that he wanted to put some distance between him and them. As he found an easy jogging pace to keep, he had a sudden thought.

That shopkeeper was on the phone right after I left. I know I didn't hear it ring, so he had to have been making a call. Then these people show up out of nowhere. What the hell is going on here? Are they the reason I lost my memories? Since they're dressed like the woman from my dreams, are they trying to finish the job?

20

"There's nothing here."

"There's gotta be. This is where this whole mess started."

Frank kicked an old wooden crate out of the way.

"We've been here for over an hour. From the looks of it, the CSI guys swept this place with a fine tooth comb, then went over it with a lint brush to make sure they didn't miss anything."

"I know, I know, but there's gotta be something they missed, something they ignored because they weren't looking for it," she said as she stood up, glancing around the area. After a few seconds, she pulled out the folder of crime scene photos. Glancing around, she scrambled across the debris to a different spot. Studying the images again, she slowly turned a full circle before stopping again.

"This is where they found Samuel unconscious, surrounded by dozens of bodies and ash."

She glanced around again.

"Why right here? From the footage we've seen of our boy in action, he has no problems moving in a fight, but in the photos, he looks like he refused to move more than a few feet from this spot. Why?"

"Maybe he was having fun? Or he was too lazy to move. Who cares?" he said, kicking another box across the room.

"Frank, be serious. Why would our guy make what appears to be his last stand right here?"

She squatted down, trying to figure out what was so special about that particular spot. Frank sighed, brushed his hands off on his pants, and walked over to where she was squatting. Standing next to her, he shrugged his shoulders.

"Still thinking he might have been bored…"

"Damn it Frank. Use your recon training and tell me why you'd want to make a last stand here."

"Fine, fine," he said as he nudged her out of the way. His expression turned serious as he slowly turned in place, pausing to glance at different spots as he slowly spun. After a few minutes, he shook his head.

"This spot makes no sense whatsoever. He's wide open, has no cover, and no way to funnel attackers. This spot would be a losing position against just about any type of organized attack."

"Yet that's exactly what he did. Based off what you saw in that video, does that sound like something our guy would do?"

Frank's face scrunched up as he focused on the question, glancing around the area again.

"Well, based off how agile our guy is, unless he was injured or fighting against some seriously well trained fighters, there's no way he'd allow himself to get pinned down here," he said, studying the spot again. "Damn it, I beginning to think you're right. This is a rank amateur mistake, getting stuck right here. Our boy is anything but that. He was standing his ground here for some reason, but for what?"

Cora nodded, studying the area again.

"There's nothing here though. What the hell was he defending?"

She pulled out the crime scene photos again, letting Frank look over her shoulder. From the pictures, it appeared that he'd been able to maintain about a ten foot diameter circle around himself before he fell. Those ten feet were what Samuel was willing to fight to the death for, from all appearances. Cora pulled out a few blank sheets of paper and tore them up into small pieces. She then proceeded to compare the photos to the floor, laying out the pieces to make a rough outline of the circle that the bodies seemed to have dropped around.

Moving back to the center of the rough circle, she looked around again. Frank followed her gaze.

"I'm telling you Cora, there's nothing here. I'm agreeing with you that there's a reason he drew his line in the sand here, but whatever it was, it's gone."

Cora sighed in frustration. Her partner was right. There wasn't anything here. She squatted back down to see if there might have been something, some scratch or trace of something that might have indicated what he was fighting for. After another minute of examination, she gave up and started to stand. Her foot slipped on something greasy, causing her to fall backward.

Frank scrambled over to her, holding out his hand.

"Are you alright?"

"Yeah, yeah," she said, dusting off her hands before reaching up to grab Frank's hand.

"I think you're right about..." she said as she glanced up at Frank, her hand slowly drifting back down. Frank gave her a funny look as she started glancing around again.

"Do you want help up or not?"

"Frank," she said slowly pointing toward the ceiling, "what the hell are those?"

"How the hell did our guys miss something like that," he said, staring toward the ceiling.

"Oh, I don't know... Maybe the several dozen bodies horribly mutilated and scattered across the floor might have distracted them a bit..." she said sarcastically, pulling out a copy of the crime scene sketch.

"Har Har..."

Cora lightly sketched in the burn pattern over rest of the diagram. Glancing back up, she noticed the burn wasn't completely circular. It appeared to have slight edges, but they weren't well defined. Ignoring it for the time being, she started to glance around the rest of the upper areas of the building. The first thing she noticed was what appeared to be a new chunk of metal, shaped into a sturdy hook, sticking out of one of the main concrete support beams. Marking it on the diagram, she glanced around at the other support beams. After a careful search, she noticed four other hooks as well spaced around the warehouse. Marking their positions as well on the photos, she studied the updated sketch.

"Holy… Are you friggin' serious?"

Frank glanced over her shoulder, staring at the drawing.

"Now what?"

She glanced back at Frank, pointing at the diagram.

"That…"

"That what? I don't know what you're looking at…"

"Maybe it's all the spookiness that caused it to stand out," she said, drawing more lines on the diagram, "but for whatever reason, it fits."

When she finished, she handed the diagram to her partner. He whistled through his teeth before looking back at her.

"You're right, it's absolutely bat-shit crazy, but it really does fit, no matter how weird it looks…" he said as he trailed off, handing the sketch back to Cora.

Glancing back down at it, Cora tried to make sense of what she'd drawn. The area that Samuel appeared to be defending, fit perfectly within the burn pattern on the ceiling, which fit perfectly within the center of the pentagram the hooks would have formed if they had been connected by ropes.

21

As they left the scene, Cora tried to make sense of the new information. What they'd found could completely change what they suspected happened, but left lots of new blanks that needed to be filled in.

"So this wasn't just a mass slaughter or body drop for an illegal fight club. This appears to be some type of ritual or cult scenario. The question now becomes, were they willing, or unwilling participants. And how did our boy Samuel fit in with the new info. Was he the leader of the cult? If not, then why did it look like he'd killed all those people around that pentagram?"

Frank shook his head.

"This looks worse than that situation with Heaven's Gate back in the late nineties. At least they just poisoned themselves. This was an absolute slaughter."

Cora nodded. She kept turning the new information over in her head. If this was a ritual of some sort, did the group responsible succeed, or were they going to find more bodies somewhere? And why now? She wasn't much up on different cult beliefs, but what little she knew seemed to indicate rituals usually seemed to happen around certain times of the year. With a start, the hairs on the back of her neck started to lift.

"Frank..." she started, waiting to make sure he was paying attention before she continued, "I think we might have a much bigger problem..."

"Great, now what?"

"Halloween is two days from now. I get the suspicion we haven't seen the worst of it yet…"

"Boy, you're just a ray o' friggin' sunshine, aren't you…?"

"Yep, and if you keep it up, I'm going to give you a care bear stare…"

"You sure this guy's gonna be able to help?"

Cora glanced down at her notebook before pulling the door open.

"According to what the info desk guy said over the phone, if anyone could give us an answer, it'd be this guy."

After conferring with a couple students, Cora and Frank walked down the hall, heading deeper into the university.

"Apparently this guy is some well-known expert on the occult. The guy kept going on and on about how lucky they were to snag him to head their philosophy and religious studies department. I nearly had to hang up on him to get him to shut up."

Finding the correct hallway, they headed toward the only office that was still lit.

Cora ran her fingers through her hair as she glanced at Frank.

"So, how much do we tell this guy, anyway?"

"At this point, we're so far outside the box, I don't think we could do much worse if we started carting him around in the car with us."

Cora chuckled slightly. Since agreeing to continue investigating the case with her, he'd seemed to have started loosening up. Stopping in front of the office door, she stood to the side as Frank knocked.

"Enter," came the muffled reply.

Opening the door, they walked in, not sure what to expect. Looking around, Cora was surprised by how large the office was, indicating how high the university's regard for this particular professor was. Going deeper, she spotted collections of assorted weird items, desiccated animals of indeterminate origin, and musty books piled up haphazardly around the room.

"Hello…? Professor Waide?"

"Yes…?"

Cora glanced over to where she thought she'd heard the voice emanated from. She could faintly make out a coil of smoke curling up from behind another stack of books. She glanced back at Frank, nodding at the column of smoke, before heading forward again, carefully walking around teetering stacks of objects that were probably worth more than they made in a month.

Circling around another stack of books, they saw the professor hunched over several books and scrolls, scribbling rapidly into a notebook with precise strokes before continuing his studies. She noticed the trail of smoke was coming out of a fancy looking meerschaum pipe he had clenched lightly in the corner of his mouth. She noticed that the bowl was a deep golden brown color, almost a dark mahogany in shade.

"Professor Waide," she asked again, "isn't there a no smoking rule in here?"

The elderly gentleman turned slowly, scrutinizing his visitors before he replied.

"The university grants me special uh," he paused, waving around the room, "liberties in order to entice me to stay."

He pulled his glasses off, wiping the lenses before perching them back on his nose. He glanced at Cora and Frank before turning back toward his notes.

"From the looks of you two, I'm going to go out on a limb here and guess you're not here to discuss why I should give you an extension on a paper you haven't turned in yet, yes…?"

Glancing at Frank, she shrugged her shoulders before turning back toward the man standing in front of them.

"I'm detective Blanchett and this is my partner, detective Giani. We were wondering if you could look at something we've come across during one of our investigations."

Without turning to look at them, Professor Waide took a deep pull off his pipe while relighting it. After a few puffs, he responded without looking at them.

"Detective, unlike you apparently, I'm very busy here. I'm not one of your public servants you can just drop in on whenever you feel like it. If you want to set up a meeting with me to discuss a case, your department is well aware of my policy. So until then, I bid you adieu."

"Old codger probably wouldn't have a clue about what this meant anyway," Frank mumbled under his breath as he turned to walk away.

The professor whirled around fluidly, a flash of anger coloring his cheeks.

"Excuse me young man?"

"I said you'd probably be useless with this case. I doubt you've been outside this room to do more than eat and sleep in the past decade…"

"Is that so," the professor replied indignantly, "I'll have you know that I've been helping your department solve 'weird cases' since before your stones dropped, I'll wager."

The professor stalked up to Frank, leaning on a simple black cane.

"I've done more for your department than you ever will," he said, jabbing the stem of his pipe into Frank's chest several times.

"Come on Frank, we're obviously wasting our time here. We'll just have to find someone else to make sense of this mess before Halloween…"

As she turned away, the professor tilted his head.

"What does Samhain have to do with your case?"

Turning back to the professor, she noticed a strange intensity in his eyes.

"Samhain?"

"Yes, the Celtic festival of the end of summer. Co-opted by other religions and turned into a festival of the dead called Halloween."

Pulling out a folder, she waved it at him.

"Right now, we're not sure if it is, in fact, related. All we know is that we had a massacre in an abandoned warehouse on the outskirts of town. When we went back there today, we noticed something that oddly looks like a pentagram at the center of where the bodies fell. We're guessing the upcoming holiday has something to do with this, but we can't be sure. So far, everything about this case has been bizarre and this is just one more piece we can't make sense of."

"All right," he said testily, "since I'm going to have to eventually look it over anyway, let me see it."

He worked his way over to another table, slightly limping as he balanced on his cane. Clearing off a large spot, he motioned for them to lay out the case file.

"So far, all we know for sure is, three days ago, a man was found in the center of a huge pile of dead bodies in an abandoned warehouse. When that person woke up in the hospital, he claimed to have no memories of who he was, but we have reason to believe his name is Samuel. He also claimed to have no memory about what happened in that warehouse. Now he's missing and we have very little to go on."

The professor shuffled through the crime scene photos, giving each one a quick look before moving on to the next one. When he came to the picture they'd taken of the ceiling of the warehouse, one of his eyebrows went up.

"Detective Giani," he said absently, waiving in the general direction of his desk, "could you hand me my notebook and something to write with.

Frank walked over to the desk. After a moment of moving and shuffling stuff, he returned, handing the professor a notebook while pulling a pen out of his pocket.

"Here."

The professor gave a vague nod, grabbing the notebook and pen. Laying the photos out, he started rapidly taking notes. Without looking up, he started talking.

"You said his name was Samuel. If he didn't have any memory, how do you know his name?"

"That's another mystery. A woman by the name of Sybil showed up at his room shortly after he escaped. She's the one who identified his name as being Samuel."

"Interesting. What did she look like?"

"Well, she was dressed head to toe in black and wore a black trench coat..."

She paused when the professor snapped his head toward her, locking his eyes on her.

"A woman dressed in black wearing a black trench coat? I don't suppose it was a leather one, was it? About midway down her shin in length?"

Cora nodded at him before glancing at Frank.

The professor turned back to the photos as he waved at her to continue.

"Anyway, she mentioned his name while looking around the room. I got distracted for a moment. When I looked back, she was gone."

The professor nodded to himself, mumbling.

Cora wasn't sure, but she thought she heard him say, "not surprised."

Picking up the crime scene sketch that Cora had drawn on, he held it up toward them.

"Nice piece of detective work there. I'm surprised any of you caught that. Might I ask if there were any mysterious piles of ash there, or maybe slashes or other marks that didn't make sense? Maybe gouged right out of the concrete floor?"

"How'd you know?" she asked as she exchanged glances with Frank.

"Just a hunch. I don't suppose you have a picture of this 'Samuel' person you're looking for do you?" he asked as he puffed on his pipe.

Cora pulled out her phone, turning it so he could see the screen. As she flipped through them, she said, "These are really the only pictures we have of him. I took these just before he woke up in the hospital. We really didn't have a chan—"

She was interrupted by the professor slumping back against the table, sucking air in through his teeth.

Looking back up at her, he asked, "You said this guy was unconscious, with no memory of who, or what, he was?"

Cora was shocked by the sudden change in the professor's appearance. Up to this point, he had seemed to be confident and robust for his age, almost to the point of being rude and condescending. Now he was leaning against the table, shaking slightly. His face had gone ashen in color, and it took him a minute to compose himself. He finally straightened himself up and walked briskly over to his desk, almost ignoring his cane in the process. Dropping down in his seat, he opened a drawer and pulled out a glass and a bottle.

Frank sucked in a loud gasp.

"Is that what I think it is…?" he asked, his hand shaking slightly as he pointed at the bottle.

"By that, do you mean a rare bottle of Glenfiddich Janet Sheed Roberts Reserve 1955?" the professor asked, a slight smile playing across his face as he pulled the stopper out of the bottle.

"I picked up three bottles of the stuff when it went up for auction back in '05. It's quite nice, actually. Would you care for a dram?"

Cora looked over at Frank to see his eyes bulge out before hesitantly nodding yes. The professor reached into his desk, pulling a couple more glasses out before nodding toward Cora.

"Would you like a dram yourself, detective?"

She shrugged her shoulders before nodding as well. She watched as he poured two fingers worth into each glass. As he handed the first glass to Frank, she continued to be confused by Frank's actions. He carefully took the glass from the elderly man's hand before slowly bringing it up to his nose, inhaling the fumes deeply. A look of bliss crossed her partner's face as the professor handed her a glass as well.

Looking back and forth between the two men, she sniffed the contents of her glass.

"From my partner's reaction, I'm going to guess this isn't your everyday swill from the local liquor store?"

The professor smiled back at her, chuckling slightly as her partner replied.

"Not in the slightest. Do you know how rare this stuff is? I remember reading about this stuff on the top ten most expensive scotches ever sold. This one," he said, taking a small sip with his eyes closed, savoring it before continuing, "went up for auction for ninety-four grand a bottle."

Cora's almost dropped her glass before she caught herself.

"Wait a minute, that means…"

"That you hold about eight grand worth of alcohol in your hand," the professor said as he took a sip, "like I said, it's quite nice."

"So you mean to tell me you keep a bottle in your desk that's worth more than some people's houses? And you have no problems just giving us a glass of it?"

"Well detective," he said as he took another sip, "I felt the reward fit the gift."

Frank glanced at the other man.

"Gift?"

"Why yes, detective Giani. A most wonderful gift. One that I might never have received if you hadn't been so rude, I might add."

Cora exchanged confused glances with her partner before looking back at the professor.

"I'm not sure I follow you," she said.

She watched as he got up from behind his desk and limped over to a colorful wall hanging. Sliding it to the side, she saw that it had hidden a six foot tall safe embedded into the wall. As he spun the dial, he started talking to them over his shoulder.

"Long before either of you were born, I was on an archaeological dig over in Egypt. We had found a partially uncovered pyramid buried centuries earlier. What made this pyramid unusual, other than the fact that the top of it barely stuck out of sand, was that the stones in it were significantly older than what was used in the Cheops pyramid in Giza. The fact that the pyramids in Giza were still pretty much at the surface while this one was almost completely buried suggested that it was built by an unbelievably old, unrecorded culture. If our guess was correct, this pyramid was centuries older than what was currently believed to be the age of the human race. This one find would have proved that humans had been around thousands, possibly tens of thousands, of years earlier than originally believed. If I would have been able to make this knowledge public, it would have changed the course of archeology."

"Anyway," he said, finally unlocking the safe and swinging the door open, "our dig lasted for several months before we were able to uncover a doorway to the interior."

As he said that, he gently lifted what appeared to be a silk-wrapped package from the interior. Holding it reverently, he carried it over to his desk before going back to the safe and carrying over an accordion file brimming with documents. Setting the file down, he glanced up at them.

"Detective Blanchett, could you please lock my office door? I don't want to be disturbed while I show you this."

Cora walked back over to the door and locked it. As an afterthought, she closed the blinds on the door as well. Returning, she watched him gently start unwrapping the object.

"So after months of careful excavations, and days of slowly mapping out the interior, we finally made it to the Kings chamber, where we found this..." he said as he finally revealed what he'd had hidden in his wall safe.

Shimmering under the dim lights of the office, Cora glanced down at a near twin of the jewelry Samuel wore on his arm.

"What! You found that in an ancient pyramid? How old IS that thing, exactly?"

Cora stared at it intently. Granted, it wasn't exactly the same as the one on Samuel's arm. For starters, this one was shades of red and gold while his was blue and silver. The head and body of this one appeared to be more powerfully built while Samuel's would be better described as sleek. She tried to spot more differences as Professor Waide gently laid it down on his desk, on top of the silk wrapping.

"Honestly, we haven't been able to determine its exact age. Every method I've tried to identify it with has come up empty. Acids, files, hammers, and more recently, X-rays, ultrasound, and lasers, have had absolutely no effect on it. I haven't found anything yet that can even scratch it, let alone test it. The best I've been able to do is estimate its minimal age, based off other things we recovered from the pyramid. Some of the pottery dates the pyramid back to around one hundred and eighty thousand years B.C., based off carbon dating."

"What! How's that possible? If all that's true, then how come we haven't heard anything about all this?"

Cora noticed the professor's face sag slightly before he took another sip of his scotch.

"Therein lies the great tragedy. Apparently, that whole structure was designed to protect that thing," he said, waving at the jewelry on his desk.

"As soon as I picked it up, there was a brilliant flash of light before the entire structure started shaking. I barely remember grabbing it and trying to get to safety before the whole place collapsed and was buried under hundreds of tons of sand and rock. We lost over thirty people that day, some of whom were buried alive in there. Others were sucked to their death in the quicksand that formed as the structure sank."

"Quite honestly, I'm not even sure how I survived. All I know is that I had somehow made it out while others didn't. When the survivors of my team found me, I was several hundred feet away from the opening, clutching that to my chest like it was a child."

"I was delirious for several days before I finally came to my senses. From that disaster, I've devoted my life to trying to figure out who could have made something like that, and more importantly, why history makes no mention of them. Sure, I've seen crackpot theories, like it was made in Atlantis, or something similar. I've even had to fend off some folk who swore it was from aliens. None of it really answers the question of who created it or for what purpose. For that matter, the biggest question is, how were they able to create it? Our currently technology can't even figure out what it's made out of, yet it's nearly two hundred centuries old. The oldest known remains of homo sapiens are around that same age, so how would a race that used rocks as advanced weaponry make something like that?"

Professor sunk back into his chair, lost in thought as he finished off his glass of scotch.

Cora stared at the piece of jewelry laying on the professor's desk. After a minute, she looked up at him quickly.

"Wait a minute, if that thing is that old, then how's our boy sporting a near replica?"

Frank looked at her, surprised by the question. His eyes widened slightly before looking back at the professor.

"That, my dear, it the million dollar question. If you can figure it out, I've got another bottle of scotch with your name on it. Out of all my years of searching, that photo on your phone is the only evidence that they still exist. The only other thing I've ever been able to determine is that they were worn by a race called Syphons, but nothing to indicate why. Even that I'm not sure of since it was based off of a translation of a translation found in some documents that were traced back to the ancient library in Alexandria. Parts of the document was damaged, so the final translation wasn't really clear. It implied they were either protectors or destroyers, but the documents were too damaged to be sure. Whoever they were, they appeared to be more technologically advanced than even we are today."

The professor shook himself slightly. He eyed the bottle of scotch before putting it back in his desk.

Looking up at them, he said gravely, "To answer your original question, I think you're quite right to be concerned with the coming Halloween. Those pictures from the warehouse are indicative of a significant ritual being performed. I would suspect that there's going to be four or five more of these rituals being performed between now and then, with the final one happening on all hallows eve, at midnight, when the curtain between our world and others are thinnest. You don't have much time to stop whatever is going to happen, but I have to believe that the results would be catastrophic if left unchecked."

23

Samuel got back to the apartment a little later than he expected. The whole way home, he kept having weird sensations when he passed by certain people or areas. He had been vaguely aware of the sensations when he had traveled to the first jewelry store, but now that he was on edge from his near run-in with the strange people dressed in black, each odd sensation fairly screamed at him, like nails on a chalkboard.

Closing the door behind him, he collapsed on the couch, exhausted. He wasn't sure why, but he felt more tired now than he did after all the sword-fighting and sparring from last night. His nerves felt raw and twitchy. It might have been his imagination, but he could have sworn that he'd seen several weird creature-type people on the trip back. Some of them were similar to the one he'd run into at the library.

When he had looked at them, they seemed to develop a double-image effect, similar to what happened at the library. When he focused on them, they looked human while their ghost image took on all sorts of fantastic shapes. It was disconcerting enough that he debated having Blythe take him back to the hospital when she got back. He knew the doctor had said he didn't have any lasting brain trauma, but with the continuing hallucinations, he wasn't so sure.

Looking up at the clock, he realized Blythe should be home within a few minutes. After a brief pause, he decided to head back downstairs to meet her, hoping to work off some of the nervous energy he'd built up on the trip back.

Closing the door, he heard arguing in the distance. As he started down, he noticed the argument was somewhere below him. With a start, he realized that one of the voices belonged to Blythe, while the other was male. As he quietly descended, he noticed the volume of the argument slowly escalating.

"It's none of your business who he is. We're not together anymore. You can't tell me what to do!"

As he turned the final corner, he noticed Blythe was cornered by the guy that had caused his weird sensations when he'd left earlier. As he approached, he saw Blythe try to get around the man, but he grabbed her and pushed her back into the corner.

"Let go of me," she yelled as she dug her nails into his hand.

"You little bitch," he said as he tried to backhand her. Making it look accidental, she lifted her hands up, deflecting his shot over her head. Samuel noticed the weird shimmering affect surround Blythe expand as she dropped her hands back down, slapping the man on the chest. The impact nearly knocked him to the ground as he stumbled back a few steps. Regaining his balance, he charged back at her while rearing his right hand back.

"That's enough."

The words slid out of Samuel's mouth like they'd been cast in iron. The razor edge in the tone he used caused the man to involuntarily stumble back a step as he'd spun toward him, giving Blythe an opening to slip past. The guy reached out, trying to grab her again, but Samuel flowed like mercury around Blythe, letting her get further up the stairs while he barred the way. As Samuel came to a stop in front of the man, he reached up and grabbed the other man's outstretched hand, locking it in a viselike grip.

"I said that's enough."

The words hissed out of his mouth like steel sliding across steel.

"Who the hell are you! This is between me and her, so get the hell outta my face."

"It would appear that she would rather not talk to you, so I'd suggest leaving before something unfortunate happens."

"Is that a threat? Are you threatening me?" the man growled.

Blythe shouted from the safety of the stairs.

"Get out of here Chris! I don't ever want to see you again."

"You couldn't wait to shack up with someone else, could you, you little sl—"

Samuel increased the pressure on Chris's wrist, causing him to gasp in sudden pain.

"Let go of me you sonofa," he said before suddenly throwing a haymaker at Samuel's head with his other hand.

Without loosening his grip, he pivoted to the left while catching the strike on his forearm. Releasing his grip, he used his elbow to direct the strike over his head as he pivoted back to the right. Chris tried to take another swing at him with his suddenly freed hand, but Samuel blocked it with his left hand while grabbing the front of his clothes with his right hand. Lifting him up one handed, he charged across the landing with Chris before slamming him into the wall, crumpling a metal access panel in the process as the air whooshed out of the other man's lungs. Chris struggled weakly against Samuels grip as his feet dangled a foot of the ground.

"Are you about finished?"

"Don't kill him!" Blythe screamed, "he's not worth it."

Samuel turned sideways to look at her, shaking Chris slightly as he did.

"Don't worry, I'm just trying to provide some friendly persuasion to convince this gentleman to not darken your doorstep again."

Blythe started to smile, but the smile quickly changed to a look of horror. Time slowed down as her hand sluggishly started to extend toward him, her other hand covering her mouth to muffle a scream. The air popped as Samuel spun back to face the man he had pinned. His eyes widened as he was suddenly confronted by the barrel of a pistol aimed at his face.

His left hand swung up, the displaced air creating an audible pop. Time slowed to a crawl as the hammer started to drop in slow motion. He felt a slight tingling sensation crawl across the palm of his hand as he got it in front of the barrel before time snapped back to normal speed. The boom of the gun discharging echoed around the room before fading away. He distantly heard Blythe screaming behind him, but all of his focus was on the man in front of him. He watched as the anger drained out of the other man's face, like wax melting under a flame, as he realized Samuel was still staring directly at him, the smoke curling out from between the barrel and Samuel's hand.

"Ow…" he said quietly, slowly lowering the other man to the ground. As the man's feet touched the floor, his legs started to buckle. Samuel caught him, propping him up before shaking his head at him before he slowly released him. In a very deliberate manner, he reached over to grab the top of the pistol with his right hand, gently taking it out of the other man's now limp hand.

Samuel's muscles swelled slight as he slowly bent the gun in half, the hardened barrel popping with a loud crack as it snapped in two. Sticking the broken gun in the waistline of the other man's pants, Samuel stared deep into the other man's eyes. Instinctively, he changed the tone of his voice, causing the other man to wet himself as Samuel talked.

"I think we're done here… Don't you?" he said, nodding his head up and down.

"Su..su.. Sure… Wha… whatever you say…"

"And you're never going to come anywhere near Blythe again, right?" he said, continuing to nod.

"Never, on my mother's grave. I swear!"

"Good, because as of right now, you've slightly… annoyed me. If I ever hear of you even buying your groceries from the same place Blythe does, then I'm going to become pissed off. If that happens, I'm going to come visit you. It won't be a nice visit. Any questions," he asked quietly, shaking his head from side to side.

The other man shook as Samuel continued to stare at him.

"Good," he said as he grabbed Chris's hand, forcing it open with his right while he placed something in the other man's hand with his left. As the man glanced down at the contents of his hand, Samuel spoke again quietly.

"Now get out of here before I regret this decision."

The man's eyes flared open, glancing between Samuel and his hand several times before he took off running, the object in his hand hitting the floor and rolling to a stop against the wall as Chris ran out the exit.

"OH! MY! GOD! HE SHOT YOU!" Blythe screamed, rushing over to him.

She grabbed his hand, turning it over as she rapidly talked.

"We need to get this wrapped fast so you don't go into shock, and we need to call the ambulance, and…"

She trailed off as she stared at his palm.

The gun had left a raggedly shaped star wound on his palm from the discharged gasses being forced under the skin and rupturing it from the underside. As she stared at it, she could see the muscles moving, rapidly knitting themselves back together. The blood flowing from the wound slowed to a trickle, then stopped as it continued to heal. Samuel stared at his hand, shocked to see the skin now starting to pull itself closed. He glanced at Blythe, who looked up at him with a stunned look on her face before they both went back to staring at his hand. By then, it had healed enough to look like an old scar that was rapidly fading. Flexing his fingers, he noticed that there wasn't any pain.

Blythe dropped his hand and backed away from him a few steps. She looked around dazedly before her eyes locked onto something laying on the floor. Hesitantly walking over, she squatted down, picking up the bullet that he'd dropped in Chris's hand.

"How…" she started, trailing off into silence.

"I wish I knew… What the hell am I?" he asked, trying to make sense of what had just happened. Everything he'd done was pure instinct. Catching the bullet, changing the tone of his voice, all of it, like he'd done it hundreds of times before.

He noticed a quick flash of fear cross her face. He put his hands up, trying to placate her.

"Don't worry, I'm leaving. There's no reason to be afraid of me. I'm sorry for the trouble I caused."

He slowly turned to the exit, walking away dejectedly.

"Are you nuts? We need to get back up to the apartment before the cops arrive," she said, roughly grabbed his sleeve as she tugged him toward the staircase.

He looked at her with a confused look.

She yanked at his sleeve harder as she tried to lead him up the stairs.

"Come on! They'll be here any minute!"

After opening the door to her apartment, she motioned him in before poking her head back out, looking both ways before closing the door.

"I'm sorry I scar—"

"That was freaking amazing!"

"Wha?"

"It's like you're straight out of a comic book or something," she said, leaping into his arms.

Before he could react, she leaned in and gave him a kiss. As their lips broke apart, she studied his face.

"That was for rescuing me. My very own knight in shining armor…" she said, trailing off as she stared into his eyes.

"You're, uh, welcome," he said, returning the gaze, "for a moment there, I thought you were scared of me…"

"No silly," she said, playfully swatting his check, "I was afraid of what the cops would do when they arrived. They kinda have a 'lock 'em up, then ask questions later' mindset for this part of town. I doubt you've noticed, being Mr. Badass an all, but it's a pretty dangerous area. My neighbor got mugged a week ago just around the corner from here."

"So, uh, is it safe to assume that tool I just dealt with was the ex you were talking about before?"

"Yeah," she said, looking at the ceiling, "he one of the reasons I'm still living in this rat-hole."

Samuel raised an eyebrow as she continued.

"I had saved up a little nest egg I was planning to use as first and last month's rent at another apartment that was closer to school and work. I'd written a check for the apartment only to find out a few days later that it'd bounced. When I went down to the bank to figure out what'd happened, I'd learned he'd forged my signature and had cleared the account out. He probably came back today to try and get more money out of me. I didn't have any proof of what he'd done, or I would have tried to press charges, but since the money was probably already gone, it wouldn't have accomplished much."

"As long as I'm around, you'll never have to go through that again. I promise."

Before she had a chance to say anything else, they heard a knock at the door.

"Hello? Miss Townsend? This is the police, can you open the door for a minute? We'd like to ask you some questions about a disturbance that just happened. We have some witnesses stating you were involved."

"Just a minute!"

She looked at Samuel, a look of terror spreading across her face. Samuel looked at her with a calm expression, holding his finger up to his lips. Glancing around, he quickly headed toward the kitchen window, grabbing a bottle of vegetable oil as he passed through the kitchenette. Squirting some of it on the slides, he softly opened it. Poking his head out, he quickly looked around before climbing out onto the fire escape.

"I'll try to be back later. If I can't, I'll meet up with everyone at the warehouse. Just tell the police that a good samaritan helped you. That should be enough to satisfy them."

"Okay," she said hesitantly, glancing back toward the door as the knock came again, "oh, I almost forgot. John got back to me. Said he found something. He should be at their store, The Shining Path bookstore."

She started to lean toward him, but the cops started knocking on the door more insistently, causing her to look back over her shoulder before looking back at him. Samuel climbed up on the edge of the railing, before looking down.

I dropped five stories without an issue, this should be nothing. At the least, it should be nothing. On the bright side, if I do break my legs, I'll just heal right back up.

He turned back to look at her one more time before he jumped off the edge, rapidly dropping down three floors before hitting the pavement silently. He looked back up and saw her leaning out the window, staring at him with her mouth open. He shooed her back in before turning around, jogging to the edge of the alleyway.

Peeking around the corner, he was surprised to see several cop cars lined up in front of the complex. Based off how Blythe described the neighborhood, it seemed to be an excessive show of force. He ducked back when several cops turned and started heading in his direction.

"We need to cover the alley and fire escape in case he tries to make a run for it."

He couldn't be positive, but Samuel suspected they were looking for him specifically, especially with the close call he had with the couple in black earlier. Glancing around one more time, he spun around and sprinted off in the opposite direction, disappearing into the shadows.

Frank banged forcefully on the door, drawing his gun out at the same time with his opposite hand.

"Ma'am, I need you to open the door right now or we'll be forced to break it down."

Cora drew her gun as well, preparing to follow her partner in. As Frank started to step back to kick the door, they heard the deadbolt slide back. The door opened a couple inches before stopping when the chain went taut. A young girl peered out from around the corner of the door.

"Yes, how can I help you officers?" she asked, glancing back and forth between them.

"Miss, you need to open the door right now. Otherwise, we're going to have to break it down."

The girl sighed, closing the door slightly to unhook the chain before opening the door the rest of the way. As the door started to open, Frank forcefully shouldered it open the rest of the way and strode in.

"Hey!"

Cora followed smoothly behind him, her eyes glancing at the surprised look on the woman's face before sliding past. Her partner moved right as she went left, each covering their quadrant of the room with their firearm as they split up, rapidly clearing the apartment before they holstered their weapons.

"What the hell are you doing! You can't just barge in here like that without a warrant!"

"Ma'am," Frank said, glancing around the room again, "we had reason to believe that a dangerous fugitive was hiding in this apartment, so we couldn't take any chances with our safety, or yours."

Cora gave the other woman a closer look, recognition dawning on her face.

"Hey, you work down at the shelter, don't you?"

"Yes…" she said hesitantly.

Cora vaguely tilted her head to the side as her brows narrowed slightly.

"I didn't get a chance to speak with you then, but you seemed awfully familiar when I saw you there. Don't I know you from somewhere else as well?" Cora asked.

The other woman stared at her for a moment before a light of recognition lit up her face.

"Officer Blanchett?" she asked hesitantly.

"Yes, that's me. Where do I know you from?"

"It's me, Blythe. You came out last year when one of my ex's tried beating me up. You found him and put him away for awhile. I haven't heard from him since."

Cora squinted at her slightly before her eyes lit up.

"It IS you, isn't it? How've you been holding up?"

"I've been better. Are you here about the run-in I had with my latest ex?" she asked.

"Yes, actually. Can you tell me what happened? Witnesses are telling us that a guy intervened in your fight with your ex. Reports are kinda sketchy, but from what we can collaborate is, the guy who helped you slammed your ex into the wall, then someone fired a gun. They also stated that you grabbed the guy who helped you and ran back up the stairs while the other man ran out the door like he was being chased by demons. What we need to know is, where did that guy go after you two ran up the stairs?"

As Cora interviewed Blythe, she watched her partner wander around the apartment. He paused at the window leading out to the fire escape, running his finger across it.

Looking back over at them, he asked, "Is there a reason why there's a puddle of oil on the windowsill?"

He held the bottle of vegetable oil up for emphasis.

Blythe looked over at Frank, a slight look of fear passing across her face.

"Even though I know that guy scared off my ex for now, I wanted to make sure I could get out of here fast if he came back. He's tried to break the door down in the past, so I wanted to make sure that window didn't get jammed again if I needed to get out of here quickly."

Frank nodded as he went back to the window. He slid it open and glanced out into the alleyway. Nodding again to himself, he closed it and came back over to stand next to them.

"As I was saying, where did this man go after you two ran up the stairs?"

"He followed me up to my door and asked if I was okay. I told him I was. He waited until I'd closed the door before leaving. I'm not sure where he went after that."

Cora pulled out a photo and showed it to her.

"Is this the man that helped you?"

Blythe squinted slightly at the photo before shaking her head.

"It all happened so fast, I'm not really sure. I don't think so though. I think the guy that helped me had lighter hair."

"Are you sure?" Cora asked.

"This man is dangerous and we need to find him quickly. He's wanted for questioning in a slaughter that happened several days ago..."

Cora trailed off, trying to let the silence pressure the other woman into speaking.

"Slaughter...?"

"Yeah, he was found unconscious, surrounded by a pile of bodies. He escaped from the hospital before we had a chance to question him."

"Sorry detective Blanchett, I wish I could help you, but I haven't seen him. Now if you'll excuse me, I need to get something to eat. I've had a long day."

Cora glanced at her partner before starting toward the door. Turning back, she handed Blythe her card.

"If you happen to remember anything else, or if you see this man, give me a call, day or night. Okay?"

Blythe nodded as she ushered them out the door.

"Have a good day detectives," she said as she closed the door.

As they started to walk down the hall, Frank looked over at her.

"I'd bet my silver star with clusters that she not only knows the guy, but helped him escape out that window."

Cora nodded.

"I won't take you up on that bet… Wait… you've got a silver star…?"

Frank looked down at his feet, looking slightly embarrassed.

"Yeah, it was nothing, really. Anyway, I think we need to leave a couple plainclothes guys here to keep an eye out, and maybe even follow her if they can."

"I agree. Since it looks like our boy is long gone, let's head back to the precinct."

"Right behind you…"

25

"Did you get a chance to read this lab report from the hospital yet?"

Cora rested her face in her hands before scrubbing them roughly across the skin, looking up at her partner.

"Yeah, and if I had read this a week ago, I would have asked the captain to have all of them checked for drug use. Now it's just an interesting footnote, hardly worthy of notice."

Frank chuckled, "an' by hardly worthy of notice you mean those broomsticks pinning Russo to the wall had to be traveling over a hundred miles an hour to do that... Or that the footprints in the sidewalk indicate someone weighing at least twice the normal weight of the average person needed to skydive out of a plane to make those impressions... Yeah... didn't even bat a eye or anything."

"Shut up, you prick..." she chuckled.

Frank started to open his mouth when she noticed he was staring over her shoulder at something. Glancing back, she noticed a beat cop gesturing toward them before he rapidly headed in their direction.

"Are you detectives Blanchett and Giani?"

"We are, officer...?" Cora replied.

"Officer Francis," he replied.

"What can we do for you?" Frank asked.

"Well, I heard you were looking for reports of strange things happening around abandoned building and warehouses. I think I found something that matches that description."

Cora spun in her chair to face the officer as she pulled out her notebook.

"Let's hear what you got."

The patrol officer pulled out his notebook, reviewing his notes before he spoke.

"We'd gotten several reports of a bunch of people going in and out of an abandoned warehouse over on the east side. I did some digging and found out it was foreclosed on a couple years back and the bank advised me that they hadn't found any renters or buyer for it yet."

"Well, that's not really all that suspicious. Do you have anything else we might be able to work with…?"

Officer Francis cleared his throat nervously before continuing.

"Well, the witnesses mentioned that there was probably somewhere north of fifty people hauling stuff in with multiple moving trucks including a really weird globe of some sort, one that everyone I talked to agreed made them feel uneasy. If the eyewitnesses were accurate, there were several people who were nearly as tall as the moving truck itself."

Cora glanced over at Frank, who gave her a slight nod. Looking back at the patrol officer, she clarified.

"You mean they could reach the top of the moving truck, like a U-haul or something."

"Well, like a U-haul yes, but the witnesses stated their heads were slightly higher than the top of the vehicle. I'm pretty sure they were exaggerating, or maybe from the angle they saw them it looked that way. I mean, come on, those trucks are what…? Over seven feet tall or something like that. You mean to tell me a bunch of people who could play for the NBA are setting up shop in an abandoned warehouse…?"

Cora flipped to a blank page in her notebook before glancing back at the officer.

"Where is this warehouse, exactly?"

"We need to check it out…" Cora said again.

"And I'm telling you, we need more to go on before a judge is going to sign off on a warrant."

"What more do you need Chief? Based off what we've been able to learn, there's a high probability that there's going to be another ritualistic massacre taking place soon if it hasn't already happened!"

"Listen, I know you want to find whoever's responsible for this mess, but you need more evidence. Especially since a case can be made that you're being reckless, what with your accident and everything."

Cora bit her tongue. She'd only told Frank about Sybil being in the car at the time of the crash. It wasn't something she could risk telling anyone about. People might accuse her of losing touch with reality, especially since the only evidence was circumstantial, like the hand print in the dashboard.

"Can we at least post a patrol officer to keep an eye on the place until we can get the proof we need, Chief?" Frank asked.

"That I can probably do. But not for long. Get out there and find more to go on and then we'll talk. Dismissed."

"But Chie—"

"I said dismissed. By all rights I should put you behind a desk at this point… Don't force my hand."

Cora got up and stalked out of the office. If this was the next site for a brutal sacrifice, they didn't have days to gather evidence, they might only have hours. Minutes even… She stalked over to her desk, angrily throwing herself into her chair.

"You know, you'd get much further with the Chief if you'd stop antagonizing him with stuff like that. Now that he's aware of how badly you want it, we're going to have to find another way to check the place out."

"Damn it, why do you always have to be so smug about things like this…?"

"Because I can get away with it while still looking good…"

"Bite me."

"Can I pick the spot?"

She stared at him for a moment before she broke out laughing.

"No, you can't pick the spot… Anyway," she said as she pulled out her map, "here's where that warehouse is located." She put a dot on the map, "and here's where the other one was," she said, pointing at a dot that was already there. What does this tell us…?"

"That you drew two dots on a map…?" he replied snidely.

"Damn it Frank, you heard the Chief… We need to find something, but all we have, as you so eloquently put it, is two dots on a map…"

Frank circled over to her side of the desk, looking the map over.

"What's this dot right here?"

"That's that library I was telling you about, where I saw that guy dressed like Sybil…"

"Right, right…" he said as he stared at the map some more.

"You got a ruler in that mess you call a desk," he asked.

"Right here Columbo… Why?"

"Wanna check something…" he drifted off as he put the ruler down on the paper. After a few seconds, he looked up at her.

"Call it coincidental or what have you, but those two warehouses are nearly the same distance from that library, give a half a block or so."

Cora came up next to him and stared at the map.

"Sonofa… you're right. Hang on…" she said, digging in her desk again.

"Always wondered if I'd have to use one of these things after leaving high school," she said, holding up a compass, "let's see what we get if we do this…"

She put the point of the compass down, centered on the library. Then she adjusted the arm until the pencil point was centered over the location of the first warehouse. Spinning it around full circle, the line intersected the center of the other warehouse perfectly.

"Damn, I think we just figured out where we need to do some extra searching."

"Your car or mine, Miss Blanchett…?"

"Why, I believe the gentlemanly thing to do is provide the lady with a chauffeur…"

Frank dramatically waved her toward the door.

"After you, madam…"

156

Cora and Frank had been driving around for several hours, investigating likely locations. They had already checked out a couple gas stations, four office buildings, and seven warehouses before they found what they were looking for. As they pulled into the parking lot of another abandoned warehouse, Cora looked over at Frank.

"I'm beginning to think it was just random chance that those two sites lined up like that. Maybe the second warehouse has nothing to do with this mess."

"Maybe, but we really don't have anything else to go on. We've still got those plain-clothes sitting on that Blythe woman, so other than that, this is all we have."

Cora sighed.

"Yeah, I know, but I'm not sure how many more places that smell like week-old piss I can deal with before I feel the urge to shoot the next homeless person on principle alone."

Frank chuckled, "What, you aren't enamored by it. I remember reading about a scientist that stated urine was loaded with pheromones… You know, the stuff that gets people all hot an' bothered."

"Yeah, well I think my nose must be on the blink then, 'cuz the only thing that smell makes me want to do is flush my nose with bleach."

As they came to a stop, Frank squinted at the building.

"Hey, what's that?" he said, pointing at the side door.

Cora squinted, trying to figure out what her partner saw. After a few seconds, she noticed that there was a broken chain dangling from a partially-opened gate leading to the back of the building.

"Well, since we're here, let's go check it out."

They both got out of the car and padded quickly over to the side of the building, trying not to make any noise. Reaching the gate, Frank squatted down, picking something up off the ground. He held it up to the light, showing a lock that was recently cut, the edges still shiny in the failing light. Frank held his finger to his lips as he stood up, slowly easing the gate open further. He carefully squeezed through the gap and glanced around again before waving her after him. The two of them made their way silently around to the back of the building, frequently stopping to listen for any sounds that seemed out of place. Reaching the corner, Frank took a quick peek before pulling his head back.

"I don't see anyone," he whispered, "but I see a door about half way down, just past the loading docks."

Cora nodded before slipping past him, sliding along the wall until she reached the door. She waited for Frank to stack up behind her before she tried the knob and found it unlocked. Glancing back at her partner, she held up her hand with three fingers sticking up. She waited for him to nod before drawing her sidearm at the same time he did. She ticked off three seconds before gently grabbing the handle with her left hand, slowly turning it until it stopped. Pausing again to listen, she gently pulled until the door opened far enough for them to squeeze through.

She paused just inside the door to let her eyes adjust while Frank did the same. As an afterthought, she pulled out her tactical flashlight and held it in her off hand, resting her shooting hand over her wrist to stabilize it. Glancing back, she nodded with satisfaction that Frank had done the same. Taking a deep breath, they slowly started to work their way deeper into the building. Turning a corner, she noticed a head-high mound up ahead. Turning back, Cora gestured toward the mound. After nodding in understanding, she slid forward again, moving more slowly as she approached. When she got to within twenty feet, she could make out the contents of the pile in the dim light.

She quickly put an arm over her face to keep from gagging.

"Jesus," she whispered.

"Well Cora," he said, "I get the suspicion that a seven foot tall stack of dead bodies qualifies as a strong enough piece of evidence to get a search warrant, don't you?"

Suppressing the urge to both vomit and slap her partner, she swallowed back the tide of rising bile.

"I'd hope to god it does, but I can't help but wonder if it'll take at least an eight foot stack to convince the Chief…"

Looking around, Frank added as he clicked on his flashlight, "I think there might just be enough leftover bodies laying around to make that an eight foot stack after all."

"Damn…" she said under her breath, trying to make sense of the carnage strewn around her. "How much worse can it get…?"

26

Samuel stopped at a nearby gas station. After a few minutes of talking, the attendant finally let him use the phone to call John. After a few rings, he heard the other end pick up.

"Shining Path bookstore, Karen speaking… How can I help you?"

Samuel cleared his throat.

"Hi Karen, this is Samuel. Blythe told me John might have found something out about my, uh, jewelry?"

"Yeah, he did, actually. He's not here right now, but he left a note about what he'd found. Apparently, a local professor by the name of Donald Waide wrote a book about ancient cultures. What caught John's eye was a sketch of a piece of armor that looks surprisingly close to what you have on your arm. He actually works up at the local university in the, uh…"

He heard the faint sound of papers being shuffled in the background.

"In the philosophy and religious studies department. John noted that if you called before three, to tell you that you might still be able to catch the professor before he leaves for the evening. Apparently he has a class until four."

"Thanks Karen, I owe you both. Hopefully he'll be able to give me some answers about this thing strapped to my arm."

"No problem. I look forward to watching you whoop the hell out of Cliff again at our next get together."

"Sounds like fun. Listen, could you call Blythe to check on her? She had a run in with her ex and the police were called. I dealt with it, but had to leave before the cops showed up. I just want to make sure she's doing okay."

Samuel heard nothing but silence on the phone.

"Karen… Are you still there?"

"Uh, yeah… So you were at Blythe's apartment today…?"

"Yeah… Listen, I gotta get going if I'm going to have the chance to catch this professor. Just promise me you'll call her, alright?"

"Sure, uh… no problem. In fact, I'll call her as soon as I get off the phone with you."

"Thanks"

After getting directions from the gas station attendant, Samuel took off running. From the directions the attendant had given him, he only had around twenty minutes to cover approximately eight miles before the professor's class got out. He had to slow down a few times when he noticed the odd sensations again, but the sensations faded quickly enough that he didn't lose too much time. He got to the university a half-hour later, not even breathing hard. After asking a secretary at the front desk where the professor's office was, he took off at a jog again.

As he approached the office, he noticed an elderly man locking up an office door. Hurrying over, he called out.

"Professor Waide?"

"Damn it, why can't anyone ever pay attention to my office hours," the gentleman said under his breath as he slowly turned toward him.

"What is it?" the professor snapped as he looked at him.

"I have a question for you about something in a book you wrote…" he started before he noticed the man growing pale.

"It's you…" he whispered, pointing a shaky finger at Samuel.

"Huh?"

The man turned back to his office door as Samuel slowed his approach. With shaky hands, he managed to unlock it after the fourth try. He glanced back at Samuel as he walked into his office, turning the lights on. The professor turned back toward Samuel, waving him in with a look of awe etched on his face.

"You really are here, aren't you? You're not just a hallucination caused by a tired mind, are you…?"

"Uh, yes…" he started off hesitantly, "I mean yes, I'm really here, and I'm really me. I was hoping you could answer some questions for me."

"Of course, come in, come in," he said, the trepidation in his voice slowly turning toward excitement. He closed and locked the door behind them. Almost as an afterthought, he turned back and closed the blinds as well.

"Follow me," he said, dropping his cane in his haste to reach his desk, not even noticing the several stacks of books he knocked over in the process.

As he reached his desk, he glance back toward Samuel before smiling broadly and hurrying around to drop heavily into his chair.

"You really are here," he said again excitedly, "you don't know how many decades I've waited and wished for this day to arrive…"

"You know me?"

"Know you, no… Know of you and your kind, oh most definitely."

"What do you mean? My kind? I don't know what you're talking about…"

"Oh yes yes, they did mention you claimed to have lost your memory…"

"They?"

"Yes, a couple of detectives actually stopped by earlier asking questions about you as well. I didn't tell them much, I promise you. They'd never believe me anyway."

"The police were here?" he asked, slowing his approach to older man's desk.

"Yes, a detective Blanchett and a detective Giani. They were most interested in you and the event that happened at the warehouse."

"Uh, maybe this wasn't such a good idea," he said, slowly backing toward the door.

"Wait! Please stay. Nobody knows you're here or that anyone's looking for you except me. I have so many questions I want to ask you."

Samuel paused, struggling with the choice of staying and possibly getting caught, or leaving and having risked coming here for nothing. He wasn't sure where he'd be able go since he wasn't sure it'd be safe to go back to Blythe's apartment, or the shelter for that matter. After a moment, he slowly sat down in the chair across from the other man. The professor breathed out a sigh of relieve, the tension visibly draining out of him.

"So what can you tell me about this," he asked sliding his sleeve up on his left arm, "and do you have any idea how to take it off?"

"Can I… Can I touch it," he asked reverently.

Samuel cocked his head to the side slightly as he held his arm out.

"Sure…"

As soon as the professor touched it, he yanked his hand back slightly before reaching for it again.

"It's flexible!"

"Why wouldn't it be?"

The old man ran his hand softly up and down the metal before he sighed, looking up at Samuel before remembering that Samuel had asked him a question.

"Wait right here for a second," he said, getting up and hurrying over to a wall hanging, snatching it aside to reveal a large safe. The man visibly concentrated as he tried to quickly open the safe, redoing it twice before it finally opened. Grabbing a bundle and hurrying back over to the desk, he haphazardly unwrapped it, revealing a match to the one on his left arm.

Samuel looked at the vambrace, feeling it tugging at his memory like he'd seen it before. Even though it was quite similar, he noticed several differences. For one, the color was different. This one was different shades of red and copper. Also, this one was more spiky, angular, and muscular looking, with fins stretching off the side of the head where the ears would normally be. This one also had horns. As he continued to look it over, Samuel's vision blurred slightly, revealing glowing lines that were crimson red in color. A slight squeezing sensation caused him to glancing down at his own vambrace. He noticed similar lines, but they were an electric cobalt blue, just like the sword sheathed in it had been when it extended at the hospital.

He suddenly felt an almost-physical thump as he saw an after image roll off his vambrace, matching and reflecting a similar response from the one in the professor's hands. The professor's feet got tangled in his chair as he stumbled backward. The vambrace tumbled to the floor as the professor tried and failed to catch himself before falling into a heap on the floor. Samuel eyes went wide as he alternated looking between the vambrace and the professor.

"You felt that?"

The professor nodded wordlessly as Samuel got up to retrieve the vambrace from where it had fallen. As he touched it, he felt a sudden surge of power drain out of him, first racing down, then flooding back up, his arm. Without warning, an ear-splitting screech/roar emanated from the vambrace on the floor. Stumbling backward, he saw the dragon uncoil, shaking its head before looking around. It glanced up at the professor, hissing at him, before its gaze locked onto Samuel. Like liquid metal, the miniature dragon leaped at him, almost too fast for him to follow. He fell backward over the chair as he tried to get away, lifting his right hand to defend himself.

The dragon latched onto the palm of his hand with one clawed grip before flowing around it in a sinuous motion, gripping his right arm tightly. Rearing its head back to look over its shoulder, it whipped its tail back, slashing the sleeve of his jacket up to the elbow. Using its hind legs to kick the fabric out of the way, it stretched backward before settling down on his forearm, the tail spiraled up out of sight around his right bicep. The dragon's head settled down gently on the back of his hand, the horns retracting slightly before laying down flat along the back of its head.

Letting out what sounded like a contented chirp, the dragon's metallic tongue flicked out, licking his middle finger before the fins on the side of its head wrapped around the edges of his hand. Finally, what appeared to be the pommel of a sword slid out of the dragon's mouth, extending down his finger, mimicking the handle position on his left hand. As the sword handle came to a stop and latched on, the dragon's glowing eyes glittered deep crimson before becoming inert, the body imitating the posture and appearance of the vambrace on his left arm. Coming back to his senses, he tried to yank the vambrace off his right arm as he stood back up, but it seemed to clamp down more tightly. He suddenly got an odd thought in his mind.

>*MINE!*<

It was like a bomb went off in his head, the pain dropping him back to his knees. Through teary eyes, he saw the eyes glitter again.

>*MINE! You're not going to leave me again.*<

Pain continued to spike across his mind, like rusty nails being pounded in with a sledgehammer.

>*Always the bossy one...*<

He heard it in a different mental voice. He tried unsuccessfully to form words as the pain continued to build. Without warning, a new pain like a roaring fire surged through him. A memory slammed into his mind, knocking him senseless as he tipped backward into unconsciousness.

27

He walked down the dusty hallway slowly as he carried Amitiel in his hands reverently. Lilith had finally won out, causing Amitiel to be discarded and left behind. Samuel couldn't bear the thought of wearing her again, not after what had happened with Genevieve. As he approached the King's Chamber, he felt Amitiel squirm in his hands, but he resisted her attempt to bond with him again. After witnessing the aftermath of her being worn by another, he feared he might succumb to the same impulses Genevieve had.

As he entered the chamber, he glanced around, noting that all the safety precautions were in place and active, only waiting on him to set her on her final resting place. With the way he'd designed it, he knew that there would be no way for her to escape by herself for all eternity. He could sense that she knew it as well. As he approached the pedestal, she mustered enough energy for one final attempt to change his mind, mewling while looking up at him.

He looked down at her with a sad expression, stroking her head one last time as he place her on the pedestal.

"I'm sorry Amitiel. If there was any other way, I'd do it. But for the safety of this world and Aerth, I can't risk it. Not after what happened with Genevieve. I wish there was another option."

A tear traced its way down his face as he stared at his friend one last time before turning away, ignoring the plaintive cries as he left the chamber. The risk of her bonding to him again was just too great a risk. One that, if it only involved him, he would have gladly taken, but the *safety of at least two worlds now rested upon his shoulders alone. Even though the Creator had given life to Genevieve for him, to help ease his burden, had instead turned her back on all of them. Now he'd have to seek another way to protect all of creation.*

As he closed up the front of the pyramid, he felt a heavy weight press down on him. Resting the palm of his hand on the structure, he sent out a telepathic message to Amitiel, letting her know that he'd always remember her, and if the Creator willed it, then maybe someday they would be reunited. With that, he sent a pulse of energy through the structure, priming all the safeguards to keep her from escaping under her own power. He glanced back down at Raguel, the Peltae and Peleus bonded to his left arm. Samuel felt him stir, sunk in his own regret at the necessary actions his master and friend had taken. He animated, his blue crystal eyes focusing on Samuel.

Samuel could feel the anger and sadness radiate off the dragon clutching his arm, and couldn't bring himself to disagree. He understood his friend's decision to take a vow of silence until the day he was able to be reunited with Amitiel. He could respect that. He might have done the same if the situation had been reversed. He patted Raguel as he stared at the pyramid for a few more moments, then he turned away, walking resolutely into the arid land, a part of himself lost forever.

Samuel gasped as he suddenly came to, glancing wildly around the room before realizing he was still in the professor's office. The professor had only just started to come around his desk when Samuel sat back upright.

"Are you alright my boy?" the professor asked, concern etched deep on his face.

Samuel slowly got to his feet as he nodded, trying to get his bearings. He looked down at his right arm, the memory washing over him again.

"Amitiel, I remember you..." he whispered.

>And I remember you too. You left me alone for so long...<

Samuel could feel the hurt/anger/pain/longing in Amitiel's mental projection. The pain from the projection caused him to collapse back on the floor. As tears of pain started streaming down his face again, he sensed confusion emanating from her.

>*Something is wrong… what has happened…?*<

New spikes of pain lanced through his mind, causing him to curl involuntarily into a fetal position. The overwhelming pain made it hard to concentrate on what was said next.

>*Samuel was injured. He has no memory of us, or much of anything past three days ago. I think it's affecting his telepathy. We might need to switch to talking verbally to him for the time being. If he could just find some ***.*<

It took a moment to regain his bearings as the pain started to recede. Samuel sensed the dragon on his left arm had been the one talking. It took a several tries before he was able to form words again.

"I don't understand what you mean…"

Samuel glanced up and noticed the professor looking at him with a concerned look on his face. He held up both arms to display the glittering, alien metallic creatures strapped to his arms.

"They're alive and talking to me. I can't really explain it, but I know this one," he said, motioning with his right arm.

"Remarkable…" a slight look of envy crossing the professors face as he continued, "and how… how do you know 'it'?"

Samuel rubbed his head, trying to decipher all the information the memory had given him. After a few seconds, he looked back at the professor.

"She… It's a she. I'm not sure of the details and reasons why, but I remember placing her in a pyramid designed to keep her from escaping for some reason. I think I was concerned about some great danger that might happen if she wasn't contained there, but I just don't remember…"

The professor nodded, then a look of confusion started to cloud his face.

"You said you remember placing it, I mean her," he amended when he saw the look on Samuel's face, "placing her on the pedestal? That you were responsible for the pyramid's construction…?"

Samuel pondered the memory again before nodding.

"Yes, I vaguely recall fragments of memory associated with the construction of the place, of how I felt the need to make it as secure as possible with the available resources of the time."

The professor leaned against his desk for balance, a distant look on his face.

"That would mean…" he said, his voice drifting off in wonderment, "you're well over a hundred and eighty millennia old…"

Samuel stared at the professor, his mouth hanging open.

A hundred and eighty millennia old… that's impossible…

"Nah, that's underestimating your age by quite a bit, actually…"

Samuel mouth dropped open as the creature on his left arm looked up at him. He noticed that the sword handle was actually attached to the underside of the dragon's chin somehow, but he couldn't tell where the rest of the blade went. Glancing at the professor, he gestured at his left arm.

"Did you hear that, or am I imagining it?"

The professor nodded slowly. Samuel looked back down at the dragon on his left arm.

"You mean to tell me that I'm older than that?" he asked in disbelief.

Nodding, the dragon continued.

"Actually, you're significantly older than that…"

Samuel dropped heavily into the chair behind him. He looked up at the professor with a questioning look.

"Professor, how is that even possible. Granted, I've got what appear to be two dragons clutching my arms, but look at me…" he said, gesturing toward himself.

"I look like I'm in my twenties or early thirties at the most. I don't understand it."

The professor jumped, the question snapping him out of his thought. As he slowly made his way back around his desk, he stared at the dragons on Samuel's arms. Dropping heavily into his chair, he pulled out a bottle of scotch from his desk. Pouring himself a good measure, he gulped half of it down without seeming to taste it. After a moment, he glanced back up at Samuel.

"As I mentioned earlier, I told you how I talked to the detectives earlier. In that meeting, I'd told them that I'd uncovered the pyramid during an archaeological dig… But what I failed to tell them was when the dig was…" he said, taking his glasses off to polish them before setting them back on his face, "you see, I was in my early sixties when I was on that dig, and to be sure, it would have been the crowning achievement to my career if I'd been able to reveal that discovery. Unfortunately, at the time I found it, there was no way to document it in a way that would have proved it had existed, at least not after it sunk under the sands."

Professor Waide fussed with his glasses again before continuing.

"You see, when I had picked that," he paused to collect his thought, "that 'creature' up, I'd told the detectives that I had witnessed a brilliant flash of light. What I didn't talk about was what that flash had done to me."

Samuel could feel a sense of satisfaction emanating from Amitiel, along with a pin-prick of pain when the professor mentioned it.

The professor continued, unaware of what Samuel suspected, "That flash of energy seemed to have changed me somehow, changed me on a fundamental level. I suddenly felt stronger, faster, and seemed to have vast amounts of energy available. More than I'd ever felt in my life, even in my youth. As the structure started to collapse around me, I felt time slow down as I rushed from the chamber, the chunks of building blocks slowly drifting toward the floor as I easily maneuvered around the falling debris, pushing stone blocks out of my path like they were weightless. It felt like it had taken me several minutes to escape the collapsing pyramid, but I know, based off calculations I did later, that I'd been able to cover several hundred yards in the space of a few seconds."

"So you're like me then?"

The professor paused as he smiled to himself.

"No… Even though I'm changed, I doubt I'm anywhere near as powerful as your kind are."

He paused to take another long sip of scotch.

"As I was saying, when I finally reached the mouth of the structure, because of my velocity and the angle of the ramp I was traveling up, I accidentally launched myself through the air and landed quite a distance from the opening. I don't remember much after that until they found me, but for several days after that, my body was racked with a burning fever and severe convulsions while I recovered. Since that day though, I've never had a day of illness, nor have I ever been permanently injured. Whatever that energy was, whatever it did to me, it now allows me to recover from most injuries within days, usually within hours."

To emphasize the point, professor Waide picked up a small dagger off his desk, pulled it out of its sheath, and nicked himself with it. Samuel watched as the wound gradually started to close. At the rate it was going, it would probably take at least another ten to fifteen minutes to completely close up.

"Remarkable, isn't it?" he said.

Samuel gestured for the dagger. The professor quizzically looked at him before handing it over.

"Yeah, not too shabby," he said as he dragged the edge of the blade over his palm. He nearly broke the blade with the amount of force he had to apply to cut himself, wincing slightly at the pain.

He held up his hand, showing the other man the bone-deep gash he'd just given himself. He watched with a slightly amused look as the professor's rapt look of attention as the wound on Samuel's hand close up seconds later.

"Simply remarkable…" he said quietly. He shook his head slightly before he continued.

"After that incident, I've devoted my life to researching everything I could about what most people would consider magic, for that's the only explanation I can come up with for what happened to me. I'm now the foremost knowledgeable expert in the world. Unfortunately, not very many people are aware of it since I have to periodically disappear and change my identity."

Samuel tilted his head sideways in an unspoken question.

"Well, the reason I have to change my identity, and the reason no one ever heard about my find, was because I discovered that pyramid nearly three hundred years ago. One of the benefits, I've since learned, of my wonderful healing ability, is that I don't age anymore."

28

The professor started to open his mouth to say more when the phone on his desk rang, startling both men. Samuel could see the professor ponder for a moment before picking up the receiver, listening intently to the speaker.

"No, I'm quite all right. No, you don't have to send anyone… No… No…" he said, getting visibly more upset as the conversation progressed.

Finally, he spat, "fine, so be it," before slamming the receiver down on the hook. Looking back up at him, Samuel could see the sadness on his face.

"It would appear that your little beastie's screech caused some concern with some of our other faculty members in the building, prompting them to call the police. The front desk was kind enough to tell me that the detectives from earlier have decided to check on my well-being, so it appears our conversation is going to have to end prematurely," he said, getting up and herding Samuel quickly toward the office door.

"I do so hope I'll have the chance to converse with you again, hopefully with your wonderful memories restored, but for that to happen, you must leave before the detectives reach us."

Samuel looked back at the man, shaking his hand warmly before replying, "I look forward it."

As the professor reached for the handle, someone pounded on the door.

"Professor Waide, open up, it's detectives Blanchett and Giani."

The professor looked at him with fear in his eyes. Without thinking, Samuel jumped straight up, performing a split as he landed lightly on the mantel ledge over the door, completely hidden from view. The professor looked up at him in shock. Samuel nodded to the elder man as he continued to perch above the door, a look of understanding crossing the other man's face.

Reaching forward, the professor unlocked the door, opening it slowly.

"Yes, detectives?"

"Are you all right professor, we got reports of a loud disturbance coming from this part of the building."

Cora roughly shouldered him out of the way as she stepped into the office.

"Mind if we come in?" she asked.

The professor replied in a testy voice.

"Fine... But I am going to have to file a complaint with your precinct. I provided you certain... leniency, when you stopped by earlier, due in most part with what you'd brought me, but now you're just being a nuisance."

"Noted," she said as her partner brushed past the older man as well, scanning the room carefully before glancing back at the professor.

"So what happened here?" she asked, "You've got quite a few piles of books knocked over."

As she asked the question, Samuel noticed that both her and her partner had placed their hands near their sidearms.

"Ah, just me being clumsy in my old age," he said as he tried to wave off the mess, "when you get to be my age dear, it happens sometimes."

"Really," she said as she moved deeper into the room, "is that why your cane is laying on the floor over there?"

The professor's eyes widened at Cora's statement. Reflexively, the professor glancing up at him. Both Cora and Frank following his gaze. Eyes going wide, both detectives spun away from the door, trying to put distance between themselves and Samuel. As they tried to pull their guns, the professor lunged at the detectives.

"Run," he yelled as Samuel dropped lightly to the floor. Samuel paused for a moment as he watched the professor physically lift detective Giani over his head in an attempt to throw him deeper into the office. Detective Blanchett paused for a split-second, a stunned look etched on her face as she watched the older man effortlessly snatch her partner over his head, before she kicked the back of his knee, forcing him to drop her partner in a heap on top of them. The professor shoved Frank off, causing him to sail several feet through the air before knocking down another pile of books. As Cora struggled to free her sidearm, the professor clamped his hand down over her's. Samuel caught her glance at him while he stood in the doorway. Their eyes locked for a moment, causing him to take a tentative step in their direction. The professor noticed the movement and yelled at Samuel.

"Run, boy! I don't know how long I'll be able to hold them."

Samuel took another tentative step toward them, paused, then spun away, vanishing out the door.

29

Cora saw concern etched across the younger man's face as their eyes locked. It surprised her when he took a tentative step toward them, unsure whether he should help or not.

"Run, boy! I don't know how long I'll be able to hold them."

Cora felt the professor relax slightly as he yelled at Samuel. As Samuel turned away, Cora took advantage of the lapse by sliding backward, causing the older man to stumble forward to keep his balance. Cora quickly reversed direction while performing a koshinage throw, dropping the professor to the ground. She quickly stepped back while she drew her weapon, pointing it at the professor.

"Frank!"

"I'm fine! GO!"

Cora glance over and saw Frank propped up against the wall, his gun pointing at the professor.

"Are yo—"

"GO!"

Cora glanced between the two one last time before she spun around and raced out the door. Hearing the sound of someone running down the hallway, she glancing in that direction. She caught a flash of Samuel running toward the end of the hall and sprinted after him, trying to eat up some of the distance between them. As she closed the distance, she noticed him looking back at her before he glanced back and forth between the exit and the staircase to the upper floors.

"Freeze," she yelled as he launched himself up the staircase, clearing three steps per stride.

Where the hell is he going?

She started running up the stairs, stopping at each landing to make sure he wasn't trying to ambush her. At each pause though, she could still make out the sound of him running ever higher.

As she reached the top floor, she took a deep breath before slowly advancing down the hallway, trying each door to see if any were unlocked. About halfway down, she noticed a door marked roof access was partially open. She placed her hand on the door and pushed quickly, peeking out the door before ducking back. Not seeing any obvious danger, she pushed the door open again, slipping out and pressing her back against the wall. She glanced around rapidly as she slowly slid her way down the wall, trying to figure out where Samuel might be hiding.

"All I want to do is figure out who I am and what happened to me, detective. That's all."

The jarring suddenness of the sound caused her to flinch. Spinning around the corner, Cora spotted Samuel looking over the edge of the building.

"Freeze," she yelled, pointing her gun at him as he started turning around.

"I said don't move!" she yelled again, her finger slowly taking up the slack of her trigger.

"Actually, you said freeze…"

She kept her gun trained on him as he stopped, then turned slowly back to look over the edge of the building.

"Place your hands on the back of your head and walk backward toward me. Slowly."

She watched as Samuel slowly placed his hands on the back of the head. Once that was done, he glanced over his shoulder.

"I'm not going to hurt you detective Blanchett."

"I don't care. Face forward and walk backward toward me. No sudden moves."

Samuel gradually approached her position. When he got to within ten feet, she ordered him to stop.

"Now on your knees, ankles crossed."

"I can't do that detective. If I let you take me in, I'm never going to get the answers I need."

"I told you I don't care! You don't have any choice in the matter. We're six floors up with a gun pointed at you… How did you think you were going to get away, anyway?"

"As you said detective, we're only six floors up."

Cora's phone suddenly rang, almost causing her to shoot Samuel in the back. Taking a deep breath, she relaxed her finger off the trigger before slowly taking her left hand off her gun. She reached into her pocket to grab her phone. Glancing down, she hit the answer button before putting it up to her ear.

"Frank, I got hi— OH SHIT!"

In the split-second that she'd taken her eyes off him, Samuel had somehow spun around and covered the distance between them. She reflexively squeezed the trigger, but he was no longer in front of her. She saw his hand blur, moving faster than her eye could track. She tried to bring her gun back to bear on him again, but he effortlessly snatched it out of her hand. Simultaneously, he grabbed the phone out of her other hand. She made a desperate attempt to grab her gun back, but he effortlessly deflected her, before slipping behind her.

"Is this detective Giani? Just wanted to let you know she'll be back down in a minute."

He's talking on my phone while fighting me!

She tried to turn fast enough to catch him, but every time she turned, he effortlessly managed to stay in her blind spot directly behind her.

"Good bye detective."

Cora heard the call end. Without warning, she felt a hand slide into her pocket. Acting instinctively, she launched an elbow backward, but felt it get redirected away again. She heard a click before the unmistakable sound of the slide being worked on her sidearm. Samuel slid back into view in front of her before launching himself at her, both arms outstretched. He moved so rapidly, like water rushing over rapids, that she didn't have time to make sense of what he was doing. She tried to take a step back to give herself room but stumbled over something and started to fall.

Unexpectedly, she felt both of his hands slide under her jacket. She couldn't tell what his right hand was doing other than tugging on something, but his left hand and arm slid around her back, arresting her fall before pulling her back upright like she was weightless. She tried to grab onto his right hand to try and perform another koshinage throw like she'd used on Professor Waide moments ago.

She felt him start to slide across her back almost effortlessly, like he knew what she was attempting to do. She felt a slight hitch in the movement. Somehow, he'd manage to rotate faster than expected by kicking his feet over, allowing him to land on his feet before springing up and backward, doing a backward flip over her head to land nearly at the same spot she had started the technique from, placing him behind her again. She spun toward him again, leading with a left straight punch to the midsection. Unexpectedly, he suddenly froze in place, allowing the strike to connect before drifting backward away from the follow-up.

It took a second for the pain to blossom in her hand and wrist. The impact had most likely sprained her wrist, possibly fracturing her knuckles.

What the hell is he made out of? I've broken bricks with that same strike, but I didn't even feel him flinch.

"Like I said detective, I don't want to hurt you, but I can't let you take me in, either."

Without warning, Samuel spun around and sprinted toward the edge of the building. She took off after him without thought.

He's going to kill himself.

His fluid strides lengthened the gap between them before launching himself off the roof. She reached the edge a split-second later, watching him drop the last couple of feet before he hit the ground. His impact shattered the sidewalk, dust and fragments spraying out in all directions. He slowly rose to his feet and stepped out of the mini-crater he'd created, brushing cement dust off his clothes in the process.

Turning around and looking up at her, he cupped his hands to his mouth.

"I'm sorry!" he yelled before turning around and sprinting away, a cloud of dust trailing behind him. She could make out a bloodstain where his left hand had slapped the ground when he landed. She stared a moment longer before she was startled again by her phone ringing. It took her a moment to realize it was in her pocket again. Shakily pulling it out, she saw it was Frank. Looking at the time-stamp, the fight, if that's what you could call such a one-sided match, had lasted less than a minute. Hitting the answer button, she put it up to her ear.

"Cora! Are you alright?"

The tension and concern in his voice brought a smile to her face.

"Yeah Frank, other than a possible sprain, some throbbing knuckles, and a bruised ego, I'm fine. I'm heading back down. He got away again."

She could hear the sigh of relief through the phone before he responded.

"Thank God you're okay… So how'd he get away this time?"

"You'll never believe it…"

As she said that, she realized there was something under her jacket.

"Hang on a second…" she said, gingerly shifting the phone to her injured left hand.

"What the…"

"Cora, you still there? What's going on?"

She slipped her hand under her jacket, feeling the heft of her sidearm resting in her holster, the catch snapped shut. Withdrawing it, she noticed that the magazine had been removed. She also noticed there was a faint smear of blood across the barrel from where Samuel had grabbed it.

"Oh, this just keeps getting better and better."

"What?"

"I'm on my way down. See if we can get into that bottle of scotch again when I get there."

She hit end before sliding the phone back into her pocket. As an afterthought, she started patting down the rest of her pockets.

"Frank is never going to believe this," she said under her breath as she headed back toward the professor's office.

"He did what!"

"Jumped off the roof. He literally jumped off the top of a six story building, hit the ground, and popped up like nothing happened."

"You're shitting me..."

"That's not all, either," she said as she pulled out her specimen bag, shaking the object inside of it around to catch his attention.

"When I answered the phone, he somehow got the drop on me. I reflexively tried to shoot him, but he moved faster than I could track. As best I can tell, he somehow caught the bullet."

"Let me see that," he asked, holding his hand out. She handed it over as she looked down at the professor.

"This thing's completely flattened. If it wasn't for the fact that it's covered in blood, I would have said it hit a rock or something."

"I know," she said as she continued to stare at the professor. "I never felt so helpless in my life. While fighting me, he was able to talk to you on the phone, remove the magazine from the gun, clear it, and stuff everything back in my pockets, including the bullet he caught."

She held up her hand that was quickly swelling.

"To top it all off, the only real shot I got at him, which I realize now he let me get, felt like punching a wall. There was no give at all."

"There's some ice in the miniature refrigerator over there under that table."

Cora glanced over to where the professor was gesturing before looking down at him again. Finally, she nudged him with her foot.

"What's going on professor? Not that BS you gave us earlier, either. Start talking or you're going to spend the rest of your short life behind bars..."

She shot a confused look at her partner when the professor started chuckling.

"What's so damn funny? You're looking at charges for aiding and abetting a known fugitive, possibly a mass murderer and/or serial killer. You'll be lucky to see the light of day after this. You'll probably die in prison."

The professor chuckled again as he slowly rose to his feet, ignoring the fact that both detectives had suddenly drawn and pointed their guns at him.

"Oh, put those away. I have no reason to do anything to harm you now that I know Samuel was able to get away."

Cora looked hesitantly toward her partner as his face screwed up in confusion as well.

"You asked why I was laughing, detective Blanchett," he said as he casually waved his hand, snapping the handcuffs like they were made of paper, "it's quite simple, really. You'd inadvertently made a joke, only you didn't realize it."

The detectives cautiously followed him as he walked back over and sat down behind his desk, their guns still pointed at him. Carefully, he poured himself another drink as he stared at them.

"This bottle isn't going to last nearly as long as I'd hoped," he said wistfully, waving his nearly full tumbler at them.

Cora tried not to clench her jaw as she slowly moved toward the professor.

"You were saying…?"

"Oh yes, the joke you'd made. See, what you referred to as the short remainder of my life is probably going to be a millennia or so after you've turned to dust, I'd wager."

Cora cast a brief glance at her partner before looking back at the professor.

"You see, everything I told you earlier was the truth, but I left out certain facts as well. As I was telling Samuel before you showed up, when I escaped with that item from the pyramid, I told you I didn't know how I made it. In actuality, while I might not have understood the mechanics of it, I do know how I escaped."

Cora gestured with the barrel of her gun.

"Go on…"

The professor took a sip from his tumbler.

"Somehow, among other thing," he said, jiggling the handcuffs for emphasis, "that thing stopped me from aging."

"What?" Cora asked, tilting her head in confusion.

"As unbelievable as it sounds, it's true. You see, you asked me why you'd never heard of what I discovered. Well, it's because I found it almost three centuries ago, give or take a decade."

Frank looked over at her, "This guy's lost his mind, Cora. We can't believe anything he's saying."

"You know Frank," she said as she holstered her gun, "I would've agreed with you if it wasn't for the fact that bullets just bounced off of someone I shot moments before he leapt off the top of a building and jogged away. Let's also not to forget that this guy…" she paused, waving toward the professor, "just tossed you like a shot-put across his office. Let's just say I'm slightly more open-minded than I was during our last visit."

Frank looked at her a moment before holstering his weapon as well.

The professor looked up at the two of them before asking, "Since your compatriots will be here soon, would either of you care for another dram before they get here? I'd really hate to drink alone while I fill you in on the parts of the story I didn't tell you about the first time around."

30

The professor cleared his throat before he began, giving them his best lecture voice.

"You see, I've learned through quite a few decades of research that there's more in this world than meets the eye. Things of magic and miracles."

Cora started to roll her eyes, but the professor caught her look in a steady gaze.

"I'm not talking about metaphorical or romantic notions detective, I'm talking about factual things."

He got up and walked over to his safe that was still slightly ajar, opening it more fully to pull several other silk-wrapped items out. Carrying the bundle back over, he set each item down gently. As he started unwrapping them, he continued to explain.

"For some unknown reason, silk seems to act as an excellent barrier to block what might be called, in layman's terms, latent magical energy."

As he said it, he finished unwrapping the first object. It was a quart-sized mason jar filled with a clear fluid. Inside the jar was a miniature floating body preserved in the fluid. As he handed it to Cora, her eyes widened at what she saw. The body inside appeared to be perfectly preserved, looking like a well-proportioned human only six inches tall. Other than the size, the most shocking detail was the gossamer wings sprouting from the back of the naked creature. Slowly handing it to Frank, she turned back to the professor.

"What the hell is that thing," she asked, pointing to the jar.

"I'm not entirely sure. It's either a brownie or a pixie, possibly even a fairy. I've never been able to isolate it since all the old legends stated they all flew through the use of magic, not wings. The wings actually makes it difficult to classify, I'm afraid."

Cora kept staring at the jar in Frank's hands as the professor finished unwrapping the second object.

"This object is most impressive," he said, catching Cora's attention. In his hand was a wickedly-sharp looking dagger, encrusted with jewels. She instinctively started reaching for her gun, but he held his hands up in a gesture of surrender before he gently laid it down on the table. He slowly slid across the desk toward her before gesturing for her to pick it up. As she grabbed it, she felt a slight thrum of power flow up her arm. She glanced back up as he slowly reached into a drawer, pulling out a short length of what appeared to be a metal rod. He handed the rod to Frank with a gesture to examine it while he turned back to Cora.

"What you hold in your hands was affectionately known as a vorpal blade. I know there was a movie recently that talked about a vorpal bunny, and surprising enough, there's a lot of truth to that skit. Now if you would please, hold that blade out before you carefully, cutting edge facing upward."

As Cora positioned the blade, he looked at Frank.

"I know this is going to sound like a silly question, but humor an old man. What exactly are you holding in your hand, detective."

Frank smirked as he replied, "well, using my amazing level of investigative and deductive skills, I have determined it to be a piece of structural rebar..."

The professor chuckled before continuing, "would you say there's anything special, or odd about that piece of metal rod?"

Frank turned it over in his hands, trying to flex it for good measure.

"Nope, plain old piece of rebar, satisfied?" he asked as he made a motion to hand it back, but the professor stopped him.

"Alright, since you're fully satisfied in the fact that that," he said as he gestured toward the metal bar, "is a 'plain old piece of rebar', what I would like for you to do is carefully hold it by each end, then gently bring the center of it down until it touches the edge of the blade."

Frank shrugged as he did what the professor requested.

"Are you sure about this? I'd hate to damage a priceless artifact and have you blame us for it."

"It's quite all right, just press down with the rebar and see if you can move your partner's hand. Slowly though."

Frank shrugged again and slowly pressed down. Cora braced her arm to resist the downward pressure, but the rebar parted around the blade like water, almost causing her partner to drop the two sections of rod in surprise.

"What the…?"

"How's that possible! I didn't even feel it touch the blade…"

"That's just it…" he said, gesturing with the sheath in Cora's direction, "scientifically speaking, it isn't possible."

"Come on," Frank said, rolling his eyes, "are you trying to tell me that's a magical knife."

"I'm not telling you anything," Professor Waide said as he handed Cora the sheath before unwrapping the final item, "use your senses. I'm showing you things that don't conform to what science allows for."

As he finished unwrapping the item, a smile broke across his face as a glimmering light started emanating from the item in his hands.

"So far, I've been slowly easing you into the world that Samuel exists in. For example, you've experienced my unusual strength, agility, and reflexes. While unusual, one could explain it away by science if you really worked at it, things like genetics, adrenaline, and so forth. Next I showed you a life-form that, without the benefit of opening the jar, could be argued that it was a prop or some form of doll. Harder to explain away is a knife that cuts through metal without resistance."

Professor Waide gestured toward them and the items laid out on his desk.

"Even with all this, you're still struggling with the idea that there's magic in our world. That's why I left this for last…"

As he said it, professor Waide dropped the silk away from the item in his hands. Cora saw that the object was some type of ring or hoop.

As she looked at it, she thought she saw something, a shimmering effect like what comes off the surface of hot asphalt, coming from inside the loop.

Frank lifted an eyebrow as he gestured toward the ring.

"And what, exactly, is 'that'?"

Professor Waide looked at Frank with a mischievous sparkle in his eye.

"This, dear boy, is a fairy ring…" he said, a smile slowly spreading across his face.

"Okay, I'll bite," Cora said suspiciously, "what exactly is a fairy ring."

"Well, according to the myths, it's usually a perfectly circular ring of mushrooms that act as a portal to the fairy realms."

Frank waved in the ring's direction.

"That doesn't look like a fungus…"

"Quite right, this is something rarer…" he said as he moved the ring around, "this is a portable one."

"So what does a portable fairy rin—" Cora started to ask, but trailed off as Professor Waide stuck his hand, then his arm through the ring, finally stopping just short of his shoulder. From their side of the ring, it appeared that his arm had been severed at the ring. Cora could make out all the muscle, blood vessels, and even the marrow in the center of his arm bone. The sight of it all flexing and pulsing started to make her queasy.

"Holy shit!"

Cora looked over at Frank. His eyes went wide in shock while his mouth hung open. Without warning, his hand shot out, reaching toward the area where it appeared the Professor's arm stopped. As his fingers reached the point where it should have touched the bloodless stump, his fingers vanished. Inhaling sharply, he yanked his hand back as the Professor did the same thing.

"Well… That was an interesting sensation…" Professor Waide said as he shook his arm out. "I've never thought to try and have something enter from both sides of the ring at the same time…"

The professor trailed off, appearing to be in deep thought. Frank's reaction was a little more animated.

"Interesting sensation?" he exclaimed, shaking his hand out, "It felt like I just shoved my hand into an electrified bucket of ice water! Damn that hurt!"

The professor came out of his ruminations with a start.

"Oh, sorry about that… My body seems to react differently to the energies that power the ring. More importantly, now you realize that this isn't some type of parlor trick. Unless you're going to be bull-headed about it, you'll have to allow for the possibility that there really is something called magic that we know very little about. I'm pretty sure it's related to quantum mechanics and string theory somehow, but since there's very few people I can discuss this with, the research needed to advance my working knowledge of it is very difficult to arrange without looking like a shyster. Just look what happened with the first public report of cold fusion…"

Cora vaguely remembered overhearing some of the science nerds in CSI discussing it once a while back, but didn't really understand it. Waving her hands at all the items on the table, she looked back at the professor.

"So what does all this have to do with Samuel?"

Taking a long sip from his tumbler, he met both their eyes before continuing.

"Why detective," he said as he gestured toward the items on his desk again, "everything…"

31

Samuel ducked into an alleyway. He'd been sprinting for the past fifteen minutes to put some distance between himself and the cops. As he slowed to a jog, he marveled again that he wasn't out of breath.

I wonder how long I could keep that pace up before I got tired…

>That's a silly question.<

The sudden pain lanced through his mind, causing him to stagger into the wall before completely losing his balance and falling on the ground.

>What's wrong with you?<

"Amitiel, talk out loud! I told you before that he'd been injured. Mind talking to him is causing him pain."

"But I can hear him fine!"

"Whatever the damage is, it only appears to be a one-way issue. We can hear his thoughts, but when we project, it's hurting him."

As Samuel's thoughts cleared again, he glanced back down at the blue dragon on his left arm.

"You're Raguel, right?"

Samuel felt a little uneasiness as the blue dragon's head swung around to look up at him.

"Yes, I'm glad you're starting to get your memories back. The surge of energy from the bonding must have helped you heal more."

"Bonding?"

"Yes, that surge of energy you felt when Amitiel here," he said, gesturing with his head toward the other dragon, "was caused by your life energies joining together. It would take a long time to explain, but the short answer is, without the bonding, you would slowly weaken her over time and you wouldn't benefit from the symbiotic link."

Samuel scratched the back of his head, trying to make sense of what Raguel was telling him.

"I don't understand… Why would she get weaker? And what's a symbiotic link?"

Samuel almost smiled as the little dragon gave an exasperated sigh.

"Okay, since the short answer won't work, let's try a slightly expanded version. You are a Syphon. That means you absorb and are sustained by Aether. In layman's terms, magical energies. That's why you're always hungry no matter how much you eat. There's not a lot of energy left in cooked food. Your body has to convert it into Aether before your body can use it. What your digestive system does… it's technically classified as a form of alchemy."

Raguel squirmed around a bit, trying to get a better position to see Samuel before huffing again.

"This is ridiculous. Hang on a sec."

Samuel jumped as Raguel uncoiled himself and leapt off his arm, landing silently on the pavement. He shook himself out before glancing up at Samuel.

"Going to give myself a kink in my neck at this rate," he said before his body shimmered. Suddenly, he expanded in size, growing until he was about the size of an English mastiff.

"Ah, much better. Now I can talk to you eye-to-eye, so to speak."

Samuel could only nod quietly as he tried to process what he'd just witnessed.

"So as I was saying, you absorb Aetheric energy. Food doesn't have very much left in it by the time you eat it. So your body breaks down the food and converts it into magical energy. A very inefficient process I might add."

"So what does this have to do with the bonding process?"

"I was getting to that. Since Amitiel and I are both magical creatures, if she didn't bond with you, you would have unconsciously started feeding off her. If your memories were back, you would be able to control that urge, but you'd still feel the need constantly at the back of your mind."

Raguel paused to scratch himself behind the ear.

"Anyway, when we bond with you, we blend our life energies together. You'll also get a significant boost to your abilities once you remember how to access them. Hopefully the added energy boost will help you get your memories back sooner."

"Why?"

"Really? You haven't put two and two together yet? That bullet really did a number on you. Basically, you're using ambient Aetheric energy to heal yourself. If you had been in a safe place, you probably would have been fine by now. As it stands, you've been unconsciously using your abilities to shield yourself from discovery, at least you were until you bonded with Amitiel. That takes a lot of energy to maintain. Hence why you've been so hungry and why your memory isn't b—"

The weird tingling feeling coming from behind him caused Samuel to snap his head around toward the alleyway opening. Raguel's head stretched up to look over Samuel's shoulder at the same time. As the tingling got stronger, Samuel saw several heavily muscled guys slowing making their way down the alleyway toward them. As he stared, the weird tingling sensation continued to wash over his body. The feeling was becoming strong enough that he suspected he could determine their exact position even if he closed his eyes. He suddenly experienced the odd superimposed image effect again, seeing the men turn into hulking, eight foot tall creatures.

"Trolls."

Samuel glanced back at Raguel before glancing back at the creatures. As they neared, he could just make out their conversation.

"Is dis da guy we were suppos'd to find? He don't look like much."

"He sure looks like what da boss said he'd look like."

"Can we eat 'im?"

"Boss didn't say, jus said ta deal wit 'im."

Samuel caught a whiff of the stench rolling off them as they continued to approach.

"Uh, what do we do? Do we run for it?"

Without warning, a strange guttural hissing noise started filling the alleyway from somewhere behind him, causing the creatures to pause. As soon as the hissing started, a frigid blast of air blew past him. Turning around, Samuel almost took a step away as he saw the glint of cold blue light glowing in Raguel's eyes. As he watched, a coating of frost and rime started forming on the dragon's scales before slowly spreading away from his clawed feet across the alleyway floor. The dragon started clawing at the pavement, leaving deep furrows behind. As the air temperature continued to drop, fog started rolling off him, almost like steam coming off snow on the first warm spring day. Slowly, his tongue flicked across his lips as he turned toward Samuel, a wicked smile forming on his face.

"Run…? Never…"

Raguel suddenly leapt at him, causing Samuel to swing his arm up reflexively.

"We destroy."

As Raguel flew at him, he spit out long flowing stream of clear liquid. Samuel flinched to the side as the spray passed by his head, frost instantly forming along the side of his face. As the dragon reached him, his body rippled and contorted, shrinking down to his normal size. Latching on to Samuel's arm, he flowed back around into position. Winking up at him, a cruel toothy smile spreading across his face, he chuckled.

"You didn't think I was going to hurt you, di— behind you!"

Samuel spun around. He barely had time to notice one of the trolls was encased in a sheet of ice. What filled his vision was the sight of the largest one swinging his clasped hands down at him with an overhead strike. He swung his arms up, trying to brace for the impact. As their arms made contact, he sensed the force of the impact, even dropping down to one knee as the pavement turned to dust under him.

A strange tingling sensation started flowing up his arms from the point of contact. It slowly changed to a feeling of warmth as he realized that he wasn't hungry for the first time since he woke up.

Pushing back against the trolls arms, he suddenly lashed out with a right palm heel strike. A loud crunch echoed off the walls as the creature flew back several feet through the air before crashing noisily into a dumpster, crumpling the side like it was made of paper.

"He's a Syphon! Boss never said he was a Syphon!"

Samuel wasn't sure, but it sounded like there was a tinge of terror creeping into the speaker's voice.

"It doesn't matter. The boss'll kill us if we don't take care of 'im. Get 'im!"

Samuel felt the itching sensation building up on his left hand again. He reached out to wrap his hand around the pommel that formed. Yanking the sword free, he dropped into an aggressive stance. As the trolls cautiously approached, he could feel the encouragement and excitement flow from Ratuel. The slight prick of pain the mental encouragement generated was forgotten as he felt the adrenaline release throughout his body.

Here we go!

The thought echoed in his mind as he launched himself at the next troll, the sound of tinkling glass trailing behind his sword as he swung it forward through the air.

Samuel's legs gave out on him. The adrenaline started flushing out of his system as he glanced around at the carnage. The nerves from the battle left him shaky and weak, making it hard to concentrate on what to do next. He started to ask Raguel what they should do with the bodies when he noticed a faint glow coming off them. As he watched, they slowly started evaporating, almost like dry ice. He could feel something coming off the bodies, but he couldn't quite describe it. Glancing down at Raguel again, he gestured to the bodies.

"What's happening to them?"

"Their bodies are slowing dispersing. Shouldn't take more than a couple hours or so."

"Why are they..."

Samuel tried to think of the words to describe what he was seeing. He waved in their general direction.

"Why are they evaporating though?"

Raguel let out a small sigh.

"Because… Their life force acts as the glue that holds them together in this realm. When extinguished, they fall apart at the cellular level, if not smaller. If they were back in Aerth, it wouldn't happen."

"Aerth?"

"Oh for the love of God. I'll be so glad when your memory returns. Yes, Aerth. The best way to describe it is that it's a mirror image of here. The main difference is that this place is based off science and technology while Aerth is based off magic and aether."

"Sorry I'm being such a bother after being shot in the face. I'll try not to annoy you anymore."

Amitiel animated and glared at Raguel, smoke and small jets of flame coming from her nostrils. Samuel could almost sense the argument going on between them. The feedback alone was starting to cause a migraine. Finally, Amitiel glanced up at him. He felt the concern emanate from her before it abruptly stopped. She glanced back at Raguel.

"You can be such a jerk sometimes. From what you just told me, it's not his fault he doesn't remember any of this. A little understanding would be in order."

Glancing back up at him, she continued.

"I'm sorry I keep forgetting to talk to you audibly. It's been so long since I actually spoke, it's taking me some time to relearn and get used to it again."

She glared back at Raguel, who hung his head dejectedly.

"Don't pay any attention to him. He can be insensitive sometimes. Once we're done sharing information, if you have any more questions while we wait for your memory to come back, you can ask me instead."

Samuel started to open his mouth when he noticed Raguel sticking his tongue out at Amitiel when he thought she wasn't looking. After the fight, the completely normal, almost human reaction caught him completely off-guard. He burst out laughing.

"It's fine, I'll survive. I know I'm probably a pain in the ass with all my questions, but I don't know how else to figure out who I am."

Glancing one more time at Amitiel, Raguel looked back up.

"Let's get out of this smelly alleyway before ghouls show up to try and snack on the bodies before they completely evaporate. That's all we need to deal with."

Samuel nodded before standing up. Getting his bearings, he turned away from the direction the trolls had come from. Unconsciously sheathing his sword, he took off at a jog. He wasn't sure where he was headed. All he knew was that he needed to keep moving before someone else found him.

"So what you're telling me is that I'm some sort of guardian appointed by God?"

Amitiel glanced up at Samuel while they ran across the rooftops, heading toward Blythe's building.

"Yeah, pretty much."

Samuel mulled over what she had told him. At some point in the past, God had split Earth and Aerth apart, and appointed him to be the guardian of both, along with the rest of the realms. That's why he'd been bonded with Raguel and Amitiel. It still didn't tell him the reason he'd been shot at that warehouse, but now it made more sense why he'd be in a place where it could happen. A thought suddenly occurred to him. Now that he knew the dragon was alive and could talk, maybe Raguel could tell him what happened. He glanced down at the dragon again.

"So why was I at that warehouse, anyway?"

Raguel glanced up at him with a sad look on his face.

"I knew this question was going to come up eventually. I just wish I had a good answer for you."

"Huh?"

"Yeah…" Raguel said, trying not to meet Samuel's gaze, "about that. Honestly, I only know fragments about what you were doing. Since taking my vow of silence, you've tried to talk to me less and less over the years. Eventually, other than the subconscious communication we have when in battle, you just sorta locked me out of your head. Don't forget, today's been the first time we've really talked in a hundred and eighty centuries. Quite a long time to go without sharing our thoughts with each other."

Samuel thought about what he wanted to ask Raguel next. He picked up a little speed as he leapt through the air and landed on the roof of the next building, tumbling forward before springing back to his feet to keep up his momentum.

"So what do you know? You had to have some idea about what I was doing there."

"All I know is that you've been trying to track down rumors over the past fifty years about Genevieve having resurfaced. Something big was supposed to happen at that warehouse, some type of ritual that you were trying to break up when that shot hit you in the face. I had to draw a lot of the aetheric energy out of the environment in order to keep you alive and to drive off the last few stragglers that remained. If the humans hadn't shown up when they did, you might have died."

Samuel slowed to a stop at the edge of the building next door to Blythe's apartment. Slowly glancing over the side, his vision adjusted to the reduced visibility. He'd been running a random pattern for the past few hours, slowly making his way back here. He wanted to make sure the sun was down before he arrived to make it easier to try and sneak in if possible. He wasn't sure what type of surveillance the police were going to set up, but he hoped he'd be able to get around it. He wasn't looking forward to sleeping outside tonight.

After several minutes of looking around, he'd been able to spot a few people that he suspected were undercover cops, but he couldn't be sure. Trying to figure out his next move, he looked down at Raguel.

"I don't know if I should chance it. I can't be sure if I spotted everyone. You got any ideas?"

Samuel jumped a bit when Amitiel spoke up.

"I can help."

"I'd almost forgotten you were there. You've been so quiet this whole time."

"I haven't been around anyone for eons. At least he's been around to hear people talking."

Amitiel gestured toward Raguel with a wingtip.

"I'm just not used to having conversations and talking is all. But to get back to your problem, I can help."

"How?"

"Like this."

As she said it, Samuel felt a tingling warmth course up his arm, then his neck, and finally coming to a stop behind his eyes. As he focused on the sensation, his vision started to take on a rainbow effect.

"What are you doing to me?"

"Sharing my thermal vision with you. You should be able to make out thermal changes in the environment once you get used to it. We used to do this all the time."

Samuel glanced around in wonder. The world looked so different when you could see heat patterns in the environment. The roof he was standing on was a yellowish color while the alleyway below was various cooler blue shades. As he looked around, he noticed a few more people than he'd noticed originally. With some focus, he realized he could actually make out the outline of their gun on some of them. After studying the area for around ten minutes, jumping between a few buildings to check out all the directions the alleyway went, he came to a decision.

"I think I'm going to chance it. There's nobody on any of the other roofs. Nor is there anyone actually in the alley itself, just at the different entrances. I think if I jump over there and climb down the fire escape quietly, I can get to her apartment without anyone noticing. What do you two think?"

"It's a pretty big risk. I think we should just go somewhere else instead. Maybe there's another homeless shelter you can sleep at."

Amitiel glanced over at Raguel.

"Homeless shelter?"

"Yes. Think of a monastery without the preaching."

"Okay," she said as she glanced forward. After a moment, she looked back over.

"What's a monastery?"

Raguel shook his head.

"Never mind."

After one more look, Samuel got a running start and leapt over to Blythe's building. He slowly climbed down the fire escape, pausing every few steps to listen and look around. After several minutes, he finally reached her window. He gently put his ear up to the glass to see if he could hear anything. He lightly tapped on the glass, but didn't hear any response. Looking around again, he checked to see if the window was locked. Silently sliding it open, he quietly slipped through the window before turning around to close it again. As he started to turn back toward the main area, his world erupted into fire as something splattered into his face, followed by a blinding light. Samuel let out a yelp of pain as he fell backward, knocking stuff over in the process.

"Oh my god! I'm so sorry!"

Through the burning pain across his face and lungs, he heard stuff getting knocked around before he heard the water start running in the sink. A moment later, something wet was shoved in his hands. It took him a moment to realize it was a wet cloth.

"I didn't know it was you. I just saw someone coming through my window and reacted."

Struggling to concentrate through the pain of what felt like razor blades skating across his eyes, he used the cloth to wipe his face down. After a couple minutes, the burning pain started to subside.

"What the hell did you hit me with?"

"Uh…" she said, pausing for a moment, "bear repellent…"

As the last of the burning sensation receded, he glanced up at her with bloodshot eyes.

"That was rather unpleasant…"

"I'm so sorry… I guess the good news is, the sales person over-hyped it. He said anyone I used it on would be, in his words, 'twitching in their own pool of vomit for the next half hour minimum,' yet you seem like you're almost back to normal."

He struggled to his feet, still slightly off-balance from the unexpected assault. He felt Blythe grab his arm and helped him up, leading him over to a chair to sit in.

She took the cloth from him, rinsed it out in the sink, and brought it back to him. The feel of the ice cold cloth felt good against his violated skin. After a few more minutes, he felt back to normal.

"I'll have to remember to knock louder and wait next time."

"What are you doing here? The cops are all over the place."

When she mention that, he glanced up in alarm. Feeling the tingle travel up his arm again from Amitiel, his vision shifted again to allow him to look through the walls of the building. Glancing both ways, he didn't see anyone making any suspicious movements. Patting his arm, the tingling faded away, letting him see normally again. He noticed that Blythe had backed away a few steps while staring at him intently.

"What's wrong?"

"Your eyes… I might have been imaging it, but they were glowing red a moment ago."

"With the way my day has gone, it wouldn't surprise me."

"Why, what happened? I mean other than the cop thing earlier."

"Oh, let me tell ya…" he said, holding up his right arm where Amitiel was attached, "this is just the tip of the iceberg."

33

Cora and Frank headed toward their car. They'd spent the past hour talking to the other officers that had shown up shortly after their fight with Samuel and professor Waide. It took a bit of work, but Cora was finally able to convince them that it hadn't been a gunshot that people heard. Instead, what they'd heard was someone dropping something heavy off the top of the building as a prank. The main reason they finally believed her was because of the impact crater Samuel had left when he landed. As they got in, Frank looked over at her.

"So what do you think? Think he's on the level?"

Cora cast a sidelong glance at him as he started the car.

"Are you serious? After everything he showed us? How can you still be skeptical?"

"About the existence of magic? No, the professor convinced me of that. I'm talking about all the other stuff. They say the best lies have a grain of truth to them."

Cora thought about what he said before she responded.

"Frank, you don't get it. When I was fighting him, it was like fighting a ghost. He could have killed me without even trying, but he actually caught me when I got knocked off balance. I'd like to believe that someone who's capable of that wouldn't be responsible for that slaughter, regardless of circumstances he was found in."

As she talked, she readjusted the ace bandage wrapped around her wrist. Thankfully, the pain was starting to go away, but for some reason, she was really thirsty. Flipping her notebook open, she listed off what they knew.

"So far, all we really know is that Samuel was found in a warehouse surrounded by bodies. We found a second warehouse with dead bodies in it as well. Based off the rough time of death that the M.E. could give us, they died while Samuel was still in the hospital. We also have reason to suspect that we've located a third warehouse. We haven't heard back from the patrol stationed out there, but I'm going to go out on a limb and suspect we're going to find bodies there as well."

"What about what happened to Russo? Based off the lab reports, he died sometime before our boy escaped. One of the nurses said she checked on Samuel sometime after the M.E. said Russo was killed, so he wasn't responsible for that death either. Think it might be that Sybil woman?"

"It's possible, but not likely. If it was her, then why'd she show up after he was gone? No, someone else is involved… Someone who doesn't have a problem killing indiscriminately. Based off the evidence, I'd suspect someone else who can use — I can't believe I'm saying this — someone who can use magic as well. How else to explain what happened without someone noticing it."

Frank chuckled.

"I think I'm going to have to talk to a shrink, or a priest, after this case."

"Or take up basket-weaving…"

They both broke down laughing for a few minutes before he glanced over at her again.

"So what's our next move?"

"We need to investigate that other warehouse, warrant or no warrant."

Frank put the car in gear and started backing out of the parking spot.

"I think we need to get better equipment first."

"Holy shit! Where'd all this come from?"

Frank smirked as he moved deeper into the room.

"Don't ask. Let's just say I still have a few friends in recon…"

Cora looked around the room wide-eyed as he turned on more lights. She always thought it was a movie trope to have an armory like this hidden in someone's house, but this looked straight out of a big budget spy movie. As she started to walk around the room, Frank motioned to the walls.

"Take what you think you'll need. Since this might be a big-game hunt, you don't want to wish you'd grabbed something and didn't."

Cora nodded as she continued to examine the guns and other weapons hanging on the wall. Turning back to Frank, she gestured toward the wall.

"A Desert-Eagle? Really?"

"Hey, it's the most used handgun in the movies. Every bad guy has one. I wouldn't suggest it though."

"Why?"

"It's hard to shoot accurately. The grip's so big and bulky, you'll have a tendency to shoot low and to the left. While stopping power is a high-priority, accuracy is more important."

Cora nodded as she started to move around the room again.

"What about this one?"

Frank glanced over and smiled.

"Can't go wrong with that. Make sure you get some speed-loaders for it."

She smiled as she pulled down the raging bull revolver. If a .454 couldn't stop whatever they came across, then not much else would. She pulled down the cross-draw holster that went with it and shrugged into it. Grabbing three speed-loaders, she also grabbed a couple of bricks worth of ammo. She grabbed a backpack off the wall as well and dropped the ammo into it. Glancing around again, she saw two handguns she wasn't familiar with.

"What are these?"

Frank walked over and pulled them down. He checked the chambers before handing them to her, one at a time.

"These are classics. They don't make them anymore unfortunately, but my god are they fun to use. The one in your left is an AMT automag 3, chambered in the .30 caliber carbine round. The other is a Calico 900, chambered in 9 millimeter."

"What's this cylinder on top of this thing?"

"That's one of the reasons why it's not made anymore."

He gestured for her to hand the Calico back over. Removing the cylinder, he showed it to her.

"This here is a hundred round helical magazine. I had my machinist friend turn this bad boy into a selective fire machine pistol. He also modified it with a buffer plate so it can handle +p+ without cracking the frame. For what we might come across, it might be a bit on the light side, but for overall output, it might make up for it."

Glancing around the room again, she smiled again.

"This room is like a candy store for gun nuts."

"Yup. But less talking, more arming."

The smile slowly faded from her face as she thought about what they might be going up against.

"Right."

When they finished loading up, Cora felt like a one-woman army. She had decided on a drop holster for the automag, the cross-draw for the raging bull, and Frank had figured out how to rig up a horizontal scout-style carry holster for the Calico that sat just under the bottom of the backpack she was carrying. To top it off, Frank had also hooked her up with an Armalite AR-10 rifle chambered for a .308 round. She debated about leaving some of it behind. Including the bullet-proof tactical armor, she weighed at least an extra forty pounds. She started to remove some of it but then thought back to how she'd been man-handled by Samuel. She also remembered how he'd caught the 9mm bullet out of the air when she'd shot at him. With that image firmly in mind, she resettled her equipment again.

"Want some?"

Cora looked over to where Frank was standing. In his hand were a couple of grenades.

"Frank, we ARE still going to be in the city limits. I think that might be a bit much."

He looked sadly down and the grenades before putting them back.

"Yeah… You're probably right. It's been a long time since I geared up for something like this. I got carried away."

She looked at him as she held her arms out to the side while she spun in place.

"You mean like this?"

He chuckled again.

"Yeah, something like that. Unless you can think of anything else, let's bring this stuff out to the car and head out. It's going to be dark soon."

"Speaking of which, you don't happen to have any night vision equipment, do you?"

"Good thinking, let me grab it and we'll get on the road."

"Sounds like a plan. Let's go."

The sun was just dropping below the horizon as they arrived. They circled the block once before pulling into the parking lot. Looking around, they spotted the patrol car off to the side. Hopping out, they walked over to see if the officer had seen anything suspicious. As they got closer, they realized nobody was in the car.

"Somethin's not right," she said as she drew the automag. She glanced over at Frank and saw that he'd done the same. Carefully approaching, Cora thought she saw something on the ground by the driver-side door. She pulled out her tactical flashlight and clicked it on. Shining it on the ground, she saw the light glitter back at her. Glancing back at Frank, she pointed at the ground.

"Glass," she mouthed.

She pointed to herself, then at the driver's side of the car. Then she pointed at Frank and gestured to the passenger side. When they finally got to the car, they looked it over.

"I've got fresh blood over here," she said quietly. "It looks like someone or something smashed the window and dragged him out. Whatever did it was strong, too. The seatbelt was snapped, not cut."

"Same over here," he said as he shined the light into the passenger seat.

"Whatever did this hit them fast. They never stood a chance. Think they're still alive?"

"Only one way to find out. Let's get suited up and find out."

"Right behind ya."

CLICK.

Cora's heart dropped. She thought back on Frank's quip about not wishing they'd left something behind when they needed it. She really wished she'd grabbed some of those grenades after all.

"Frank! I'm out," she yelled as she backed into him, dropping the rifle and pulling out the revolver.

"I've got one mag left, but it's not going to be enough! Head for the door, I'll cover you!"

"I ain't leaving you Frank! We either both get out of here together or we don't! End of story!"

She could hear his ragged breathing behind her as she cocked the hammer on the huge chunk of metal in her hands. She couldn't help but wonder how useless it was probably going to be against whatever these things were. At first glance, they looked like really ugly, muscular men. When they smiled though, she could see what could only be described as gnarled tusks instead of teeth.

"Aim for their head. That seems to be stopping them," he yelled as he let off another controlled burst, followed by a low grunt from one of the creatures. Without warning, one of them dropped down from the catwalk above them, landing only a couple feet away from her. Spearing her arms out, she jammed the barrel of the gun against its head before it got up and pulled the trigger. The sound was deafening as the creature's head exploded, the body falling over backward.

"Got one!"

"Aw shit."

The tone in his voice told her something was wrong. As she started to turn, she heard a wet thump a split-second before Frank's body slammed into her, launching them across the floor, sliding to a stop about ten feet away from where they'd been standing. The impact had knocked the big revolver out of her hands, leaving her defenseless. Looking back, she saw the monster pick up the gun off the floor. Showing her a ragged smile, it easily bent the barrel in half before tossing it to the side.

"Looks like yur luck just ran out human. I'm going to enjoy making a stew out of da two of ya."

Cora desperately tried to get to the automag on her leg or the Calico strapped to her back, but she was pinned in an awkward position due to Frank's limp body pressing her down into the floor.

"Frank! Wake up!"

All she got was a low moan from him.

At least he's not dead. Not that that's going to be the case for much longer.

"Who are you?"

"Doesn't matter. If ya wanna call me sumfin', ya can call me yur cook."

As he smiled, Cora heard a whistling sound. A puzzled look crossed the creature's face before its head slid off its neck, making a wet splat as it hit the ground. The head bounced once before rolling to a stop a few feet away. Its body spasmed a couple times before collapsing forward lifelessly.

"Didn't I say this probably wouldn't turn out well for you two?"

"How…?"

"I knew you couldn't leave well enough alone, so I had someone follow you. Good thing, too. What orcs lack in the brains department, they more than make up for it in toughness."

"Behind you!" Cora yelled.

Sybil slid slightly to the side as the punch slid past her head close enough to tousle her hair. Reaching up one-handed, she quickly levered its arm down over her shoulder, dislocating its elbow before doing some type of throw that launched it straight up in the air.

"Don't mess with my hair. And you," she said as she pointed at Cora, "stop yelling. I'm right here."

As she said that, she ducked down. It was the first time Cora noticed that Sybil was holding a sword in her hand. Taking a double-handed grip, she continued.

"I could smell that cretin from a mile away."

With a sickening crunch, Sybil's whipped her sword upward as she stood, neatly slicing the creature in two as it fell past. Shaking the blood and gore off the blade, her eyes got cloudy, emitting a pale phosphorescent glow. A moment later, her eyes went clear again as the glow died.

"Looks like that's all of them," she said as she walked over. She glanced down at where Cora was struggling to get out from under Frank.

"Ready to admit it yet?"

"Admit what?" she gasped. The weight of Frank and his armor was starting to make it hard for her to breathe.

"That you're out of your league."

Cora glared up at the other woman.

"Fine. You're right, I'm wrong. Happy?"

Sybil smirked down at her.

"That's all you had to say."

Cora watched as the other woman shoved the blade of her sword into the dragon-shaped jewelry on her arm. With a stunned look, Cora watched as the blade disappeared before the handle shrunk and latched onto Sybil's finger. Once it was sheathed, she reached down and grabbed the front of Frank's armor one-handed, effortlessly lifting him off her and holding him dangling in the air. Cora scrambled to her feet, looking between Sybil and Frank.

"Be careful with him, he's hurt."

"Don't worry, he'll live. He just got knocked unconscious. Probably has multiple cracked or broken ribs though. It's a good thing he had armor on or it would have been much worse. We'll take care of him when we get back."

"Back where?"

Sybil raised an eyebrow as she looked at her.

"Uh… Back to base…"

"Base? And where would that be?"

"You should already know that detective. You've been there."

Cora looked at her with a puzzled look.

"We're heading back to the library."

"Where am I?"

Cora hurried over to Frank's side. As he struggled to sit up, she gently pushed him back down before grabbing a glass of water.

"We're safe. Here, drink. It'll help with the healing process"

He groaned as he reached for the glass. Taking several large gulps, he handed the glass back before sinking further back onto the cot.

"What happened? Last thing I remember was one of those things punching me in the chest."

Cora nodded to the people walking around in the other room.

"If you can believe it, we got rescued by that Sybil woman. Apparently she followed us with a small team and rescued our asses without even breaking a sweat."

"Yes, indeed we did. You should both be thankful of that. Otherwise, you would probably have wound up in some horrid dinner party as the main course."

Frank glanced up at the fiery redhead that entered the room.

"Where are we?" he asked, trying to prop himself up on an elbow.

"More importantly, who, or what, are you. We unloaded enough rounds to make hamburger out of a grizzly and it barely slowed them down. Yet your team shows up and makes short work of them. How?"

"Let's just say that, while you might have been armed for bear, we're armed for dragons. Or more aptly, armed with dragons, among other things."

"Speaking of which, not that I'm not grateful or anything, but how exactly were you able to ride in on your white horse and rescue us right in the nick of time, anyway?"

Sybil gestured toward Cora.

"You can thank your partner. If she hadn't been so stubborn, I might not have assigned a detail to follow her. As it was, once you arrived at the warehouse, they were able to detect high levels of aether radiating from the warehouse and called it in. We've actually been trying to track down that group since the incident with Samuel was reported."

"What, you mean you were watching for something like this? This is the third one we've found this week. And what's aether?"

"Third? Shit…"

Sybil sat down heavily, running her fingers through her hair before looking back up at them.

"Are you sure? We've been searching for something like this since we learned about Samuel's arrival. As far as we knew, that was the only one so far. This doesn't bode well… Not well at all."

Cora stared at Sybil.

"Why, other than the fact that there's three huge piles of dead bodies stacking up at different locations?"

Sybil glared at Cora before standing back up.

"Never mind. It's no longer your concern. You'll stay here until you're healed, then we'll get you out of the city and help set up a new life for you both. Until then, you're not to leave this facility. For your own safety."

Cora leapt up and started to stomp toward Sybil.

"Wait a damn minute. What the hell do you mean relocate? I'm not going anywhere. I'm staying ri—"

Sybil snapped out her hand, placing one finger against Cora's chest before walking toward her.

"Enough," she snapped, effortlessly pushing Cora backwards toward the bed, "I've humored you long enough. I've had to save your life twice so far. When this is over, your department is going to 'find' your bodies, end of story."

Cora grabbed the other woman's finger with both hands, attempting to bend it backward. No matter how much force she applied, it was like trying to bend a steel bar. To emphasize her point, Sybil raised an eyebrow slightly before jabbing her with her finger, almost causing Cora to flip over the bed.

"How much clearer do I need to be? I can manhandle you with one finger," she said, holding up the finger she had pushed Cora over with, "One finger… Let that sink in for a minute. The things we go up against? They've managed to kill our members in the past. Even with all our strength and abilities, we're not impervious to injury and death, just look at Samuel…"

Sybil trailed off for a moment, her head hanging down, looking lost in thought. Shaking her head, she spun on her heel as she strode away.

"If you want to live through the remainder of the week, you'll do well to stay put."

Cora watched as she walked away. She wasn't sure, but she thought she saw Sybil angrily swipe at her eyes just before she disappeared through another door.

"Interesting…"

"Are you insane!"

"Keep you your voice down Frank," Cora hissed, looking around as she did, "they'll hear you."

"And that would be a bad thing how?" he asked, lowering his voice slightly. "The other option is to let you kill yourself."

"I'm not going to get killed. If I see anything out of the ordinary, I'll beat it."

"What do you hope to accomplish then, huh? What makes you think Samuel's gonna show up there?"

"Nothing, other than a gut feeling that he's going to show up there sooner or later. It's the only thing that ties back to him. All I know is that if I lost my memory, if someone told me I'd definitely been somewhere, I'd go there to see if it helped me remember something."

"If you're too stubborn to know when to quit, then I'm coming with you. Someone needs to cover your ass."

As he attempted to get up, he groaned in pain before slumping back again, his face draining of color.

"You're not going anywhere Frank. You're too injured."

Frank struggled to catch his breath before he spoke again.

"Then you're not going anywhere either. How many times do you think you're going to be able to cheat death?"

Cora sighed. She stared at Frank quietly for a moment before responding.

"I can't just sit here, waiting for them to make us disappear. If I'm wrong, then I'll be back before nightfall. Otherwise, we have a chance to tie this all together and maybe still have our own lives."

He made one more attempt to sit up before collapsing back in exhaustion. Reaching a hand out, he rested it on her leg.

"At least wait until morning. Since I can't stop you, then at least be safe and come back in one piece, partner."

Cora placed her hand over his, giving it a gentle squeeze.

"I promise."

35

"I still can't believe it. It all sounds like some type of fantastic dream."

Samuel looked at Blythe.

"It feels like it too. Since waking up in the hospital, I've gone from nobody special to being God's chosen protector of at least two different worlds. I feel woefully inadequate."

Blythe jumped slightly as Raguel spoke.

"Nonsense… You're still a force to be reckoned with, just ask those trolls."

"I think it's going to take a bit to get used to that," she said, gesturing toward the dragon on Samuel's left arm.

"You think that takes getting used to, try imagining what it's like having him talk in your head unexpectedly."

Raguel glared at him.

"Yeah, yeah. Pick on the little dragon that's been protecting your ass…"

"Sorry. It's just been a really long day."

The dragon's expression softened.

"It's fine. I suppose if I was in your shoes, assuming they'd fit, I'd probably be the same way."

Samuel smiled down at him, giving him a pat before turning his attention back to Blythe.

"So what are your plans for tomorrow?"

"Well, apparently this magic stuff helps me heal faster. Raguel thinks the warehouse I was found at might have some residual traces left. Plus, he thinks the traumatic experience I had there might be strong enough to jog my memory. Maybe I'll get lucky."

"Do you think it'll be dangerous? After all, that's where you almost got killed."

"Well, the thought did cross my mind," he said before holding up both arms, "but I'm hoping that, between the two of them, I'll be safe enough. Really, I don't have a lot of options left. Now that I know they're not actually jewelry and professor Waide is probably under arrest, the warehouse is all I've got left. Otherwise, I'd have to hide out for an unknown length of time before I have the possibility to talk to the professor again."

Blythe stared into his eyes intently.

"Would that be so bad?"

He reached out and gently grabbed her hands. Squeezing them softly, he returned her gaze.

"No, it wouldn't, but until I recover my memories, I'm putting you and everyone around me in danger. I don't know how those creatures found me, so I don't know if they can do it again. I probably shouldn't even be here now, but I had nowhere else to go. So either I go and possibly recover my memories, or I leave the city to keep you safe."

He gave her hands another squeeze as he finished.

"I'd rather see if I can get my memories back so I can stay..."

Samuel snapped awake. It took him a moment to realize what had startled him awake. Glancing down, he heard very quiet snoring coming from Raguel. He smiled as he realized the little dragon hadn't frozen himself before he fell asleep. He reflected on the conversation they'd had the night before. She'd wanted him to spend the night with her in case he didn't come back, but he'd finally convinced her that it'd be safer if he stayed on the couch. That way, if something found him again, he'd be able to protect her better. For reasons he couldn't put his finger on, he'd grown to feel incredibly close to her.

Maybe she reminds me of someone I loved before I lost my memory.

After a few minutes, he quietly slipped off the couch and headed toward the kitchen to get something to drink. He felt Raguel jerk awake and clench his arm before realizing he was still mobile. Slightly relaxing his grip, Samuel could feel him revert back to his metallic state. Getting a glass of water, he sat down at the kitchen table to discuss his plan. Blythe had given him a map of the city the night before that she'd picked up on the way home. He studied the layout of the city for a few minutes, but for some reason, he'd realized he'd memorized it with just a glance. Going by the legend, he figured it would take him a couple hours to walk to the warehouse

"So how likely is it that going to the warehouse will help me get my memories back, anyway?"

Samuel felt Raguel move his head to look up at him.

"Honestly, it depends on how much residual energy was left behind. I absorbed a lot of it to channel into you to keep you alive, but there should be some left. Whether it's enough to heal you the rest of the way remains to be seen."

"That's not very encouraging."

"Did you want the truth or just something that sounded good? Who knows? The shock of being there might do more to help you remember than any residual energy would. There's really no way to tell until we actually get there and see what happens."

"What do we do if this doesn't work?"

Samuel looked down at Raguel, noticing the concerned look on his face.

"I don't know."

Samuel watched as the sun slowly rose above the horizon. Even though he couldn't remember it, he found it comforting to just sit and watch as the world slowly came alive. As the sky went from nearly black, to slowly shifting through varying shades of red, then yellows, and finally the beginnings of blue, Samuel marveled at the beauty of such a simple event happening thousands of times throughout a person's lifetime. He couldn't help but wonder if his old self even noticed the Sun rise after having lived as long as he had.

"Good morning."

Samuel glanced over and smiled at Blythe as she came out of the bedroom, her hair all mussed up from sleep.

"Good morning yourself. Did I wake you?"

Samuel watched as she raked her fingers through her hair, trying to untangle some of the knots that had formed while she slept.

"No… As much as I'd like to sleep in, as soon as the light hits my eyes, I wake up. The only way I ever get to sleep in is to wear a sleeping mask. I didn't put it on last night. I didn't want to miss my chance to say goodbye."

"I wouldn't have left without saying goodbye, unless I didn't have a choice.

Blythe grabbed a bowl and poured some cereal before sitting down at the table with him.

"So how long do you think you'll be gone for?"

Samuel turned the thought over in his head again. Once there, he had no idea how long he'd need to stay. It'd all depended on what happened when he arrived.

"I wish I knew. I really don't want to be there past nightfall, but I also don't want to leave too soon. The longer I stay, the better chance I have of at least remembering something."

As she put her bowl in the sink, she cast a worried look at him.

"Be careful. I know you can take care of yourself, but without your memory…"

"I know. I promise I won't do anything dangerous or stupid."

Blythe glanced away from him. After a minute, she turned back to him with tears in her eyes.

"What if you do get your memories back? What if you already have a girlfriend? I don't want you to go!"

Samuel walked over and held her in his arms. She shook in his arms for a few minutes before she grew quiet. Backing away slightly, he tilted her head up with his finger.

"I'll come back to you, I promise."

After a few minutes, he held her at arm's length, looking into her eyes.

"I have to do this. If I don't and something happens to you or other innocent people, I'll never forgive myself."

Wiping a tear away, she nodded.

"I know… That's one of the reasons why I'm falling for you."

Samuel slowly approached the warehouse, watching for anything out of the ordinary. It had taken him a lot longer to get here than he'd originally estimated. He had had to change direction and hide several times as he kept coming across more and more of the people dressed in black. Because of them, the Sun was only a short distance above the horizon now. He thought back to how he'd decided to wait until after noon to depart.

Even though he knew it was important, he just couldn't seem to bring himself to leave Blythe. Instead, they had spent the morning just enjoying each other's company. Since he couldn't really leave the apartment, Blythe had gone to the corner deli and brought back bagels, cream cheese, and jelly for an early lunch. He hadn't really been hungry, but he enjoyed just spending the time with her quietly. Finally, he realized he was just putting off leaving. After giving her another hug, he headed toward the window. Glancing around outside to make sure nobody was watching, he blew her a kiss and slipped out the window.

Now that he was here, he was having second thoughts about going in. While he wanted to remember who he was, he worried that, if he did get his memories back, would he still go back to Blythe. Part of him kept trying to convince himself to turn around and head back, meeting her at the warehouse with her friends. The memory of sparring with Cliff brought a smile to his lips. He glanced down at Raguel.

"Would it be so bad to just make new memories and forget about trying to recover my old ones?"

"Yes, I think it would be. Your primary job is to protect everyone. Turning your back on that because of one person is just selfish and wrong. I think, deep down, you know that."

Samuel was quiet for a moment.

"I'm scared. I don't want to remember and find out I don't like who I really am."

Raguel smiled up at him.

"I'm pretty sure that won't be a problem."

Amitiel glanced at the two of them.

"I don't know… Look what happened to me."

Samuel could hear the bitterness in her voice. Even though she did her best to hide it, he still felt a prick of pain in his mind as her emotions washed over him.

I wonder if she'll ever forgive me for what I felt I had to do…? I just wish I knew why I did it in the first place.

Taking a deep breath, he took one last look around before heading in.

36

Cora pumped her fist in triumph.

I finally caught a break for once.

She watched Samuel enter the warehouse through the binoculars she'd grabbed from her apartment before setting up her impromptu stakeout. It had been nearly impossible for her to sneak out of the library, but after some hairy near-misses, she'd been able to sneak out without getting caught. Catching a cab, she'd stopped at home to grab some supplies before headed to the warehouse. She'd discussed with Frank about the best place to observe the warehouse without being seen. After some thought, they'd both decided on the roof of an abandoned building about a block away. It was close enough for her to get to the warehouse relatively quickly while being far enough away that it would be nearly impossible to be spotted from the ground.

As she headed back down to the ground floor, she checked over the AMT automag and Calico, making sure both had a round in the chamber and the safeties were on. Why Sybil's people hadn't taken them after arriving, she wasn't sure, but she wasn't going to look a gift horse in the mouth.

Then again, after watching how ineffective they had been against those creatures, maybe they just didn't feel threatened enough to take them. After all, they probably figured we'd be easier to deal with if we thought we had some protection. Guess I'll have to ask when I bring Samuel back.

Cora smirked to herself. After witnessing everything Sybil and her group could do, she was still able to find Samuel before they could.

Bet it'll piss her off pretty good.

Getting to the ground floor, she looked around to make sure nobody was around before jogging down the block and over to the door where Samuel had entered the building. She felt an odd tingling behind her, but when she looked back, she didn't see anything out of the ordinary.

That was odd.

Drawing the automag, she turned back and put her ear to the door to see if she could hear anything. After a minute, she pulled her head away before quietly pulling on the door, only opening it far enough to slip in without making noise. She stuck a piece of cardboard she'd brought with her in the door to keep the latch from clicking home and possibly alerting him to her presence. Standing just inside the door to let her eyes adjust, she listened intently, trying to catch any scrap of noise Samuel might make. Hopefully, she'd hear him before he heard her.

"Anything yet?"

Samuel slowly walked through the empty warehouse. Glancing around, he shook his head.

"Nothing. Not a single thing is coming back to me."

Raguel sighed. After a minute, his head perked up.

"I know, head over there."

Samuel looked down to see where the dragon was pointing. Peering back up, he slowly started working his way over to where the dragon was indicating.

"How about now?"

Samuel concentrated on where he was standing. As he made a slow circle, he noticed all the different rents and gouges in the pillars and floor. He started to feel like something was just on the edge of his consciousness, but every time he tried focusing on it, the feeling of a memory slipped away.

"There's something… I don't know. It feels like I might be getting ready to remember something, but it just won't come."

"Draw your sword."

"Huh?"

"Pull out your sword. This is where you were standing when you got shot. Maybe drawing your sword and going through the motions will help."

Samuel cocked his head to the side slightly before reaching for the handle. All he managed to do was grab his finger.

"Uh… How do I draw it, exactly?"

"Sorry, forgot again. It's controlled by need and desire. You basically will it to and it happens."

"Huh, very Jedi-like, eh?"

Raguel smiled up at Samuel.

"Where do you think they got the idea from?"

Samuel chuckled for a moment, then focused on the pommel.

Let's see… If I had a handle…

He tried again, but nothing happened.

Okay, this is stupid. It can't be that hard, otherwise, someone would die if they couldn't draw it fast enough. Plus, I had no problems pulling it out at the hospital and the alleyway.

Samuel stared at his finger. He tried to remember what it felt like when the sword formed in his hand the last time he drew it. As he concentrated on the memory, he started to feel the familiar itchy sensation in his hand. Focusing on the sensation, he tried reaching for the handle again. As he grabbed for it, he felt the handle solidify under his grasp. With one smooth motion, he tugged the blade free. As it left its sheath, he heard a sound like a cross between electrical arcing and glass wind chimes.

Wow… I never got the chance to really look at this thing before. This thing is awesome.

As he examined the blade, turning it back and forth, he noticed first condensation, then a sheen of ice start forming on the blade. A few drops of liquid fell from the tip, striking the floor with a sizzling sound. Looking closer, he noticed the liquid had frozen the concrete so quickly that it had formed spidery cracks in it. Standing straight again, he gave it a few experimental swings through the air and marveled at how well balanced it was. As he swung it, he noticed more drops of liquid spraying off the blade, freezing instantly wherever they hit. He couldn't help but think that, compared to this, the LARP weapons he'd used felt like swinging a broom around. Going through the form he'd used at the meet-up, he slowly lost himself in the flow of movement. Suddenly, the memory of getting shot in the face smashed into him, causing him to stumble off balance. Staggering forward, he accidentally buried the blade into the cement pillar, nearly shearing it in half.

"I remember," he whispered, supporting himself on the stuck blade.

The force of the memory caused his legs to start buckling under him. As he tried to maintain his balance, images of his fight in the warehouse started flashing through his mind. He could feel himself sliding effortlessly through his opponents, hewing off limbs and heads without thought. Then the memory of a vampire trying to choke him. As he slammed his sword into it, its head exploded and then… darkness.

"Don't move!"

The sudden voice shocked him out of his trance, causing him to search for the source. He realized he was gasping for air from the force of the vivid memory. Looking around, he gaze finally stopped on the last person he wanted to see. His anger started to rise as his attention focused on the gun she had trained on him.

"Detective, not now! I'm finally starting to remember something. I need more time."

"I'm sorry Samuel, I can't do that."

Samuel angrily yanked the sword out of the pillar, causing the pillar to groan ominously. Chunks of frosted cement clattered to the floor, the impact making the chunks shatter like glass.

"I don't want to hurt you Cora, but I'm too close to getting some answers. You know I can take that gun away from you if I want. Just go away."

He watched as Cora held her hands up in a non-threatening manner before she holstered her gun.

"I'm not here to arrest you this time. I met some people who've been looking for you. I think they can help."

Samuel slowly lowered the point of his sword toward the floor. As the tip touched, it carved out a small notch in the concrete. Distractedly, he watched as rime ice starting forming on the floor around the tip as super-cooled water dribbled off the blade. He had another flashback to a time when he had used that property to freeze a slow moving stream, allowing a caravan he was protecting to cross. The sound of Cora taking a step toward him broke his concentration again.

"GO AWAY, DAMN IT!"

Cora paused before moving back a step.

"I can't do that. From what these people are saying, it's too important. You need to come with me and meet them."

"Not until I'm finished here."

"We can come back lat—"

"I knew if I gave you enough slack, you'd come through for us again. You've got an amazing ability to find what you're looking for it seems, even better than our own trackers."

Samuel watched as Cora spun around, snatching her gun out of her holster, aiming in the direction of the new speaker. For some reason, the voice sounded familiar. It was part of another memory that seemed to be slipping away from him. Trying to locate the source of the voice, he slowly started easing around so he could get a better angle.

"You followed me again?"

"Of course. I was hoping you'd lead me to Samuel. Time is running out."

As the woman came into view, Samuel sucked in his breath.

"Hello Samuel, do you remember me? I'm —"

"You," he hissed as he launched himself at the fiery red-headed woman… the one that had tried to kill him in his memories.

37

Cora only had time to catch a slight shimmer of movement from the corner of her eye before she felt the blast of frigid air as Samuel blurred past her. The sudden look of shock on Sybil's face was instantly replaced by fierce concentration as she whipped her arm up to block his sword from splitting her in two. She lashed out with a kick that he easily dodged by skipping backward before launching himself at her again. The split-second pause allowed her to draw her own blade while trying to deflect the onslaught.

Cora quickly backed away from the wildly swinging blades. Even though she'd seen footage of him fighting, the sheer speed and ferocity of his attach left her breathless.

I actually thought I'd stand a chance against him… He was taking it easy on me when we fought.

Trying to track the combat, she had to continuously move to keep from being accidentally cut down by the two combatants.

It's almost like watching a kung-fu flick on fast forward.

As the fight wore on, Cora noticed that, imperceptibly at first, Sybil appeared to be gaining the upper hand in the confrontation. As she slowly started to force him back, Cora noticed that it looked like Sybil was trying to say something, but every time she started to open her mouth, Samuel would press his attack, trying to regain his momentum.

After several minutes and narrow misses, Sybil made a series of quick feints and ripostes, finally ending with a hard downward strike/grab combo that left Samuel's sword pinned against the floor under her foot. A coating of frost began forming across the edge of her sole where it touched the blade.

"Samuel!" she gasped. "Stop fighting me! I'm trying to—"

Cora could see Sybil's eyes bulge as Samuel made a quick motion with his left hand.

"I'm not going to let you kill me!"

As he yelled, he suddenly yanked another sword from where it was sheathed on his right arm. As the blade came clear, Cora felt a blast of heat hit her. A smoldering chunk of Sybil's trench coat landed on the floor as she sprang backward, a grimace of pain on her face. Looking back at Samuel, she saw a look of absolute rage painted across his features. Then, for the first time, she could clearly see both swords he was holding.

The one in his right hand was forming a coating of glittering ice. As she watched, it dripped what appeared to be water onto the floor where it sizzled and fogged up. The sword in his left hand, however, was the source of heat blast she'd felt. Flames licked up and down the length of the jagged-edged blade, rippling between various shades of blues, yellows, and reds. The air shimmered from the intense heat radiating off of it, causing a mirage-like effect to ripple around him. Something akin to napalm started dripping off the teeth of the blade, spalling the floor where it hit. The intense heat and cold caused the fog rising from the other blade to begin swirling around him. Glancing back at Sybil, Cora was shocked to see what appeared to be terror forming on the other woman's face.

"My God! It's not possible…"

Without warning, Samuel lunged at her, rapidly swinging both blades in intricate patterns. Sybil was forced backward as he continued to pound at her defenses. As the battle continued, Sybil's clothing started to show burn spots and sections that had fractured due to the rapid freezing of the material. Cora suddenly realized that the other woman wasn't going to last much longer due to the injuries she was starting to accumulate. Unexpectedly, Samuel ducked down and whipped out a leg, causing Sybil to fall heavily to the ground as he sprang back up. As he started raining blows down on her, her blocks and parries started slowing.

I hope I live to not regret this.

"Hey Samuel," she yelled, "catch!"

As he turned his head, Cora squeezed the trigger. The sudden boom of the gun echoed around the room.

Almost as an afterthought, he swung the flaming blade up, melting the bullet in flight.

"Why—" he started, but Sybil was already moving. Swinging back around, he tried to deflect the object she flung at him. The blue dragon on his left arm came alive suddenly, throwing off his swing and causing him to miss the object. As it shattered across his chest, Cora could hear the shock in his voice as he screamed at the now animated dragon on his left arm.

"WHY?"

"I had to. It's for your own good."

Samuel started to scream as he staggered backward, a luminescent fog forming on his chest.

"Thank you Raguel."

The miniature dragon looked up at the woman.

"You're very welcome, Lady Sybil. I hope this works."

Sybil barely got her sword up in time to deflect the blade that suddenly flew at her face. As she ducked away, Cora looked back at Samuel again. She watched as he collapsed to the ground, writhing in pain. She stumbled backward as the dragon on his right arm animated as well.

"How could you betray him like that!"

Cora saw the blue dragon duck his head as if the red one had physically struck him.

"You'll understand in a few minutes, you have to trust us."

"I trust nobody at this point," she hissed before expanding in size, her wings wrapping protectively around Samuel. Cora saw the sword blades change into something similar to a barbed whip or rope ladder. Instead of wooden rungs, however, one had glowing, jagged metal teeth and the other had what looked like shards of blue glass. They slowly started to undulate and wave in the air around him, poking out through a gap in the red dragon's protective embrace.

"LOOK OUT!"

Cora didn't even have time to turn before Sybil barreled into her, picking her up like a rag doll and sprinting away from Samuel. She had a good view over Sybil's shoulder as the blades suddenly started whipping around, shredding and destroying everything around him. Cora watched in horror as the sphere of destruction started rapidly expanding, leaving nothing intact. One of the blades whipped out and effortlessly slashed through a support, causing part of the roof to collapse. Before it had gotten within ten feet of him, it had been turned into chunks no larger than gravel.

"What's happening!" she yelled, trying to catch her breath as her ribs kept bouncing on the other woman's shoulder.

"He's healing," the other woman huffed, finally reaching the farthest point she could carry them in the enclosed space.

"I just doused him in enough aether to heal an ancient dragon. It should let him heal completely if it doesn't kill him first from overdosing. Unfortunately, it feels like being covered in acid."

Cora started to open her mouth but the other woman interrupted her.

"Shit," she said, whipping her blade up to deflect a couple blade strikes, "how the hell is he getting his blades to do that?"

Sybil reached out and pulled her into a tight embrace. Before Cora could say anything, Sybil swung her arm up as the dragon on her arm started moving. It kicked at the sleeve until its wings were uncovered. Ballooning out, the wings wrapped around the two women the same way Samuel's had wrapped around him. Just as the wings fully engulfed them, Cora could hear the blades hit, first slowly, then picking up speed. She heard Sybil's dragon grunt in pain as the impacts continued.

"I'm not sure how much longer I'll be able to hold off this barrage," the dragon said in a masculine voice.

"Hold on for as long as you can then."

Cora could hear the concern and worry in the other woman's voice as they felt the wings continue to shudder from the sword impacts. Cora flinched as the dragon cried out in agony as a small rent appeared near her face. As the onslaught continued, more and more cuts appeared. As the sound of the dragon's cries of pain started to get weaker, Cora realized that the assault was slowing down. As the dragon's wings started to droop and unfurled, Cora got her first look at the carnage. The warehouse looked like a large bomb had gone off with Samuel standing at ground zero. Most of the roof was missing along with a significant number of support pillars. All the debris was piled around Samuel, making it look like he was crouched in the center of an impact crater.

Looking back, she stared as the dragon lost its grip and slipped off Sybil's arm as she searched for something in her pocket. She saw tears streaking Sybil's face as she sprinkled her dragon with what appeared to be the same stuff she'd splashed on Samuel. As she watched, she saw the wings of the dragon relax. The physical damage he'd sustained was slowly starting to close up as his wings shrunk back down to normal size. Sybil sniffled as she gently helped the little dragon fold his wings up correctly. After a few seconds, it slowly latched back on to her arm, shuttered, and went still, looking like an intricate piece of jewelry again.

As the two women looked around, Cora noticed the wings slowly starting to unfurl around Samuel. She noticed Samuel starting to turn his head toward them. As their eyes met, Cora almost took a step back away from the intensity of the glowing electric blue eyes staring back at her.

"I remember everything!"

How could he betray me…

That was the last coherent thought Samuel had as he tumbled backward. The burning pain quickly spread across his body. It felt like someone had poured lava on him. As the spreading agony reached his head, an explosion went off behind his eyes. He actually felt the movement in his head as his brain healed, causing an avalanche of memories to overwhelm his senses. At the same time, he could feel his body getting heavier, his muscles bulking up and getting denser.

Without warning, the memory of who he was slammed into him, taking his breathe away again. Gasping for air, he felt the weight of millennia wash over his mind, confusingly at first, but rapidly resolving into something that made sense. As he became whole, he realized there were still large gaps in his memory, some that might never be repaired. As the pain slowly died down, he mentally commanded Amitiel to unfurl her wings.

"Are you sure?"

Samuel mentally smiled at her.

>*Yes my friend. I'm fine. I've been made mostly whole again.*<

>*What was that stuff, anyway?*<

>*It's something I came up with some time after I was forced to leave you behind. It's condensed Aether. It's like bathing in the waters of Aerth, except significantly more potent. I'm surprised it didn't kill me, actually. But yes, it's safe to let me out. Sybil's a friend.*<

>*Okay…*<

Samuel could feel the hesitation as she started opening her wings. Glancing down at Raguel, he smiled.

>*Next time, a little warning?*<

>*I'm sorry. I couldn't think of any other way to get your memory back. It was a split-second decision.*<

>*I understand, friend. You did what you needed to do to help me. It just hurt like hell is all. I've missed you.*<

>*Missed you too.*<

As Amitiel unfurled, Samuel glanced around.

Gee, that was some party we had. That's one memory I'd actually LIKE to forget.

Samuel felt Raguel's mental chuckle. After a few seconds, he spotted the two women at the far side of the building.

He watched as they started to cautiously approach, still too sore to move from the massive dose of Aether he'd just been given.

"I remember everything!" he managed to hiss out, his throat raspy from the rapid healing process. As he struggled to stand on shaky legs, he sheathed Hoarfrost and Brimstone.

"Samuel?"

"Yes Sybil, it's me."

"Are you —"

Samuel suddenly remembered why he had been in the warehouse when he'd been shot. There was one more location they had to activate. Now he knew why it seemed familiar at the time.

"Oh, no… Blythe," he whispered.

He swung his right arm over his shoulder, soreness and fatigue instantly forgotten.

>*Amitiel, we need to fly. Now!*<

>*On it.*<

The red dragon quickly slithered off his arm, tearing his shirt and jacket off as she repositioning herself on his back like a backpack. Expanding in size, her wings unfurled to generate a nearly twenty foot wingspan. Her head and neck extended up until it rested on top of his head, looking forward. At the same time, her tail extended out several feet as well. Giving a few tentative flaps that lifted him off the ground a couple feet before gently dropping him back down. He glanced back over at the women and noticed the mixture of awe and fear on their faces as they stumbled backward from the wind buffeting them from the red dragon's wings.

Squatting down, he tensed his legs before springing upward, wings trailing behind him. As he cleared the roof-line, Amitiel's powerful wings launched him further into the air, heading toward the LARP group's meeting place.

Please don't let me be too late.

Cora watched in disbelief as Samuel launched himself skyward, easily clearing the thirty foot vertical distance before the dragon's wings spread out, causing Samuel's form to shrink rapidly into the distance. She turned back to Sybil to ask a question when she noticed the look of dread on the other woman's face.

"Uh… What's wrong? Samuel finally got his memories back…"

The hairs on Cora's neck lifted as the other woman looked back at her.

"I think I just made a horrible mistake…"

38

Cora tried catching up to Sybil as she stormed up the library steps. She'd tried unsuccessfully to get Sybil to tell her what horrible mistake she was talking about on the ride back but the only thing she'd been able to get out of Sybil was her mumbling, "how could I have been so stupid?"

Reaching the top of the steps, Sybil slammed the doors open before storming through. As Cora followed inside, she saw Sybil heading back toward a door behind the main desk. Jogging to catch up, she caught the door Sybil had swept through before it closed. Without warning, Cora got stuck as the door frame squeezed in from the sides to pin her. In the distance, she could hear Sybil yelling.

"Where's the Archivist? I need him, now!"

Cora started to panic slightly as she looked around the library over her shoulder. She noticed that most of the patrons glanced at her before going back to what they were doing. Squirming to try and free herself, she watched as the librarian moved from behind the desk and approached her.

"Miss Renault, isn't it? How the hell do I get this door frame to let go?"

The librarian smiled as she touched Cora and the door frame at the same time, Cora noticed a slight shimmer form in the other woman's eyes before going normal again. At the same time, the door frame relaxed, letting her go.

"You better hurry and catch up to her detective. I've never seen her this upset before."

Nodding at the other woman, Cora turned and ran down the stairs. She caught up to Sybil just as she yelled again.

"Where's the damn Archivist!"

"You bellowed for me?"

"I need answers, and I need them fast. I just fought against Samuel, and he had a pair of peltae's with matching peleus. How's that possible?"

Cora watched as the man stroked his chest-length beard before replying.

"Oh dear, that doesn't sound very promising. Can you describe what the other dragon looked like?"

"Yeah, it was a freaking red dragon. Samuel placed his arm on his back and the damn thing crawled off his arm and attached itself to his backside. Then they flew off."

The archivist's eyes widened slightly at the description before he turned around and hurried back through the door. Looking over his shoulder, he motioned for them to follow.

"You need to see something before I'll be able to give you the answers you seek."

Cora looked around the large room. The shelves were jammed with thousands of books in various states of decay and disrepair. As the Archivist led them across the large chamber, she ran her fingers over the spines of some of the books. One of them looked vaguely familiar, causing her to stop and pull it off the shelf. Flipping it open, she realized she'd seen something like this on a science show several months ago. As she stared at the pages, she kept catching movement out of the corner of her eye. When she focused on that part of the page, it appeared to be like any other normal page.

"The Voynich Manuscript?"

The Archivist turned back toward her with a twinkle in his eye.

"Yes, that's one of the originals. There were three original volumes. It was somewhat comparable to an encyclopedia, but for

Aerth. That's why nobody can decipher it. Without mystical energy running through your veins, the text won't animate and flow into a readable script."

Cora shuddered slightly before replacing the book on the shelf. She didn't want to think about why she'd thought she'd seen movement on the pages.

"Come along now."

She glanced back up and saw the archivist pulling down a massive book and laying it down on a nearby table. Hurrying over, she glanced down at the ancient-looking tome. The book looked like it was made out of some type of leather cover with grayish-tan looking pages. As the Archivist opened the book, she reached out to touch one of the pages. She suddenly realized it was some form of animal skin instead of paper. Stroking her fingers across it, she looked up questioning toward the archivist.

"It's a very old tome, written on vellum. This one was a copy of a copy I'm afraid, so some of the information from the original was lost along the way. Thankfully, I believe the important bits are still readable."

Cora watched as he flipped gently through the pages. She glanced over at Sybil and noticed she had her arms crossed and was impatiently tapping her foot.

"How much longer?"

"It's in here somewhere Sybil, you just need to learn patience like I keep telling you."

"Archivist, we almost died because I didn't know anyone beside Genevieve ever had two peltae bonded to them. And the things he was getting peleus to do… He got them to change into some type of chain-sword form that I've never heard of. I've got a sinking feeling that the set that's strapped to his arm is the same one she used to nearly destroy the realms nearly seventy-five millennia ago."

"Ah, here we are," he said as he finally flipped to the right page, "is this the set you saw?"

Cora glanced down at the page. The gilded artwork was beautiful, but what caught her eye was the image of a statuesque platinum blond-haired woman with a flaming sword in her hand, along with a dragon attached to her back just like Samuel had. Another image below it showed the two engulfed in flames.

"That's the one! Shit! I just helped him regain his memories and now I find out he's working for her."

Cora looked up at Sybil.

"What do you mean her? Samuel got that one from a guy."

"What? Are you sure?"

"Absolutely, my partner and I just saw it a few hours before it decided to make itself at home on his arm."

Sybil looked back and forth between Cora and the Archivist.

"That doesn't make any sense. How the hell could Samuel bond with another peltae in the space of a couple hours?"

"Well, one possible way would be if he'd been bonded with it before."

"Then that brings us back to Genevieve. That's her peltae… or at least it used to be ages past."

The Archivist flipped the page as he answered.

"That's not entirely true. Based off what we've been able to recover, there's records of at least one other person who's had two peltae. They also happen to be the original bond partner to Amitiel."

Cora watched as the other woman tried to hide her shock.

"There's another person who's had that thing bonded to them besides Genevieve and Samuel? Who?"

The archivist gave Sybil as guarded look before he flipped the page again.

"I didn't say that exactly. I said one other person has bonded with that dragon… Genevieve's husband."

He punctuated the statement by tapping on the page in front of him.

Both women looked down at the book at the same time. Cora heard the other woman gasp.

"How is that possible…?"

>Can we go any faster?<

>*Sorry Samuel, I'm flying as fast as I can. There's something wrong with the air in this era. It's not as alive as it used to be.*<

>*Yeah, it's called pollution. Just do the best you can then.*<

>*I already —*<

The sudden wave of Aetheric energy slammed into them without warning. The blast-wave tumbled them like scraps of paper in a windstorm.

>*Amitiel, we're heading toward the water!*<

>*I'm trying!*<

>*Samuel, face me downward!*<

Samuel swung his left arm in some semblance of pointing toward the water below.

>*Let's hope there's enough moisture in the air!*<

Raguel let out a blast of supercooled air, causing a block of ice to form and rocket toward the surface of the river. The impact caused a plume of water to splash up toward them.

>*YES!*<

Raguel let out another blast of supercooled air, forming it as they plummeted toward the quickly rising geyser of water. Twisting aetheric energy, a ice ramp formed beneath them.

>*Retract your wings, now!*<

As her wings folded up, Samuel continued to direct the blast of subzero air at the water ramp. As his feet hit, he skated down the ramp.

>*Aim it back upward!*<

Samuel followed Raguel's directions, forming a U-shaped ramp. The momentum of the fall caused him to launch back into the air before Amitiel unfurled her wings, rocketing toward the rapidly approaching warehouse.

>*We're too late!*<

Cora felt a weird sensation wash over her, causing her to grab the table for balance. Before she had a chance to ask, Sybil and the Archivist were flung several feet across the room before coming to a rest in a heap.

"What the hell was that?"

Sybil got shakily to her feet, holding her head with one hand while reaching over to help the Archivist to his feet. As Cora looked at them, she noticed a trickle of blood coming out of Sybil's nose while blood dribbled out of the Archivist's ears.

"What the hell is going on?"

Sybil looked back at Cora, struggling to focus on her face. Slowly, the other woman made her way back over to the table before dropping heavily into a chair. The Archivist stumbled back over to the book, placing one hand on the table to keep his balance. Flipping through a few pages, he ran his fingers across several passages before looking back up at the two women, a deep furrows forming across his forehead.

"Unless I miss my guess, that was the completion of a ritual to weaken the weave of the world."

Cora glanced between the Archivist and Sybil. She noticed they'd both gone deathly pale.

"Can I get that in English?"

The Archivist sat down slowly in a chair.

"In layman's terms, it's the end of days. The start of Armageddon."

39

>*There it is.*<

Samuel hovered over the warehouse, Amitiel's wings scooping big slices of air to keep them aloft.

>*Thermal-vision.*<

Samuel's vision rapidly changed to a landscape of blues, yellows, and reds. As he focused, he slowly started to identify the thermal outlines of humans and what appeared to be a mixture of orcs, goblins, and trolls. As he tried to formulate a strategy, one of the human shapes launched themselves at the group before being snatched up by one of the trolls. He could tell the person's thermal outline was different than everyone else's.

"Blythe!"

>*Amitiel, two fireballs and meteor strike pattern, now!*<

With a powerful flap, Samuel was flipped over backward before his entire body burst into flames. The yellowish orange flames rapidly spread across his body as more flames erupted along the length of Amitiel's wings. Dropping into a rapid freefall, she spit out two gouts of fire, striking the roof and causing it to instantly glow white hot. As they approached the roof, Amitiel wrapped her wings tightly around Samuel's body.

>*Hang on tight!*<

The last thing he saw before Amitiel's wings blinded him was the brightly glowing roof rushing up to meet them.

Blythe stared as the now dead body of Hazel was tossed on the floor, her body making a heavy thunk as it hit. The creatures had swarmed into the place while her friends had been practicing with live steel, rapidly surrounding them. They hadn't even had time to register what was going on when the huge creature had slowly come into view, his weight causing small items to bounce off the concrete floor.

"Wot d' we have here? More bodies to add to the ritual, eh?"

Blythe had heard one of her friend's whimper in fear as more of the nightmarish creatures came into view. Reaching over the rest of the group, the monster had plucked Hazel up and held her effortlessly in front of him.

"Oi, wot's with da mewling, eh?"

As he held her, the monster glanced over his shoulder.

"Hurry up, boyo's, we gotta get dis set up quick. The syphons's 'r on ta us. We can't lallygag around here."

Blythe felt lightheaded as the creature slowly licked the side of Hazel's face, causing her to cry out in fear.

"Wot a shame we won't get da chance ta eat ya, but the boss was very clear on it. No eatin' da sacrifices."

As the girl shivered in the monster's grip, Blythe noticed a trickle of fluid start dribbling off her dangling feet.

"Oi, she sprung a leak, she did."

"We 'is all set boss."

"Good, then let da fun begin."

As he said it, Blythe had watched as he'd carried Hazel over to the center of the area the other monsters had cleared and set up a globe shaped device. They'd somehow driven metal spikes into the support beams around it and had a tangle of cables connecting to the globe, suspending it a few feet off the ground. Without warning, he'd stuck his thumb against the side of Hazel's head and pushed, snapping the frightened girl's neck before dropping her on the ground. As the body landed, a glow started emanating from the globe as smoke started to rise from it.

"Next."

As one of the creatures grabbed John, Blythe felt something break loose inside. An uncontrolled flood of rage began to course through her system.

"NO!" she screamed as the world slowed to a crawl.

She leapt up, rushing toward the thing holding John. As she bore down on them, she instinctively snatched up a longsword, whipping it forward and lopping off the arm of the creature holding John. With her free hand, she pushed John back toward the rest of her friends, causing him to fly backward and knocking several of the others down. Continuing her assault, she lashed out with a vicious kick, launching the wounded creature halfway across the warehouse before it struck with a meaty thwack, embedding itself into the wall several feet off the ground.

As her rage continued to climb, she threw herself into the closest group, gouging, ripping, kicking, and slashing her way rapidly through the slow moving monsters. Without warning, she was grabbed in a vice-like grip from behind, pinning her arms tightly against her sides. She struggled for a moment before going limp, the rage draining out of her as suddenly as it had appeared.

"Wot da we got here, a wilder? Oh, dat'll help the ritual a lot. Might even let us take sum of da sacrifices we brought back ta eat after all."

Blythe nearly gagged as the creature breathed in her face, the smell of rotting meat and sulfur causing her eyes to water and burn.

"Guess you jus volunteered ta be the next one, eh?" he said as he started carrying her toward the globe.

As he approached, a loud splattering sound struck the roof before the room was bathed in a bright yellowish-white light. Blythe felt the creature's grasp relax slightly as it shielded its eyes with its other hand as it glanced at the now-glowing roof.

"Wot's dat?" was all it managed to say before the roof exploded in a shower of molten metal and bright sparks.

Almost everyone was knocked off their feet by the sudden impact of something striking the ground on the other side of the room, showering those closest in razor sharp splinters of metal rebar and concrete. As the dust settled, Blythe could barely make out a ball of flame flaring up from the crater.

"Hurting them was your first mistake. It's also your last mistake!"

Something about the voice sounded familiar, but the voice was distorted by the roaring flames rolling off the winged creature. Without warning, something moving too fast to discern came slithering out of the flames. All she had time to make out was something that sounded like tinkling glass before the object wrapped around the creature holding her with blinding speed. As it stopped moving, she could make out what looked like rippling bolts of lightning held together with sharp chunks of blue crystal. As she watched, she could see the monster's muscles start to bulge as it strained to move. She gasped in pain as it start to squeeze her tighter.

"No," the fiery creature rasped, a ripple forming in the chained lightning flowing from it. Without warning, Blythe dropped to the ground, the hand that was holding her flopping lifelessly on the ground next to her. She glanced back up and saw the fiery mass clearly for the first time. A man slowly strode toward them as his flaming wings flared out to his sides, a wave of heat washing over them.

"You're not going to hurt anyone else here today."

Blythe watched as ice rapidly started spreading across the monster's body, causing it to whimper in pain and fear.

"Who's mewling now, asshole…"

As the creature stopped moving, the weapon flexed, causing the monster to shatter into frozen chunks that tumbled across the floor. Then it rapidly flowed back toward the man, forming into a glittering crystal sword.

"Now you all die."

Samuel caused the blade to retract into a sword again.

"Now you all die."

Without warning, he blurred forward, lashing out with both swords. As he flowed through the creatures, he rapidly switched from long sword to chain sword forms, carving a path through them. Moving as if alive, his blades sought out targets, slashing, burning, and freezing their way through them like wheat. Accentuated between sword strikes, Amitiel and Raguel took turns freezing and roasting orcs and goblins at will. Flapping her wings, several of the creatures were blown off their feet while Raguel froze them to the ground moments before Samuel slaughtered them. Within moments, the only sound left was the crackling of small fires and heavy breathing from his friends huddled at the far corner of the warehouse. Looking around, he spotted Blythe lying on the ground. Without thought he rushed toward her, flaming wings folding up behind him.

"Blythe!"

Her gaze snapped up and he felt the surge of Aether well up inside her as her eyes began glowing neon blue. Slowing down, he carefully approached her.

"GET AWAY FROM HER!"

An unexpected impact across his back knocked him off balance slightly. As the blows started coming faster, he realized he was being attacked by multiple people. Amitiel instinctively swished her tail, knocking the swords out of his attackers' hands before tripping and pushing them backward. Spinning around, he saw the fear in their eyes.

"Guys, it's me!"

Cliff tried to scramble to his feet, eyeing where his partially melted sword had fallen.

"What's wrong with all of you?"

"You look a bit different than the last time they saw you."

Samuel turned around to see Blythe slowly standing up, her eyes fading back to their normal color.

"Huh?"

"Uh, you're on fire and have wings you dummy."

Looking down at himself, he nearly slapped himself in the forehead before realizing he was still holding his swords. Sheathing them, he looked back at her.

"You have a point."

>*Amitiel, kill the flames.*<

With a whump, the flames extinguished themselves while Amitiel's wings shrank down behind him.

"Sorry about that guys, didn't mean to scare you like that."

"Samuel…?"

Samuel glanced over at Karen as he held his right hand behind him, allowing Amitiel to scurry onto his arm and wrap around it before becoming still.

"Heh… yeah, it's me. I, uh, finally remembered who, and more importantly, what I am."

Cliff tentatively started to approach him.

"Holy-ee shit. What the hell are you? And what the hell were those things!"

"Well, that's kinda a long story, one I don't really have time to explain right now. All I can say is that I need you guys to get out of the city as fast as you can. Something really bad's about to happen."

"Something bad's going to happen! Something bad's already happened. Hazel's dead!"

Samuel looked sadly down at Hazel's body before looking back up at his friends.

"I'm sorry I didn't get here sooner, and I know this sucks, but you all need to get out of the city. Otherwise, there's a real good chance you'll all die."

Turning to look at Blythe, he continued.

"You need to leave as well, but once this is over, we're going to need to talk about what's happening to you."

He watched as she nodded without saying anything.

"If this city is still here tomorrow morning, I want you to meet me at the Miskatonic library. Do you know where it is?"

"Yes, but where are you going?"

"I need to stop what's happening, or there won't be a city, possibly a world."

Blythe stepped toward him.

"Then I'm going with you."

"You can't. I can't do what I need to do unless I know you're somewhere safe."

He turned toward Cliff.

"Make sure she stays with you guys."

"What if there's more of those creatures?"

Samuel looked at Cliff for a second before turning back toward Blythe. Gently holding her hand, he nodded toward her.

"I'll come back for you. Just stay safe."

>*Amitiel, keep her safe for me. Would you do that for me please?*<

>*I'm not leaving you again.*<

>*You have to. I need her to stay alive until I can come back for her. I promise I'll come back for the both of you.*<

Samuel felt the hurt feelings before she animated and rapidly slid off his arm and wrapped around Blythe's.

Blythe's eyes went wide as she looked up at him.

"I can hear her in my head."

"Yes, her name's Amitiel and she's going to help keep you all safe. Now go!"

Spinning around, he got a running start before leaping through the hole in the roof. Landing outside, he sprinted off, leaping over buildings as he headed toward the library.

40

"Sybil! The outer perimeter alert's gone off. It's detecting demonic and aetheric energy building up to dangerous levels."

"Acknowledged. Get everyone ready. Expect a full assault any minute."

Cora watched as Sybil nodded before the other person rushed off.

"What can I do?"

As Sybil looked her up and down, she felt an eerie sensation pass through her.

"At this point, nothing. You haven't progressed far enough. Stay down here with your partner. With any luck, it'll be over quickly."

"Progressed enough? Progressed enough for what?"

"I don't have time to explain. If we survive this, I'll answer any questions you have. But for right now, you'll only get in the way."

Before Cora could say anything else, she felt a vibration rock the building.

"They're testing our defenses!"

Sybil grabbed Cora by the shoulders and stared in her face.

"Stay with Frank. Under no circumstance leave his side. To do so will mean death."

As Cora opened her mouth, Sybil spun and blurred away, the whoosh of her sprint causing loose papers to get pulled into her wake. Cora headed back to Frank's room.

"Damn it!"

"What, you don't like my company now?"

Cora looked down at Frank.

"I thought you were down for the count. They'd told me they'd given you something to rest."

"Yeah… Tasted like crap, too."

"Well, I guess I could think of worse places to be for the end of the world. How you feeling?"

Cora felt herself smile when he chuckled.

"Like twice-hammered, reheated crap, but thanks for asking. Could you help me sit up?"

Cora walked over and gently pulled her partner into a seated position, placing extra pillows behind him to prop him up.

"So what'd I miss while I was out? Did I hear you say something about the end of the world?"

"Frank, you'll never believe me. We've moved into biblical references now."

Frank patted a spot on his bed.

"Take a seat. Looks like we'll be here for a bit, so fill me in."

Cora sighed as she sat down, taking Frank's hand into hers.

"Well, for starters, I know who our boy is finally…"

"Oh really? Who?"

"Where do we stand with the centurions?"

"They're almost fully charged. They'll be ready within the next five minutes."

Sybil shook her head before running her fingers through her hair. Pulling out a leather thong, she tied it back into a ponytail.

"Remind me if we make it through this to keep them at least at eighty percent charged. That miscalculation might cost us today."

"Noted."

Sybil looked at the battlefield map.

I'm glad we spent the research time to make this thing. Seeing the entire battlefield in real time might just help us get out of this alive.

As she watched, she could see the massing supernatural creatures starting to pile up around the shield in three places along with a few fliers that were testing the inner perimeter before being turned into cinders. What appeared to be the main force was to the front of the building several blocks off, along with two skirmisher groups flanking left and right. The strategy made sense. The library had been made by dwarves and titans. Their ability to create structures that repelled nearly any supernatural force was well founded. Short of Leviathan himself showing up, the only way in was the front door. A door guarded by some very powerful sentinels that had been here since long before she took over.

"Fully charged!"

"Good. Everyone ready?"

Sybil looked around as everyone murmured about the coming battle, casting uneasy and nervous gazes back and forth. Taking a deep breath, she squared her shoulders and hopped up on a table.

"Can everyone hear me okay?"

After a few seconds of everyone nodding, she continued.

"I'm sure all of you are aware that something major has happened. As best we can tell, a ritual that unknown parties were trying to perform appears to have been completed, or at least progressed far enough that we might not be able to stop it. We haven't been able to get in touch with the other garrisons around the world, so we don't know how widespread this is or if it's only us.

"At this time, we don't know how large a force is coming against us. What I do know is this, we cannot let them succeed. I don't know what their aim is, but with all the relics we have in storage, allowing them to get inside could spell the end of the world. End of story. I know you won't let me down just as I know I won't let you down, either.

"Take this remaining time to prepare yourself for battle. I know most of you here haven't experienced a major conflict since becoming a syphon, but take heart. I've broken you up into groups led by someone who has. Trust them and their decisions. There's a bigger picture here than what you may personally understand. If you can keep it together and follow orders, we stand a good chance of seeing the Sun rise tomorrow. God bless and stay safe."

Sybil hopped off the table to the sound of awkward sounding cheers and clapping.

How the hell do they come up with those motivational speeches in the movies? Do they practice them beforehand on the off-chance they'll need to give one? Hopefully I'll get the chance to practice if I ever have to give another one…

A loud gong went off, accompanied by the feeling of the floors vibrating. As Sybil listened, she could hear the sound of heavy impacts echoing around the building.

"The centurions have moved to engage!"

"Syphons! Move out!"

The impact jarred her teeth as she swung her arm up at the last second to block a sword the size of a steel girder. Sliding forward while keeping her arm in contact with the metal, she shoved the blade upward, throwing the giant nephilim off balance. Before it could recover, she leapt forward, burying her blade into his chest and twisting before kicking off backward. Doing a backflip, she landed gracefully with her sword up, looking around for the next target.

"LOOK OUT!"

Sybil turned in time to see one of the centurions start to topple off-balance toward her. Throwing herself to the side at the last second, she narrowly avoided being crushed under the weight of the guardian. Ripping off the section of her armored duster that was pinned under the sentinel, she glanced around her.

"Fall back and regroup! Wedge formation!"

Sybil got her feet back under her before leaping over a knot of orcs, landing forty feet away. As she landed, several other syphons formed up behind her, creating a V-shape.

"Forward! Let's see if we can break up some of their formations!"

Driving forward, Sybil swung her blade side to side. She trusted the people to her left and right would deal with the wounded she left in her wake as she plowed ahead. As the first group of orcs broke and ran, she quickly scanned the battlefield for her next target. A loud grinding sound caught her attention.

Glancing over, she saw the fallen centurion slowly dragging itself back to its feet. Continuing her survey, she finally caught a glimpse of who was leading the attack.

Heaven help us, it's Damien.

Sybil focused her energy for a moment before sending out a telepathic blast.

>*There! That's who we need to stop. If he falls, we have a chance of stemming the tide.*<

She watched as everyone glanced her way before looking in the direction she was pointing. Several of the older syphons gasped and stumbled backward as they recognized who was leading the attack.

>*If we work together, we can end this. If he's here, then it's even more important we stop them before they get to the library. The steps are the line in the sand if humanity is to survive. Molon labe!*<

Letting out a primal scream, they all charged at the archdemon commander.

The air was blasted from her lungs as the kick launched her half the length of a football field before getting embedded in the engine block of a pickup truck. She tried weakly to claw her way out as she watched the archdemon slowly drift through the air toward her. She half-heartedly tried to raise her sword in defense before noticing the blade was snapped off a couple inches above the guard.

"Now now Lady Sybil… is that any way to treat an old acquaintance?"

Trying to draw in a breath around her fractured ribs, she sneered at Damien.

"Go to hell," she gasped before launching into a coughing fit.

"Really my dear? That's the best you can do? Where do you think I'm headed after this little scrimmage? Not some human amusement park to hang out with an oversized mouse…"

Without warning, Damien dropped from the sky, stomping one foot onto her broken ribs and grinding at them as he leaned in close.

"When I'm finished here, I'm going back to my condo next to a lovely lake of fire. The brimstone fountains are to die for. Those damn HOA fees to keep the souls screaming are hell to pay for though…"

Sybil pushed against his foot helplessly as he flipped his sword around, the tip creasing a spot on her forehead.

"I guess this is goodbye then. It was such a nice massacre you arranged for me to have."

As the blade slowly started to dig into her skin, she squeezed her eyes shut.

"Really… Is that any way to treat a lady?"

"Wha—?"

Without warning, the pressure of Damien's foot vanished with a loud thump. Opening her eyes slowly, she tried to understand what she was seeing.

"Last time I saw you, you couldn't count to ten on your fingers…"

"You asshole. Do you know how hard it was to regrow this thing?"

"Apparently not hard enough."

Sybil watched as Samuel turned his head in her direction.

"Sorry I'm late. You okay?"

Samuel watched as blood started to trickle from the spot where Damien's blade started to press into Sybil's forehead.

>*Cruel bastard, isn't he?*<

>*Yeah… Let's go wipe that smirk off his face a second time.*<

"Is that any way to treat a lady?"

Samuel launched himself through the air, kicking the archdemon in the side of the head, propelling him into the side of another vehicle. The impact almost ripped the vehicle completely in half.

"Last time I saw you, you couldn't count to ten on your fingers…"

As he watched Damien extract himself from the wreckage, the archdemon brushed chunks of metal and plastic off like it was dust. He shook his new hand at him.

"You asshole. Do you know how hard it was to regrow this thing?"

"Apparently not hard enough."

Samuel heard Sybil's labored breathing starting to ease up slightly. He glanced over at her while keeping Damien in his peripheral. He spotted several compound fractures, but since she was still breathing, she'd pull through if he could beat Damien.

"Sorry I'm late. You okay?"

He winced slightly as she tried to look at him. Her one eye was nearly swollen shut from the beating she'd taken.

"Sa… Samuel?"

He slowly approached her as he kept Hoarfrost between himself and the creature.

"Oh go on. A few more minutes won't matter anyway. I can wait. Just hurry up with this sappy shit."

Samuel nodded to the archdemon.

"That's very sporting of you, sir."

"Why thank you. I see your manners are back. Am I to take it your memories are back as well?"

Samuel nodded slightly as he crouched over Sybil. He gently ran his hand over Sybil, realigning her broken bones while she gasped.

"I… I thought… you had gone… over to Genevieve's… side."

"Huh? Why would you think that?"

Samuel found her vial of aether and opened it. He dripped a few drops in her mouth before sealing it. Sybil shuddered before she responded, her bones snapping as they quickly started healing.

"You had that other peltae on your arm. The one that She used to crack the firmament the first time."

Samuel looked down at her sadly.

"Yeah… I should have never given it to her. It was a bad idea."

Sybil winced as her ribs snapped back into place.

"That's an understatement."

"At least she didn't have it the second time when she caused the flood."

"Not very reassuring."

As the pain lifted from her eyes, Samuel noticed her glance at his arm.

"You don't have it anymore? Where is it?"

"I let a friend borrow Amitiel to keep her safe."

"Oh bravo! You might have actually stood a chance if you had held on to her…"

Samuel glanced back up at the archdemon.

"My patience is at an end. Time to die Samuel. Rest easy knowing that your girlfriend here will be following along shortly."

Samuel barely got Raguel up in time to block the vicious strike.

Raguel screeched in pain.

>It cut me!<

Samuel leapt backward to put distance between them before looking down. A gash was slowly closing up across Raguel's back.

"Oh, you like that? It's amazing what you can do with this old thing."

Samuel looked back up as his opponent stalked toward him, casually waving his sword in front of him.

"Excalibur?"

"Precisely. Did you know this was an actual angelic weapon? Now you get to have a wonderful dilemma… Do you protect yourself at the expense of your little dragon there? Or do you take it on the chin for him instead."

Samuel sprang at the archdemon, his blade locking up his opponent's. As his face came within inches of Damien, he snarled.

"I vote for option three."

As Damien started to respond, Raguel spat at the fiend, causing a block of ice to form in his mouth and throat. Rotating his sword around Excalibur, Samuel slammed the pommel of Hoarfrost into his opponent's temple, causing the archdemon's head to snap sideways. As Damien tried to swing his head back, Samuel reared his blade back while sliding his right foot behind Damien's feet before simultaneously sweeping his opponent's legs out from under him while slamming the pommel straight into the creature's forehead. Taking a double handed grip, Samuel whipped his blade around, trying to decapitate the arch-fiend as he fell backward.

At the last second, Damien swung his blade up to deflect Hoarfrost. Instead of having his head removed, Hoarfrost only left a gash on his forehead. Before Samuel could riposte, Damien swung his arm up and sprayed a swarm of stinging insects into Samuel's face, forcing him to stumble backward.

"Did you really think it was going to be that easy?"

As the swarm fell to the ground, frozen by Raguel, Samuel tilted his head side-to-side, causing his neck to pop several times.

"Hey, I can hope, can't I?"

Damien wiped the back of his hand across the gash on his forehead as maggots dripped out of the wound.

"Haven't you heard," Damien asked as he reared back, "hope is highly overrated."

Lunging forward, the ferocity of the attack slowly forced Samuel backward. Sparks sprayed off both blades as they repeated clashed against each other. Locking blades again, Samuel tried to rock his blade around Excalibur to try and strip the sword away by hooking his pommel around it and yanking, but Damien held firm, yanking back and throwing Samuel several dozen yard through the air before he landed smoothly.

"Didn't you know? The wielder of Excalibur can't drop the blade while in combat. Guess you'll have to try and fail at something else…"

>Give me two ice blasts when he charges us again. I want you to encase his feet and head in blocks of ice. See if we can slow him down some.<

>Say when.<

>NOW!<

As Damien sprung in again, Raguel spat out a huge globule of liquid nitrogen, striking him in the face. As he stumbled, the second blast lodged him in place, his feet frozen to the ground. Samuel sprang in, swinging his blade in an overhand strike in an attempt to cleave the archdemon in half. At the last second, Damien burst into a swarm of insects before reforming several feet away.

"Well that's new…"

"Oh, you like it? I've been wanting to try it out for ages now. I know lots of new tricks."

Without warning, Damien's arm changed into a writhing mass of insects that lashed out at Samuel. It slammed into his chest like a wrecking ball, knocking him through a lamppost and causing him to leave a furrow in the asphalt as he slid to a stop. Springing to his feet, Samuel shook the chunks of road off.

"Well this is going to take longer than I expected."

Sizing him up again, Samuel charged the archdemon. As he approached, Damien gestured toward him.

"Come get some!"

44

Sybil tried to make sense of what she was seeing. Samuel and Damien were moving so quickly that she was tracking them more by sound than sight. Flashes of light kept strobing as their blades crossed over and over, sounding like thunder in the distance.

"How the hell is Samuel able to fight like that?" she whispered to herself as she slowly tried to get back to the library steps.

The better question is, how come his sword hasn't broken? All it took was one swipe for Damien to shatter my blade like it was made out of glass. If we survive this, I've got a lot of questions for him.

Sybil winced as she saw Samuel get kicked in the chest like Damien had done to her, but unlike her, Samuel was able to back-flip out of it and slide for several yards before charging at the archdemon again. Sybil couldn't help but notice that, while the archdemon still was moving effortlessly, Samuel was starting to slow down.

If he falls, we're done for. There's nobody else who's even going to come close to fighting like Samuel is. I wish there was something more we could do to help.

"Excuse me… are you Sybil?"

The unexpected voice startled her, causing her to spin around and bring her broken sword up in a defensive position. Standing before her was a very out of place looking, petite, blond-haired girl. She was startled when an arc of electricity sparked between her eyes before turning green again.

A wilder here, now? This can't be a coincidence.

Lowering her broken blade she nodded.

"Yes, I'm Sybil. Have we met before?"

"No, but Amitiel suggested I look for you. She thought you might know where I could find Samuel."

Sybil's eyes widened as she realized who the woman was.

"Are you, by any chance, the friend that Samuel gave his Paltae to?"

"Peltae?"

"Yes. You might…"

She trailed off as the other woman cocked her head slightly to the side.

"Yes, he sent his dragon with me, but I couldn't leave the city without knowing he was safe."

Sybil gestured behind her.

"Safe wouldn't be the word I'd use. He's all that's stands between us and destruction, and at this point, it doesn't look like he'll be able to hold out much longer."

Sybil watched as the other woman looked beyond her, observing her eyes go wide as the fighting continued behind her.

"I've got to help him!"

Sybil barely reacted in time to keep the other woman from sprinting past her.

"Hang on, miss…"

"Let me go. He needs me!"

The other woman struggled against her before going limp.

"Let me go," she whispered, her voice barely heard above the fight raging beyond them. "He's the only guy that ever saw me as a woman and didn't hurt me. I can't lose him."

"You can't help him, miss…"

"Blythe. My name's Blythe. Can't you do anything to help him?"

Sybil glanced down at the other woman's arm, gently lifting it up in between them.

"We can't, but she might…"

Samuel barely deflected the rapid flurry of strikes. Without warning, Damien lashed out with a vicious axe kick to his face, knocking out several teeth as he was slammed into the pavement. Stomping on his chest, Damien smirked down at him.

"Gee, this seems kinda familiar, doesn't it?"

Samuel pushed up against Damien's foot, lifting it several inches off his chest before the archdemon flexed, slamming his foot down on his chest again.

"Uh, uh… You're not going to get out of it this time. You might've gotten lucky at the hospital, but it's not going to happen again. Any last words?"

"Bite me."

"What is it with syphons and stupid comebacks? Why can't you just die screaming like everyone else? Oh, well, guess I can't have everything… Oh wait, I can. Now die!"

Samuel watched as Damien swung his arm back to deliver the fatal blow. Suddenly, Damien was launched backward by a ball of flame. Looking behind him, he watched as Amitiel, now nearly the size of an eighteen-wheeler, came charging across the battlefield toward him.

"MINE!"

Samuel kipped back to his feet an instant before Amitiel shrunk down and latched onto his back, bonding to him and bursting into flames. As she fanned her wings out, superheated air blasted dust and debris out in all directions. Energy surged up in him as all his wounds instantly healed. The air started shimmering around him as his energy levels continued to climb.

>*Am I glad to see you, but is Blythe safe?*<

>*She's with Sybil. I like her. She wouldn't leave without you.*<

>*Thanks for the save. You need to be careful. His blade can cut you.*<

>*Understood. Let's show this piece of offal what we're really capable of.*<

>*Lovely idea.*<

Samuel reached up with his left hand, grabbing ahold of Brimstone's handle. As he drew the blade, another blast of superheated air erupted around him.

"Seriously! I get interrupted twice in one day while trying to kill a syphon. What is this world coming to?"

As Samuel watched, a look of understanding washed over Damien's face. Looking up toward the sky, he screamed in anger.

"You're not going to stop me! It's too late!"

His gaze dropped back toward Samuel.

"And you," he said, stalking toward Samuel, "are going to die. No more games. It ends here!"

Charging in, Damien took a vicious two-handed strike at Samuel's neck. Blocking it with Brimstone, he smiled cruelly at Damien.

"My turn!"

Samuel ducked under the blade as it passed over his head. Without warning, Damien reversed the direction and height of the strike, slashing out at Samuel's legs instead. Samuel cartwheeled over the blade, using Brimstone to drive it into the ground as he thrust out with Hoarfrost. Damien barely got Excalibur up in time to deflect the strike, causing it to nick his shoulder instead of impaling him.

"Let's see how you deal with an aerial attack!"

Samuel watched as Damien launched himself skyward before unfurling his wings and chasing after him, flames trailing off the tips of the wings.

"You're not going to get away that easily."

As he approached, Samuel reared his arm back before swinging forward, Brimstone snaking out before him and wrapping around Damien's leg.

"Get over here!"

Samuel yanked back hard, snatching the archdemon out of the sky. He spun him around several times before swinging him downward, slamming him into the pavement. The impact caused several cars to flip over from the shockwave. Samuel took off, flying toward the library while dragging Damien across the ground and slamming him through several vehicles along the way.

Damien twisted around and knocked the blade off his foot, causing Samuel to tilt off balance momentarily before righting himself. Doing a loop, he bore down on the archdemon before flipping over and drop kicking him in the chest, launching him across the battlefield and bouncing off the wall of the library steps.

"This isn't over yet!"

>*Give him both barrels!*<

As Damien launched himself back at Samuel, Raguel and Amitiel alternated blasting him with ice and fireballs, slowing his approach. Getting close, he hissed in Samuel's face as he locked blades with him again.

"You really think you can win, don't you?"

Freeing his blades, he lashed out and nicked Damien in the throat, before kicking him in the chest.

"Yeah, I do."

Samuel slowly forced Damien back across the battlefield again. For every attack the archdemon tried to muster, Samuel would lash out with a vicious counter, striking several times for each attempt Damien made. Without warning, Samuel launched a powerful kick at his opponent's chest, blasting him back through the air to slam into the stone wall beside the library steps again, causing spidery cracks to form in the stone. Before he could move, Samuel thrust his blades forward, driving them into the archdemon's chest. Excalibur dropped to the pavement with a loud rattle.

"And so it ends."

Samuel's muscles rippled as energy surged through them. Twisting the blades horizontally, he pressed against them, crossing the blades in front of him, leaving deep gouges in the stone as he sliced Damien in half. Stepping back, he watched as the upper and lower parts of the body started sliding away in opposite directions. Turning away, he started searching for Sybil and Blythe.

He sensed movement behind him as he tried to dodge to the side, but realized he'd been too slow as Excalibur appeared jutting out of the front of his chest.

"You still don't get it, do you?"

Samuel gasped at the pain, blood misting out of his mouth as the sound of mocking laughter came from behind him. Damien slowly started twisting the blade as he whispered in Samuel's ear.

"You can't banish me from this world now. Can't you feel it? As we fought, the amount of aetheric and demonic energy was gradually increasing as the weave of the world slowly unravels. There's enough here now that I'm immortal."

Damien grabbed his head as he forcefully twisted it from side to side.

"Look around you. It's only a matter of time before the realms start to merge. I don't have to beat you to win. I just have keep you busy."

As Samuel looked around, he noticed it starting to get darker. Glancing up, he watched as the moon slowly started to take on a reddish tinge as more demonic energy gathered in the area.

"Why don't you just give up now and save yourself the pain and suffering of losing. I promise, if you drop your swords now, I'll kill you quickly. Just for old time's sake."

To accentuate the point, Damien twisted the blade again before putting his foot on Samuel's back and kicking, causing him to fly through the air and landing in a heap on the ground. Slowly forcing his way back to his feet, he faced the approaching archdemon.

"She didn't tell you, did she?"

Damien paused, coming to a stop with a haughty sneer on his face.

"Tell me what exactly, hmmm?"

Samuel dropped his head forward. Sighing deeply, he raised his head back up.

"You know, it's funny."

Damien cocked his head to the side quizzically.

"Funny…? What's funny?"

"The fact that you keep telling me that I don't get it."

"Huh?"

"It's kinda ironic since it's really you who doesn't get it. God forgive me for this…"

As Damien started to swing Excalibur at him, Samuel slammed the pommels of his swords together.

Blinding light flared out from the swords, slamming Damien back into the wall a third time and pinning him in place. Small chunks of granite fractured off and tumble into the air as the ball of light continued to expand. As the light intensified, the sound of trumpets ripped across the landscape.

"What are you doing?" Damien gasped as the light started to dim.

Samuel held both blades aloft, now joined at the pommel. As he held them overhead on his upraised palms, they started spinning rapidly. A small vortex formed and rapidly grew in size above the spinning blades. Abruptly, the handles pivoted and started spiraling around each other, twisting together into a single handle. As the process continued, the guards fused together into a large crossbeam ending in a trefoil pattern. Both blades launched out in chain form before coming back together, interlocking with each other, forming a massive blade. Finally, the transformation finished, leaving behind a seven foot long, crystalline purple blade. Purple energy rippled up and down the blade like flames.

Bringing the blade down in front of him in a guard position, he watched as fear slowly spread across the archdemon's face.

"Look familiar?"

"How...?"

"Michel entrusted it to me after paradise was divided. Since he no longer had to defend it, he gave it to me for safekeeping. He figured I might need it for the next Armageddon."

Samuel watched as Damien dropped to his knees.

"Have mercy. It wasn't my idea, I swear..."

"That might be, but you went along with it anyway. So now you'll have to pay the price."

Screeching, Damien launched himself forward, swinging Excalibur toward Samuel's neck. As the blade approached, Samuel casually reached up and caught the blade by pinching it. Then he swung the massive blade down. The blade hit Damien on the top of the head and traveled down before embedding itself in the ground.

As the blade cut through him, a ghostly image of Damien soul was split as he was slain in the spirit. The threads of his soul drifted away as his remains dissolved into a bunch of insects that scurried away.

"May God show you the mercy I can't afford."

"Samuel…? Are you all right? Is that what I think it is?"

Samuel turned to watch Sybil and Blythe slowly approach, the purple light cast from his blade causing their skin to glow.

"Is it over?"

Samuel stepped forward to embrace Blythe.

"Unfortunately, no. The demonic bubble that he created with that ritual is still weakening the weave. If I don't stop it soon, this world and Aerth will both be destroyed."

Turning toward Sybil, he gently pushed Blythe toward her.

"Take care of her. If I fail, I want you to train her in my place. It's been several generations since we've come across a wilder of her caliber. She's too important to lose."

Before either woman had a chance to respond, Samuel leapt up, Amitiel's wings unfurling around him before propelling him skyward. As he strove higher, his vision shifted, allowing him to see into the spirit realm. Turning in a slow circle as he hovered, he noted the major ruptures located at the five warehouses around the city. He also noticed small rents starting to form in the weave as well. Taking the blade and holding it aloft, he spun it clockwise around his head, slowly gathering speed. As the wind rose, the sound of trumpets gradually got louder.

"Blessed be his name!"

As he uttered the words, the bladed flared out in five directions, the sound of unspooling chains echoing across the landscape as the rotating vortex of air above him drew in the demonic energy. With the sound of a huge gong, the five-fold blade slammed into the rifts in the warehouses, shattering the spiritual locks that the rituals had formed, holding the rifts open. With a loud, sub-sonic thump, the rifts closed, sucking energy back into them. Spooling back up to form a single blade again, Samuel swung the blade down in front of him, slicing a rift into the weave in front of him. Thrusting the blade through, the vortex of demonic energy was dragged into the rift, the sound of damned souls echoing out from the gash. As the remainder of demonic energy was finally shunted back into the demonic realms, he withdrew the sword, allowing the rupture to reseal. Looking around one last time, he noted all the little rents and folds left behind in the weave, like pulled threads. Separating the blades, he sheathed them back in their respective dragons.

>*Well, that was fun.*<

Samuel started to nod at Raguel before passing out.

43

Blythe watched as Samuel slowly started to plummet out of the sky. Without thinking, she took off at a sprint with Sybil slowly falling behind. As Samuel fell closer to the ground, she redoubled her efforts, running faster than she ever thought possible.

Please God, let me get there in time.

As she got closer, she felt a burst of energy. Instinctively running up the side of one of the centurions, she launched herself off its head, stretching her arms out as far as she could. Miraculously, she caught Samuel in her outstretched arms, the impact slowing his decent slightly. Pulling him in tight, they both dropped toward the ground. She felt a tickling sensation as Amitiel quickly slithered across her back before latching on and flaring her wings to try and arrest their fall, but they were too close to the ground and bounced heavily off the surface. Blythe felt the familiar sensation of having her bones break as they skidded to a stop. She tried to block out the pain as she gently stroked Samuel's head, noting that he was still breathing softly.

She gradually realized the pain was lessening as she felt her body start to knit itself back together.

>*What's happening to me?*<

>*You're a wilder. Your life is only going to get more interesting from here.*<

She felt Samuel start to stir in her arms. Looking at his face, she watched as his eyes fluttered open.

"Nice catch. I owe you one," he whispered.

"Well… I had to return the favor," she said softly, "and I still owe you one."

Smiling back at her, he reached up and gently pulled her toward him.

"No, I think we're even."

Smiling, Blythe leaned forward and kissed him.

Samuel slowly walked toward the library, his arm around Blythe's shoulders. Glancing around, he noticed the bodies of several syphons laying broken on the ground while others tried to help the ones who were still badly injured but alive. As he got closer, Sybil finally caught up to them. Giving him a strange look, she nodded at them.

"Are you both all right?"

"Well, we're fine enough for now."

"Was that really the archangel sword?"

Samuel scratched the back of his head before responding.

"Yeah, that was actually his sword. We kinda go way back."

Sybil looked at him suspiciously.

"And you… Are you really who I think you are. There's a picture in the archives that looks suspiciously like you."

Samuel sighed. He'd hoped that info would never get out, but these were strange days indeed.

"Yeah, it's me. I'm Adam."

"So that would make Genevieve…"

"Yup… Eve."

"How…?"

"It's a long, long story. For now, let's get this mess straightened up. The forgetfulness caused by that much aetheric energy spilling out will only go just so far."

Sybil glanced around before nodding.

"Well, you're the boss. At least it's over with."

Samuel shook his head slowly while looking at Sybil.

"I wish that were true, but this is just the beginning…"

Hank watched as Samuel and his friend slowly started cleaning up the devastation caused by Damien. Unfocusing his eyes, he glanced toward the heavens, noting the various pulls and tears in the weave of the realms. Waving his hand, a steaming bacon, egg, and cheese biscuit appeared. Looking back at Samuel, he shook his head slowly as he turned around.

"That boy has a lot on his plate now. I just hope he's up for the challenge… For the sake of all the realms."

Taking a bite of the biscuit sandwich, he gave it an appreciative glance as he started walking away.

"I really need to rethink my edict about eating pork," he said as he slowly started breaking up into sparkling motes, "bacon has got to be on my top ten list of best things I created, somewhere just behind light…"

Within seconds, all that remained was the slight scent of bacon.

44

"So what are you saying, exactly?"

Sybil glanced around the table before looking back at Samuel.

"What I'm saying is, Armageddon has started. It's just not off to as fast of a start as prophesied."

"And you know this how?"

"Unfortunately, this isn't the first Armageddon I've had to stop. This time though, Genevieve planned this attack pretty well. By drawing the sword of Michael, I helped weakened the weave between realms. I'm suspecting that, if Damien had gotten inside, he would have gotten to the Arch of the Covenant."

The Archivist gave him a confused look.

"Don't you mean the Ark of the Covenant? And what do you mean if he got to it. Nobody knows where it's at since the Levites hid it."

"Nope, I meant Arch, but it's mostly semantics. The Arch actually looks like the description of the Ark in the bible, but it's actually a arch that opens a doorway to the Akashic records. If Damien had been able to reach that plane, he could have rewritten history in any way he chose."

Sybil gestured toward him.

"That still doesn't answer the question about why you think the Arch is here somewhere."

"Well, that's easy enough to answer. I buried it here before I had the library built."

Samuel watched as everyone stared at him.

"Well, now that we know who you really are, I'll step down so you can lead us."

"Uh, no. As far as I'm concerned, you're still the commander of this garrison. I gave up that role a long time ago and I really don't want it back."

Sybil shook her head.

"You're the one who started our order. You need to lead us again in this time of tribulation."

Samuel gave her a firm stare.

"No. End of story. You've done a good job up to this point and they trust you. Besides which, I'd rather not have everyone learn who I really am. I worked hard to bury that secret long ago. Plus, I'm going to be busy training Blythe for the foreseeable future along with trying to remember how to repair the weave since this isn't the first time it's happened. Hopefully the rest of my memories will return soon so I can remember how I fixed it the last two times."

"Fine, but this particular discussion isn't over. Now what about this other syphon you said you came across?"

"Yes, a professor by the name of Clarience Waide. We'll need to bring him into the fold. I think him and the Archivist will get along great."

"But what group is he from? And why is he teaching at a university?"

"That's what makes him unique, actually. As far as I know, he's the only person who's ever been turned into a syphon by a peltae before."

"What? How?"

"That's what I hope to find out."

Cora watched as Samuel and Sybil walked toward them. Glancing down at Frank, she squeezed his hand before looking back up. Looking at Samuel, she noticed something different about him. As he got closer, she realized the way he carried himself was different.

He tood taller, more sure of himself. As they stopped, Samuel gave them a warm smile.

"Detectives Blanchett and Giani, please allow me the opportunity to apologize for the run around I gave the two of you over the past few days. I'm sure by now you realize there was a good reason for it, but it's still inexcusable. As for you," he said, looking directly at Cora, "I'd especially like to apologize for the way I treated you on the rooftop of the college. You were only trying to do your job. Please accept this gift as a token of my apology."

As he said it, he extended his hand out, gently grabbing her left hand before sliding something around her middle finger. Releasing her hand, he took a step back. Looking down, she saw that he had slipped a large, plain silver ring with a flat, round top on her finger. Looking at it more closely, she noticed it had a faint starburst pattern radiating from the center of the circle.

"Um… Thank you? You really didn't need to—"

Samuel held up his hand with a smile.

"This is to help keep you safe until we can get you trained in the proper use of your own peltae and peleus. To use it, do this."

She watched as he gestured to her arm before curling his arm like he was hiding behind a shield. As she started to mimic the movement, she looked at him funny.

"My own who and what?"

As her arm came into position, she heard something similar to a transformer arcing as a large, transparent glowing blue field surged out of the ring, forming into a shield approximately three feet across. Tapping on it with the finger on her other hand, she felt a slight electric tingling run down her hand.

"That's an aegis shield. It can withstand most anything up to the force of a peleus. So as long as you can get it up, it'll stop just about any physical force in this world. With a little practice, you should be able to get the hang of changing the size of it along with keeping it from opening on accident. Sybil can fill you in on the details."

Cora watched in fascination as the shield shimmered and shrank back down, disappearing into the ring as she straightened her arm. Looking back up, she noticed Samuel turning to walk away.

"Wait! I have so many questions for you…"

Turning back, he gave her what appeared to be a mischievous smile.

"Don't worry. You'll have plenty of time to ask me questions throughout your training."

"Training?"

"Yep, because of what we had to do to keep the both of you from dying, you're both going to become syphons. Welcome to the family."

Cora's mind went blank as Samuel walked away. She jumped slightly when Frank cleared his throat.

"Uh… Syphons?"

Samuel gently knocked on the open door. Glancing in, he noticed Blythe looking down at her hands, shoulders slumped forward.

"Mind if I come in?"

Samuel waited a moment for her to respond, but after she made no response, he slowly entered her room. Quietly bringing a chair over, he slowly sat down in front of Blythe, waiting for her to respond.

"It's not fair," she whispered, not looking up.

"What's not fair?"

Her head snapped up, tears running down her face as she met his surprised look.

"You don't have to pretend. They already explained that it wasn't love you were feeling before."

Samuel tilted his head to the side in confusion.

"Huh?"

"Sybil told me why we were attracted to each other. It's because I'm this wilder thing, or whatever it's called. I was 'pulled' to you because of the aetheric energy flowing through you, so you don't have to pretend anymore."

Samuel leaned back in his chair with a sigh as she went back to staring at her hands.

"See, it's true, isn't it!"

Samuel reached out and gently lifted her hands in his own and gave a light squeeze. When she tried to pull away, he held them more firmly.

"Look at me," he said softly.

Looking back up, he could see the sadness along with a longing in her eyes.

"I'm beginning to think Sybil only gave you part of the story."

He lifted one of her hands up and lightly kissed her palm before continuing.

"Yes, because of our physiology, we were unconsciously drawn to each other, but," he said as she tried to pull away again, "that feeling only makes you want to be near me. As in my general vicinity. It's not an emotional thing."

"I don't understand…"

He paused for a minute to gather his thoughts.

"Would you want to walk down the street naked?"

"What! No! Why would you suggest that?"

"Would you feel more comfortable wearing clothes to walk down the street?"

"Well duh…"

Samuel smiled slightly.

"It's like that. You'd just have a feeling of comfort being near me. The way we feel for each other, on the other hand, is entirely real."

He watched as he saw the hope blossom in her eyes before a look of confusion set in.

"Then why would Sybil say something like that?"

"It's a long story… but to make a long story short, we used to be a couple not too long ago."

Blythe's shoulders slumped slightly when he said that.

"So I'm what, your rebound?"

"No. I keep forgetting this is all new to you. Sybil and I broke it off nearly seventy years ago, give or take a decade."

"That's what you call not too long ago?"

"Comparatively speaking, yes. Suffice it to say, there's nothing between us anymore."

"Are you sure?"

Samuel smiled as he leaned forward to kiss her.

"Absolutely."

Samuel held Blythe's hand as they walked into the library. Looking around, he saw people milling around the area. On the other side of the room, he saw Sybil giving Frank and Cora a tour of the place. As he made his way over toward them, he noticed Sybil give them a slight frown before heading in his direction.

"Blythe? How'd you get tangled up in all of this?"

"Hi detective Blanchett. I kinda lied to you earlier when I said I hadn't seen him before."

Samuel smiled at her as she looked at him. Looking back, he thought he caught another frown on Sybil's face, but it was too fast to be sure.

Cora looked at Blythe with a stern look.

"Uh huh, thought so."

"But—"

Cora's stern look changed to a smile as she continued.

"No buts. Looks like this time you found yourself a good one."

Blythe smiled before looking back up at Samuel.

"Yes I did."

Samuel squeezed her hand slightly before looking back at everyone.

"Did Sybil fill you in on everything?"

Frank nodded at him.

"I'm still a little hazy on the how's and why's, but for the most part yes. I guess the next question is, when do we start?"

Samuel looked at all of them seriously.

"As soon as possible. This is only the beginning. Genevieve knew that either Damien was going to access the Arch, or that I'd have to pull out Michael's sword. One way would have allowed direct access to the Akashic records, the other would just weaken the weave between worlds. Either way, she's one step closer to her goal."

"What goal is that?"

Samuel glanced over toward Cora.

"Basically, she wants to merge the realms back together and restore Eden to its former glory. And we have to be ready for her next move."

www.ingramcontent.com/pod-product-compliance
Lightning Source LLC
Chambersburg PA
CBHW070901180626
46817CB00003B/863